To the Heart of the Rainbow

Gareth Knight

Illustrated by Libby Travassos Valdez

SKYLIGHT PRESS

© Gareth Knight 2004, 2010

Illustrations © Libby Travassos Valdez 2004

First published in 2004 as "Granny's Magic Cards" by Sun Chalice
Books, PO Box 5355, Oceanside, CA 92052, USA.

This edition published in Great Britain in 2010 by Skylight Press,
210 Brooklyn Road, Cheltenham, Glos GL51 8EA

Designed and typeset by Rebsie Fairholm
Printed and bound in Great Britain

www.skylightpress.co.uk

ISBN 978-1-4461-6607-9

Dedicated
to the memory of the original granny
Daisy Frances May Berryman,
for whom the cards were friends,
and to her real life great-grandchildren,
Gabriella and Gregory

Contents

Chapter 1: The Fool and his Dog

IT all began when Richard and Rebecca told their Granny that they were bored.

They were sitting in the upstairs room which she was using while she stayed with them. The day was dark and dull and all day long the rain had beaten upon the glass of the windows and the slates of the roof, and they could not play outside.

Granny sat at the little baize table beside the window that looked down over the garden wall and onto the Tewkesbury road. The children sat either side of her and between them all lay spread a pack of cards, where they had been playing Snap and Beggar My Neighbour and even Pontoon. This was a special Granny secret because it was a gambling game and children, and even grown-ups, she said, were not supposed to play it. Terrible things could happen to you if you played such games for real money. Kings had lost their kingdoms, rich men their fortunes, when gripped by the gambling fever that could come through the cards. But Granny said it was all right if you played with something not worth very much, like dead matches. But you had to be careful. Even playing for matches could be dangerous, unless they were all given back after the game was over.

This made Pontoon very exciting but even that grows boring in time. And now Richard had won all the dead matches off the others and it was still only ten to three and the rest of Sunday afternoon stretched before them and still the rain came in sheets down the grey window pane.

"What can we do now?" sighed Rebecca.

"Would you tell us our fortunes?" asked Richard.

This was a favourite question whenever Granny arrived for a holiday. It was well known, but again not talked about very much in front of grown-ups, that telling fortunes with the cards was another of Granny's secrets.

Sat on the beach when she herself was a little girl, an old gypsy had come along, so she said, and taught her how to lay out and read the cards. Dad said that it was nonsense. And Mum did not really approve of Granny doing it, but she herself sometimes had her fortune told. "Only to please Granny," she said, though the children didn't really believe her.

But Granny had to be in the right mood to tell the cards, and after an hour or so of playing games like Snap (which with Rebecca could become quite riotous) she felt the time was not quite right to try to consult the future.

"Oh what are we going to do till tea time then?" complained Rebecca.

"You'll have to ask the cards yourself," said Granny, getting up and plumping up the pillow on her bed, which was a sign that she was shortly going to ask them to leave her to rest.

"But we can't tell fortunes," said Richard, "no gypsy ever told us."

"Will you teach us to tell fortunes?" asked Rebecca.

"Some day my dear, perhaps, some day," said Granny, taking off her glasses and putting them in their case. "But you have to have the second sight – or at any rate a bit of it."

"Have I got it? Have I?" exclaimed Rebecca.

"I don't know yet my dear. I expect you have if you are grandchildren of mine; but time will tell."

"How will it tell?" asked Rebecca.

"You will have to wait and see," said Granny firmly, "and now you will have to leave me because I am going to have forty winks."

"Can't you make it only twenty?" asked Rebecca.

"No my dear, I've got to have my beauty sleep."

"Oh!" moaned the children. "What can we do now?"

"I'll let you into a little secret," said Granny. "You go and ask the cards if they will play with you themselves. They will if you've got the second sight, and it's one way to find out if you have. Here you are, I will lend you my special pack of cards so you can go away somewhere quietly and try it."

"Oh yes please," cried the children. "What do we do?"

"Listen carefully," said Granny, "and lay them out as I tell you."

*   *   *   *   *   *

Later, in the quietness of the loft, which they used sometimes for a play room, the children sat upon a rug on the floor and did as Granny had told them.

They took the cards of all the four suits, and laid them out in order; the Ace to the Ten and the Jack, Queen and King all in a line.

The Spades on one side of a square, behind which Richard sat. The Hearts in a line making the opposite side of the square, behind which Rebecca sat. And between them, to Richard's left and Rebecca's right, stretched a line of Clubs. And in another line to Rebecca's left and Richard's right stretched a similar line of Diamonds. The cards were in clockwise order going round the square, Ace to King of Spades, Ace to King of Clubs, Ace of King of Hearts, and Ace to King of Diamonds. And in the centre of all, between Richard and Rebecca, was placed the fifty-third card, the Joker.

"What do we have to do now?" asked Rebecca.

"We have to use our imaginations," said Richard, "and then say the magic rhyme."

"Can you remember it?"

"I think so."

"First of all we have to build up the pictures. I'm the king of a castle here, and I have a magic wand, which I hold out over the cards."

"And I am a beautiful queen, and I have a golden cup, shaped like the Ace of Hearts, and I hold it up towards the centre to catch the Wisdom of the Joker."

"Are you imagining like mad?"

"Yes."

"Eyes closed?"

"Yes."

"All right, I'll begin."

Richard began to recite the little spell that Granny had told them.

"*Jolly jesting joker, lord of the dance,*
  Say the word that will give us en-trance.
  With my magic sword I open the ways ..."

"Go on, Rebecca."

"Oh, I nearly forgot it," stammered Rebecca, and then continued. "*Into the magic cup we gaze.*"

"Now we walk round it three times," said Richard. "No, not that way, clockwise, to your left."

The children did so, stooping below the low roof beams.

"And now we sit and think of our magic sword and our magic cup, and on the side where the Clubs are, we imagine someone sitting, just like me, a fairy prince holding a magic wand."

"And," said Rebecca, "on the side where the Diamonds are, someone just like me, but like a fairy princess, sitting in piles of gold and precious gems and holding a brilliant jewel."

"And in the centre," said Richard, "we have to see the jolly, jesting joker in his coat of many colours and his cap and bells."

They sat in silence solemnly for several long minutes. All was quiet. The buzzing thoughts in their heads slowly stilled, so there was an inner quietness too.

"Oo-er!" said Rebecca suddenly.

"What is it?" asked Richard.

"Can you hear something?"

"No. What is it?"

"I think I can."

"Yes – wait a minute, so can I."

"It's little jingling … "

"Bells!"

"Oh, do you think?"

"The bells on the joker's cap!"

"Let's look."

They opened their eyes and looked. But the cards still lay on the floor between them, the pasteboard emblem of the Joker staring blankly up at them.

"Oh, we should have kept our eyes shut."

"Oh but Richard, I can hear more things."

"Yes. I hear footsteps."

"And look at the secret doorway, it's getting lighter."

The secret doorway in the loft led into darkness, and beyond it nobody went because there was no floor-boarding laid down, and if you went in there you had to walk on the beams only, for if you did not you would fall through the ceiling into one of the bedrooms below, or even the well of the stairs. They were forbidden to go in there, but anyway it was very dark, and full of dusty hanging cobwebs, so neither of them were ever tempted to go through the rickety little wooden door then closed off from the boarded, windowed part of the loft where they were allowed to play.

"And there's a scrabbling sound, like animal's feet."

"You don't think it's rats?"

"No."

But there was now a very bright light coming from within the darkened part of the loft, and then a scratching, and the door, which was always ajar, for it had no lock, and very old hinges, swung open a few inches, and a little face peeped through, near the bottom of the door jamb.

"Why Richard, look! It's a dog! A little dog!"

They gazed astounded at a rough-coated dapple coloured dog, which gazed expectantly at them, its tongue lolling out of its mouth, and a mischievous look of enquiry on its face.

"It wants a walk. Or to play. Come on then," coaxed Rebecca.

"Thank you kindly for the invitation," was the reply in a clear strong human voice, and the door swung open, and there ducked into the room, the dog running after him, a merry looking young man with yellow hair, and coat and breeches of many colours, not unlike that shown on the Joker's card. He had a kind and merry face, and over his shoulder a staff on the end of which hung a knotted bag such that you might see Dick Whittington carrying in a pantomime, holding all his worldly goods when he went off to seek his fortune.

"I've not been asked into a children's upper room for many a long year," he said, and sat down cross legged between them in the middle of the cards. He threw down his bag, which seemed very full of lumpy objects, and his dog sat down as well and let Richard and Rebecca tickle its ears.

"Well, now that I'm here," he said, "what do you want with me? You have to ask the questions. Otherwise I can't tell you anything."

The children stared at him, wide eyed.

"Are you the Joker? Really the Joker? From the middle of the pack of cards?" asked Richard.

"In a manner of speaking, yes." he replied. That's what they often call me nowadays, and there's nothing wrong with that. What is life without a jest or a joke? It would be a very dull game wouldn't it? But in other times and other countries people who know the cards called me lots of other things – the Poor Man who had nowhere to lay his head; the Beggar Man who wanders the roads seeking charity from strangers; the Fool – because what sensible practical person would do such a thing? Even the Madman because some people see no sense at all in what I have to tell them!"

"I'm sure you are not a madman or a fool," said Rebecca, and the dog nuzzled her hand and wagged his tail.

"You must be very wise to see I'm not," said the Fool, "but that is because, like me, you are an Innocent."

"What's that?" said Rebecca.

"Ah, you only know what an Innocent is when you are one yourself. It takes one to know one," said the Fool. "When you are young you have innocence, but most people lose it when they grow up."

"How horrible," said Rebecca.

"Oh, it's what growing up is for," said the Fool. "You have to lose something to find out what it is and how much you miss it."

"Like having a tooth come out," said Richard. "You never think about it until it starts wobblng and then there's a gap in which you keep putting your tongue."

"Exactly," said the Fool, "and it's only a misfortune if you don't grow another grown-up tooth in place of the baby one. And there is a grown-up kind of innocence too, but it's wise as well."

"I think I know what you mean," said Rebecca, "Granny has a lot of it. That's why she knows such interesting things and likes playing games with us."

"Is that what is called second childhood?" asked Richard.

"In a way I suppose it is," laughed the Fool, "and that's why she knows about me, for childhood is a time for playing, and my real name is Lord of the Games."

"What games?" asked Rebecca.

"All games," said the Fool.

"You mean football and cricket and chess and ludo and …" said Rebecca.

"Yes, and much more besides," laughed the Fool.

"Do you know lots of games?" asked Richard.

"I know all games," he replied.

"Oh tell us them, teach us them!" the children cried.

"I think that would take rather too long," said the Fool, "even if I took you outside of time."

"Can you go outside of time?" asked Richard, "Like in science fiction stories?"

"Of course I can," said the Fool, "that's one of my favourite games."

"Is it better than being in time?" asked Richard.

"Being in time is another game," said the Fool. "Or perhaps I should say games, because there are lots of different spaces and lots of different times, and each one has its own kind of games. So you see there's no end to it really, you could go on playing different games for ever."

"How jolly super!" said Richard.

"Oh, I don't know," said Rebecca, "some games are horrid."

"Only when those who play them make them so," said the Fool.

"Yes," said Rebecca, "Richard always cheats at Snap."

"I don't!" cried Richard. "And anyway Rebecca always sulks if she thinks she's losing."

"You see what I mean?" said the Fool.

"Well, if you show us some new games we promise we will play them ever so quietly, and be very well behaved, and not cheat either," said Rebecca.

"That's what people always say," smiled the Fool, "and I'm always foolish enough to believe them, and then to keep on giving them another chance."

"Oh do try us," said Richard. "Show us how to play a game outside of time."

"Is that what you really want?" asked the Fool.

"Oh yes, yes please!" the children cried.

"Very well, but you will have to follow me," he replied, and stood up, while the dog scurried excitedly round him and jumped up, pawing at his back.

"Where do we go?" asked Richard.

"Through there," said the Fool, pointing at the dark open doorway, through which he had come.

"Oh but we are not allowed in there," said Rebecca. "It's all dark and spidery, and you will fall through the ceiling and hurt yourself."

"Only if you stay in your own space and time," said the Fool, "but there are lots of other times and spaces you can move into, if you know how to go through the door the right way."

"And how is that?" asked Richard.

"Wait a moment and I will show you," said the Fool, and he rummaged about inside his dark bag and drew out four shining and golden objects, and poured a pile of leaves upon the floor. They looked as if they had been picked from the laurel bush that grew by the front gate. They were dark and green, but seemed much bigger and had a shiny heavy look as if they came from a very special bush such as you only see displayed at a prize flower show.

The Fool poured a pile of leaves on the floor

"You must help me," said the Fool. "First we must make a circle of leaves around the door. Here are some silver pins to help you," and he held out to each of them a packet of shining pins that seemed to glow with their own light.

The children set to with a will, and starting from the top, above the door, soon had constructed, under the Fool's directions, an oval wreath of laurel leaves all around the dark opening.

"Now go and sit at your places," said the Fool.

The children did so, and watched as he took the four shining golden objects and placed them at the four corners of the door. Each was a little plaque and on each was a different creature. To the top and the left there was a shining angel, to the top and right there was a golden lion, to the bottom right there was an eagle, and to the bottom left a golden bull.

"Now," said the Fool, standing by the doorway, "it is time to use your imaginations again. For you cannot come through here in your ordinary bodies, otherwise you will still be in your own space and time and fall through the floor. You remember you were told to imagine yourselves as a King with a Sword and a Queen with a Cup? And that beside you, you had to imagine there was someone else looking just like you – a Prince with a Wand and a Princess with many jewels and treasures?"

"Yes," said the children.

"Well, imagine that you are no longer sitting in your own bodies as the King and Queen, but that you have moved round to sit in the imaginary bodies of the Prince and Princess." He paused a minute. "Have you done that?" he asked.

"Yes, I think so," said Rebecca.

"It's a bit difficult," said Richard. "I can still feel I'm sitting in my real body, even though I'm imagining like mad I'm in this other one."

"Never mind about that," said the Fool. "With practice you will improve. And it doesn't matter if you are still aware in the background of sitting here in the loft, as long as you have enough faith to believe that you are also coming in your other body with me. Are you ready?"

"Yes," breathed the children excitedly.

"Now open your inner eyes and follow me."

The children opened the eyes of the imaginary bodies of the

Prince and the Princess, he holding a slim silver wand and she holding a golden circular disk.

They looked towards the door, to find that the Fool had gone through.

"Follow me!" came the echoing cry, as if from miles and miles away in a space like a vast cavern.

Their movement was as quick as their thought and they found themselves almost immediately through the oval wreath and the door.

Chapter 2: The Lobsters and the Moon

THE Fool had gone far into the distance but was still visible as a tiny silver figure receding rapidly from them. There was an echo of laughter all about them, and they found themselves drifting in what seemed to be a dark blue infinity of space in which there were millions of shining stars.

"Gosh, do you think we are in outer space?" said Richard. "But then we can't be, or we wouldn't be able to breathe. Not without space suits and things. Perhaps this is some kind of inner space."

"I think we'd better try and catch him up," said Rebecca. "Before he goes out of sight."

"But he's going like billy-o," exclaimed Richard. "Look, he's so far ahead of us he's dwindled to a point of light – in fact you can hardly tell him from any of the stars."

And this was so. For if for a few moments the receding figure did at least seem brighter than the background of stars and constellations, it soon became indistinguishable from the whole host of the heavens.

"He could be any of them now," said Richard.

"Should we try and go back to the attic?" asked Rebecca. "There must be some way to tell us where to go. He seemed such a nice Fool, he wouldn't just go away and leave us."

"Well it certainly looks as if he has," said Richard.

"What's that funny noise?" asked Rebecca.

"What noise...?" began Richard, and then he heard it too. It was a regular puffing noise, a bit like a steam engine. Then both children found themselves being scrabbled and licked by a jumping galumphing bundle of excited fur.

"Oh how lovely," cried Rebecca, "he's left his dog!"

And for a few minutes they careered around rolling over and over in space in the starlight, because just like the pictures of men in space they had no weight, it seemed, and were in complete freedom to go up, down, forwards, backwards, sideways, to roll over and over, or do cart wheels, with the minimum of effort. They seemed also to generate their own light. For although there was a clear light given by the heavens, they themselves were surrounded by an aura of silvery light that lit up the space immediately around them.

"Good dog! Good dog!" they cried, until eventually they finished romping and chasing around in circles, and sat cross legged in the empty air, a position they found very comfortable because having no weight it did not make their legs ache. In fact Richard found that he could sit cross legged upside down just as easily, but decided it was best not to do so too much, because there was a danger, being in free space, of losing all sense of what was up or down, and then they would be well and truly lost.

"What shall we do now?" sighed Rebecca.

"Where do you want to go?" asked the dog.

"Who said that?" the children cried.

"I did, of course," said the dog.

"Do you mean to say that you can talk?" gasped Richard.

"Of course, why not?" said the dog. "Just because all beasts are dumb in your little corner of the universe, doesn't mean to say that all the rest of the worlds are in your sorry condition. And maybe you'd all be a lot better off if animals *could* talk to you and tell you a bit more plainly what you are doing wrong."

"Oh yes, perhaps people wouldn't be so cruel to animals, if they could speak," said Rebecca.

"Maybe not," said the dog, "but people are sometimes cruel to children, and to other people, so it doesn't seem to make much difference whether they can speak."

"You can sometimes get into more trouble because you *can* speak," said Richard. "Our headmaster at school calls it impertinence."

"Anyway, now that you know I *can* speak," said the dog, "what would you like to know?"

"What's your name?" asked Rebecca.

"I thought you would never ask," said the dog. "Names are very important. You can tell a lot about someone if you know their real name. But I believe where you come from people don't often have their real names – which is perhaps just as well, because if someone knows your real name they can use it to gain power over you."

"How horrible," said Rebecca. "Do you mind telling us your name then?"

"Oh I don't mind," said the dog, "I know you are not wicked. Perhaps a bit naughty sometimes, but my master would not have brought you here if you were not to be trusted. Actually we have different names for use in different times and places, but underneath, everyone has their *one true name* and that's the Essence of our Goodness."

"What should we call you?" asked Richard.

"You can call me Canis," said the dog, wagging his tail. "And that's because I'm canny. I know lots of things and the word 'cunning' comes from that. And that word originally meant 'wise', but some humans in your world have made it mean something underhand. And also because I *can* do lots of things, such as guide people to where they want to go, and keep out those who have no business to go into private special places. So I also let people know whether they *can* go somewhere or not, either by leading them or driving them away. That will do for the moment. Only my master knows my full and secret name."

"Your Essence of Goodness," said Rebecca.

The dog nodded gravely.

"What are *our* full and secret names?" asked Rebecca.

"Do you really want to know?" asked the dog.

"Oh yes!" the children cried.

"I thought that was why my master might have left you here," said Canis, "because it is a difficult journey to find that out. You have to do it on your own, but you need a canny creature to guide you – someone who knows the ways."

"Do you know the ways?" asked Rebecca.

"I can open them all to you," said Canis, "but you will have to tread them."

"It sounds exciting," said Richard. "When can we start?"

"As soon as you like," said Canis. "Are you ready?"

"Yes," nodded the children in excitement; and the dog suddenly raised his snout high into the air and let forth a great long doggy howl, like some dogs sometimes do.

"Ow............ow.............oo.............oo......oooooooooooo!"

The children felt their skin rise up in goose pimples, so eerie was the sound. And their hair fairly stood up on end when, from nowhere it seemed, there came an answering howl.

"Ow............ow.............oo.............oo......oooooooooooo!"

And then there was a gradually growing pale radiance coming from behind and above them, like somebody turning the lights up slowly in a theatre, and there was a sound of deep and slow movement of great waters, like when you put your ear to a large shell and it sounds as if you can hear the sea breaking. And turning, they saw that the light came from a great disk of pale yellow silvery white that hung in the sky and which they had not seen before – in fact it could not have been there. And they themselves were standing, not in empty space any more, but on a sandy, pebbly strand, with their feet barely beyond the water line, for now there was to one side of them, as far as the eye could see, a great calm, heaving, grey-green ocean; and on the other side, under the moon, a pathway leading to distant hills, that first led between two ancient, high and massive, crumbling stone towers.

Before the towers, on one side of the path stood their friend Canis, baying at the moon, and on the other side, a sight to make your blood run cold if you had met it on your own, a lean grey wolf, with slit eyes and slavering mouth of fierce fangs, that also bayed at the moon.

"Oh dear, I don't think I like this very much," said Rebecca, her lip beginning to quiver.

"Are they going to fight, do you think?" said Richard, looking toward the dog Canis and the grey wolf baying on either side of the path. "Are we meant to go along that path I wonder?"

"I don't fancy walking between the two of them," said Rebecca. "That wolf looks very fierce. And even Canis, although he was very friendly before, seems as if he might have gone a bit wild."

"And I wonder who lives in those dark towers," said Richard. "Or even if there are wandering packs of wolves running in those hills. Wolves don't usually go alone. At least, I don't think so, though I have heard adventure stories about lone wolves."

"Adventure stories are different when you find you are actually in them," said Rebecca.

Their deliberations were interrupted however by a sound in the shingle at their feet. It was a slow scraping sound, like pebbles sliding against shells, although it was not caused by the slow swell of the sea, for it had a different, more rapid, purposive sound. They looked down and started back in surprise.

The shingle beneath their feet was heaving up as if some creature were burrowing beneath it, to get to the surface.

"I think it's a mole," said Rebecca. They had many of them in their garden at home and father said he was at his wits' end on how to get rid of them, for they dug up all the lawns and the flower

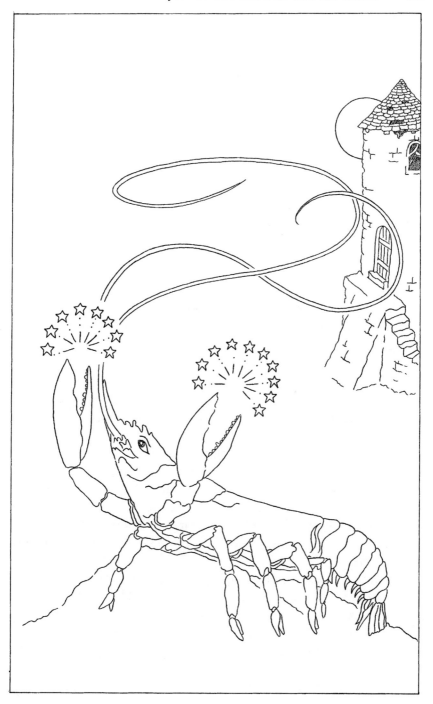

"An elixir is a liquid that has strange healing powers"

beds and left great piles of earth all over the place. Though Rebecca thought them rather jolly.

"You don't get moles so near the sea, silly!" said Richard.

"I'm not silly!" said Rebecca. "I should have thought it obvious that anything could happen here. Who heard of talking dogs?"

But Richard was soon proved right, for a hole appeared in the ground before them, and out of it came a large claw.

"Oh!" cried Rebecca, jumping back in fright, as it went "Snap, snap-snap!" in the air.

They stood and watched as the claw was followed by a scaly arm, or leg, and another large elongated claw, just like the first one. Then by a strange looking, fierce bewhiskered grey-green face, and finally, with much heaving and shoving, eight scaly legs and a long scaly body.

"It's a shell fish," said Richard in amazement. "A great big lobster!"

"I thought lobsters were bright red," said Rebecca.

"Shh!" said Richard. "Only in the shops – when they've been cooked."

"Yes, I expect *you* would look pretty bright pink if you'd been cooked," said the lobster, swivelling its eyes back and forth between the two of them.

"Oh, I'm terribly sorry Mr Lobster," said Rebecca, "I didn't mean to give offence."

"No, I don't suppose you thought," said the lobster, "about other creatures' feelings. People never do. It's lucky for me I've a thick skin," and he rattled his scaly armoured tail swiftly from side to side. "And," he continued, "that we've met in my world and not yours. I've no wish to be cooked and eaten by ignorant humanoids."

"We're not ignorant!" said Richard. "We came from a highly civilised country."

"That's a matter of opinion," said the lobster. "But I bet I know more about your world than you do of mine. That's why I'm here and not there."

"It doesn't look very nice here," said Rebecca. "It looks very dangerous and spooky."

"That's what shows your ignorance," said the lobster. "When there's howling between dog and wolf it's a time of great opportunity. Think yourselves lucky to be here."

"Why, what happens?" asked Richard.

"Observe and follow," said the lobster, in a superior manner. "That is the beginning of wisdom." And he reared himself up on his tail, on the path before him, and snapped his claws together, in a strange, irregular but rhythmic way.

"It sounds as if he is playing castanets," giggled Rebecca, who often got a bit giggly when she was frightened.

"I am signalling to my fellow crustaceans," said the lobster, "that all is well and that they can follow. Despite the presence of biped intruders."

"What does he mean – 'biped'?" asked Rebecca, "and who are the intruders?" She looked round nervously.

"He means us," said Richard. "Biped means 'two legs', like we've got."

"I'd rather have two than eight," sniffed Rebecca.

"I shouldn't say that too loudly," muttered Richard, as all about them, along the shore, more piles of sand began appearing, followed by pairs of claws and then more lobsters. And even in the sea, lobster heads and claws were appearing over the waves and snapping in the air, taking up the rhythm of their leader.

"You don't think they are going to dance do you?" said Rebecca, who had read about a lobster quadrille in 'Alice in Wonderland'.

"We came to collect the moon dew," cried the lobster who had first appeared to them. "It is a great elixir."

"What is an elixir?" whispered Rebecca to Richard.

"An elixir," said the lobster, who had very sharp hearing, "is a healing liquid that has strange and wonderful powers. In the world you come from, men in olden time spent their lives searching for the secret of making it, though I believe that now it is a forgotten art. Here, in this superior world, we can collect it, at the right time and place, from nature. If you are bright enough to know what is good for you, and few humans are, you will join us in collecting the falling magical dew."

And as he spoke all the lobsters advanced from the beach onto the path and the surrounding grass and formed up in lines and curves and circles in odd geometric patterns, snapping their claws in time and shaking their scaly armour to give a rhythmic rattle to their swaying dancing as they gyrated up and down in their dance all around the baying dog and wolf, and all about the two towers.

"Oh look at the moon," said Rebecca in a hushed voice.

They had not looked up at it in all the time they had been talking to the lobster and watching the strange sight of the lobsters dancing.

It remained hanging there, huge in the sky, much bigger than any moon seen on Earth, but it began, like the ordinary moon seen from the Earth sometimes does, to grow a halo round itself – like a great disk of silver mist all about it. And then its own shining silvery light shone onto and into the mist, so that there appeared beautiful delicate rainbow colours all around it. And behind the veil of mist it appeared almost as if there was a face on the great disk of the moon; a broad, gravely smiling, almost loving face. And then, from the configuration of circles of silvery rainbow lights around the moon and the straight rays of similar rainbow colours spreading star-like from it, where the lines and rings intersected there appeared silver-golden drops in the sky, which became bigger and bigger, and then, like drops of water on a twig or leaf in rainy weather, or like a melting icicle, gradually became too heavy for themselves and dropped to the ground beneath. Whereupon the lobsters broke the formation of their dance with outstretched front claws and sought to catch the great dewy drops as they fell.

"Come along, come along! Catch your own!" cried the lobster to them, whom they had spoken with before. "You will need it to catch your Essence of Goodness. Otherwise you will have to go back to your own world empty handed. Such a chance as this only happens once every ten thousand years."

"Oh dear," cried Rebecca, "we haven't claws like them. We've nothing to catch them in. Haven't you got a tin or something in your pocket, Richard?"

Richard started to try to search through his pockets but then realised he wasn't wearing his ordinary clothes. When they had changed to their imagination bodies they had changed to a fairy tale kind of clothes. He was dressed in tight fitting doublet and hose like a fairytale prince, and Rebecca was in a flouncy kind of party dress.

"Use your wand! Use your talisman!" cried the lobster, rushing backwards and forwards catching more of the falling drops in his uplifted claws.

"Oh what does he mean?" cried Rebecca, "They're not much good at catching things – are they?"

But she held out her golden disc, that was on a long chain round

There appeared great silver-golden drops in the sky

her neck, before her, and sighting a large and beautiful drop of the precious moon liquid falling towards her, it seemed from an enormous height, she caught it. Of course in normal circumstances one would have expected a great splash and for the drop to have bounced off. But with Rebecca's disk this did not happen. There was a high pitched "ping", like a little silver bell, and when Rebecca looked at her golden disk she saw that it was not plain any longer, but that the impact of the moon-drop had made a pattern upon the gold, as if it was inset with hundreds, even thousands, of little diamonds and rubies – and in a most beautiful complex six-fold pattern – just like a magnified picture of a snow-flake seen on Earth.

She showed it in amazement to Richard, who, turning with a sudden inspiration, held his wand up high above his head. A silver golden moon-drop fell towards him. He pointed his wand towards it. There was another silvery "ping" as he caught the dew on the end of his wand, and instead of shattering and splashing all over the place, he found, to his amazement, that at the end of the wand there now sprouted a most wonderful perfectly formed red rose that shone and sparkled like crystal fire.

As they stood there in amazement looking at these beautiful objects that the moon dew had formed, the lobsters had also filled their claws with gold and silver liquid light and were streaming in an excited long chattering column along the pathway between the two towers toward the distant purple hills. The silver liquid in their upheld claws seemed like flaming torches in the distance and their whole concourse like a great triumphal procession.

"Do you think we should follow them?" said Richard.

"What is our friend Canis doing?" asked Rebecca.

But when they looked, the wolf that had been with Canis was racing off, his fur blazing like silver frost, to race to the head of the procession, but Canis was standing up on his hind legs looking expectantly up at the moon, which no longer dropped dew as the mist about its face cleared. Now that they could see the face more clearly it had a strangely familiar look.

"I've got a feeling I've seen that moon's face before," said Richard.

"Yes," said Rebecca. "Isn't it rather like ... the Fool's?"

And as she said so, it smiled again and gave a slow wink.

"Oh it is, it is!" cried Rebecca, jumping up and down excitedly.

Canis was also jumping up and down, like a great bouncing furry ball and as he did so, the last remaining clouds of the moon mist formed into a bright straight moonbeam, and Canis leaped upon it, as if it were a solid path, and raced away along it up towards the moon's disc.

As he did so the face on the moon slowly faded away but in its place there remained a shape left on its surface that had the rough appearance of a man walking with a bundle on his shoulder and followed by a dog.

"What shall we do?" cried Rebecca. "We're going to be left alone."

Indeed they were. The last of the lobster procession had departed and they now stood alone on a desolate looking moor before the two dark crumbling towers.

Chapter 3: The Transforming Angel

"I'VE got a feeling," said Richard, "that we should follow." And as there seemed nothing better to do, they started along the path after the procession of lobsters, whose few lights were twinkling along the path and over the moors and hills.

But before them between the two towers there remained, slanting down to the path, a ray of moonlight.

"Have we got to go through that?" said Rebecca. "It looks spooky and spider webby."

As she spoke they heard echoing around the countryside three great blasts as from some mighty hunting horn.

"It's either that or be left behind near those horrible towers," said Richard, and holding her hand, rushed forward.

As they entered into the slanting column of moonlight however, everything suddenly changed. There was a great ringing trumpet call, and the moonbeam turned into a golden upward path at the top of which was, not the moon disk, but a great winged angel, in red and gold and silver, whose wings spanned the heavens. It was she who was blowing the horn. Three more great blasts she blew, and then smiling, looked down towards them and beckoned.

Needing no second bidding the children raced up the golden hill, which was like a bridge, for it had a parapet each side over which they could see. And they did pause to look, for far below them they could hear the sounds of great cheering. And there, far into the distance, they could see the whole torchlight procession of lobsters, who were looking up and waving and cheering. But now the procession seemed to have grown in size and diversity for it was not just comprised of lobsters. It contained every creature you could imagine – bears, horses, dogs, cats, lions, lambs, giraffes, monkeys, all proceeding in a long column toward the distant hills. Whilst immediately below them, light was coming from the previously dark towers. Soon they were transformed into great bright structures as perhaps once they had been when they were first built. Light shone from their windows, and on their battlements crowds of richly dressed men and women waved excitedly up towards them, whilst others scattered from the towers, dancing and singing with joy, making their way to the end of the golden pathway bridge –

following in the footsteps of the children.

Full of exhilaration the children looked back up toward the smiling angel, who stood resting on her long trumpet, from which there hung a long unfurling banner upon which they saw a combination of their own moon jewels. It had a beautiful complex snowflake pattern in gold, and in the centre a red rose.

"Come on!" they cried, and raced on excitedly up the hill, to the sound of excitement, music and revelry below, as the crowds from the towers followed far behind them.

When they arrived at the top of the long golden staircase, for that is what the bridge in fact became, they cautiously approached the angel with the trumpet, because she was of great size, and there was all about her a great blaze of light that also, as you approached it, had sound within it as well, so that as you stepped into the radiance around her you heard great choirs singing beautiful melodies, and orchestras and organs playing, and harps, and there were other winged beings floating around and about the angel. But so great was her radiance it was difficult to see what they were, whether birds, or other angels, or little cherubs or little heads with wings like you may have seen on old fashioned maps showing the winds.

They were encouraged to approach the angel however by the sight of Canis who was cavorting excitedly before the angel's feet, in and out of her flowing draperies, and around the stem of the golden trumpet and the furls of the banner which fell about it to the ground.

"Come along," barked Canis. "She won't hurt you."

The children approached and found they came barely to the knee of the angel, who stretched forth above their heads like a mountain.

"Who is she?" shouted Richard, and he had to shout because of the background of music that surrounded the angel when they stood close to him.

"She is the great transforming angel," said Canis.

"What does that mean?" asked Rebecca.

"She changes things," replied the dog.

"What things?" asked Richard.

"All things," said Canis. "People and creatures."

"What does she do that for?" added Richard.

"To help them grow."

"Will she change us?" asked Rebecca nervously.

At the top of the path was a great winged angel

"She's been doing so all your life," replied Canis, "otherwise you'd still be a little baby. She's changed you a lot since you got out of your pram."

"But I've never seen her."

"You don't have to. She works from the inside."

"From inside what?" asked Richard.

"From inside the world. From inside you. From where we are now."

"Oooh!" cried Rebecca, somewhat in alarm, "are we inside out at the moment?"

"In a manner of speaking," replied Canis, "although more strictly speaking you are outside in. Outside is Myrtle Cottage where you live, and Tewkesbury where you go to school, and some people think that that is all there is, but as you can see, there is a lot that goes on, on the inside."

"Whoever would have thought it?" cried Richard.

"It should be obvious I would think," replied the dog. "Where else would the outside come from it there wasn't an inside? It's like people thinking the world is flat instead of round. What do you think makes things grow? The seed starts to sprout, to change into a plant, and then grow into a tree, any kind of tree, with its own kind of leaves and fruit. Think of the big apple tree at the bottom of your garden. All of that came out of a little pip inside an apple core. And every little pip has a great tree inside it – with other pips and trees inside them. And the same applies to all seeds, including eggs and things. Just think when you hold a handful of packets of seeds when you are at the seedsman's what a huge garden you hold in your hand. There's not room for that in the packets is there? Or in those tiny little seeds. It's all here, on the inside, where there's plenty of room, where all the patterns are held of all the different things that grow, and also the strength and power that makes them grow."

"But things die too," said Richard.

"Yes, my pet hamster died not long ago," said Rebecca, "and it was horrible."

"That's because you live in such a small place," said the dog. "There wouldn't be room if everything kept growing and a-blowing. It's very crowded on the outside. So after things have had a chance to look around and grow a bit they come back on the inside where there's plenty of room."

"Is my hamster here then?" asked Rebecca.

"I expect so," said Canis, "unless it's gone onto the outside again. These little creatures hop back and forth so quickly it's difficult to know where they are most at *home*."

"Can we see her please?" asked Rebecca.

"Are you sure you want to?" asked the dog. "It might make you all sad and weepy again. It's bad enough to be parted once, and you've got over all that. Making the little grave for her at the bottom of the garden helped you do that didn't it? Now if you meet her again it will only be as bad when you have to leave her once more."

"I just want to see if she's all right," said Rebecca.

"All right," said the dog. "My master said I was to show you what you asked for. But I don't think we shall find her here."

"Shall we have to go back down to the moonlit moor?" asked Richard. "There were lots of little animals going along the pathway, on towards the misty mountains."

"No, you can see them over the parapet," said Canis, "those animals have not yet become individuals."

"What does that mean?" asked Rebecca.

"Nobody has given them a name," replied the dog. "That is why you have pets at home. It is so that you can love them and help them to grow into something more than dumb animals, by giving them a name."

"But what about all the animals that don't become pets and don't have a name?"

"They grow in different ways," said Canis. "Look over the parapet and you will see."

They walked over to a golden balustrade that was just beside the angel and looked down.

They found they were at a great height. Such that the ground was so far below them that it was spread out like a map. And they could see the long road leading from the sea toward the distant mountains, with all the creatures with their lights moving along it.

And looking toward the mountains they saw what at first seemed to be a great city. But on closer inspection it was seen to be a number of great towers similar to the ones they had seen at the beginning of the path. These however were newly constructed and in pairs at distances along the roadway. And they saw that they were inhabited, or being built by, not humans but animals. And that around them animals were tilling the fields and going about their business, holding markets and even driving in little machines like motor cars. In fact it was just like looking down on the ordinary world they had come from except that instead of human beings there were animals moving around.

"What are they doing?" asked Richard.

"What does it look like?" asked Canis. "Building worlds like you have come from. Each of those towers will have a round ball in space called a planet, upon the outside of things. Millions and millions of miles away from your own world of course, and with a different sun. And there they will build a civilisation."

"Just like our world?" gasped Rebecca.

"Oh yes. And they'll as likely make a better job of it," replied the dog. "There's a lot that's poorly done in your world. The way you treat animals, to start with – but I won't go on – it wouldn't be polite."

"And what happens to them in the end?" asked Richard.

They hear the trumpet call of the Transforming Angel when their planet has lived out its useful life, and they all come up here, like this lot, " said Canis, as the first rank of people from the towers immediately below reached the top of the staircase.

As they drew close the children were startled, for although they had looked like ordinary human beings like themselves from a distance, closer to them it was plain to see that they were far, far different. They were much taller to begin with, and thinner, and their faces were a pale bright yellow colour, they had pointed ears, blue hair that stuck up straight into a point behind, and their eyes were green.

"Where do they come from?" asked Richard.

"I don't think you would know their world," replied Canis. "I am not sure that its star would be visible to you, even with a good quality telescope. It is to be found more or less in the direction of the constellation you call Centaurus."

"I don't much like the look of them," said Rebecca.

"I expect they think you look a little odd too," said Canis, "dumpy and round headed and with funny coloured eyes, hair and skin."

"I haven't!" cried Rebecca.

"It all depends on what you are used to," said Canis.

"I'd rather see my hamster," said Rebecca.

"Very well, come along then," said Canis, "we'll see what we can do. And we don't really want to get mixed up with this great crowd. We might find ourselves caught up in the rush colonising another planet somewhere, if that's what they've a mind to do. Maybe in a different space and time, and then we'd have a dickens of a job getting you back to your own world. Quick, do as I tell you. Close your eyes."

Chapter 4: The Sunflower Garden

THE children closed their eyes as they had been told. "Now think of the sun," said Canis. "A great big golden sun in front of you. Feel its warmth on your hands and face. Are you seeing it? Can you feel it? Then open your eyes."

The children opened their eyes and then blinked them very rapidly, for the great angel and the milling throng had gone, but hanging in a clear blue sky before them was a great golden sun. And it had a face on it just like the Moon that they had seen earlier – big, broad and smiling, and with a distinct resemblance to the Fool, but with the rippling flames and heat haze that passed over its surface continually, so that it was difficult to make out its exact features.

Before them was a sward of bright sparkling green turf, with a garden wall, over the top of which tall sunflowers were nodding. And in a circle on the grass before them lots of little animals were gambolling and playing – mice, gerbils, hamsters, guinea pigs, rabbits.

"Oh how lovely!" cried Rebecca, "Where is this?"

"This is the pets' garden," replied Canis. "Or a part of it. In other parts you would find cats, dogs, ponies, even quite odd animals, from stick insects to sheep. Its surprising what some people have as pets.

"Is Pinky my hamster here?" asked Rebecca.

"You'd better look," said Canis. "Or call her."

"Hamsters can't answer to their names," said Richard scornfully.

"Up here they can," said Canis. "You try it."

Rather doubtfully, Rebecca began to call "Pinky, Pinky, Pinky…" and sure enough, from out of the ruck of tumbling animals a little hamster leaped forth, hesitated, wobbling its nose, and threw itself into Rebecca's waiting arms.

"Oh it is! It is! It's Pinky!" cried Rebecca, beside herself with surprise and joy.

"Hello Rebecca," said Pinky, in a little squeaky voice, "fancy meeting you again."

"You can talk?" cried Rebecca.

"Of course I can," said the hamster. "I always could, but you could never understand me."

"Oh I didn't know," said Rebecca ruefully.

"Never mind, never mind," cried the hamster gaily. "You can't help natural ignorance. Though sometimes I wished you could understand me so that I could give you a good telling off when you forgot to change my sawdust."

"Oh I never did ... very much ... did I?" said Rebecca.

"The less said about that the better, perhaps," said the hamster. "I suppose you weren't too bad for a human child. They are generally a very forgetful species."

"Oh I'm sorry if I ever neglected you sometimes," cried Rebecca.

"Never mind. Least said, soonest mended," said the hamster. "It doesn't matter very much now. Up here we do not need to be fed, watered or to have changes of sawdust. There aren't any cages for a start."

"Did you mind your cage?" asked Rebecca.

"Oh no, it wasn't too bad," replied Pinky. "Reasonably roomy, as cages go. And the big wheel stopped things getting too boring. Gave us something to do at night. That is when it didn't get jammed up with that nesting material you sometimes put in – and didn't change any too often either," she added darkly.

"I thought you liked it old and smelly," said Rebecca.

"Yes, it's nice for it to have a 'lived in' feeling," said the hamster, "though there are limits. However I did not mean to spend all the time complaining, and I hope you do not take offence, but up here is a funny place, it's all very pleasant but it's a place where the truth will out. Animals don't mind that too much but it seems to be a bit hard on humans."

"Are there human children up here with you?" asked Rebecca.

"Oh yes, we go and play with them sometimes," said Pinky. "They live in another part of the garden. Haven't you met them? I expect you will be joining them soon. How did you get here by the way? By illness or accident?"

"I don't know what you mean," said Rebecca.

"Well, here is the place where all children come who leave the outside world so they can finish growing up."

"She hasn't come to stay," chipped in Canis. "They are only visiting."

"That's very rare, isn't it?" said Pinky.

"Yes, apart from dreams," said Canis, "I suppose it is."

"Hello Rebecca," said Pinky. "Fancy meeting you again"

"Oh you can always tell dreaming worldlings," said the hamster, "because they look vapoury, like ghosts, and also as if they are asleep."

"That's not surprising I suppose, because that's what they are in their own world," said Canis, "and very often they don't remember they are dreaming. Or only confused bits. But these two are special visitors, they are having a *waking* dream, and they will remember all of it."

"Good," said Pinky. "Will you remember that I am all right and having a good time – and also I hope that you will clean out your next hamster more regularly."

"Can't you come back with me?" asked Rebecca.

"Oh no, that's not so easy," said Pinky. "You just have to stop your waking dream to return, but I haven't got an outside body yet. I may come back when I feel like getting a bit more experience on the outer side of things, but life is very pleasant here and I'm not bored yet. By the time I come back you might be grown up even, and then who knows where I'll be born? Perhaps I might be owned by one of your daughters. It's a very chancy business getting born again. Quite easy to do – but you are never sure when or where you

are going to find yourself. But we can always meet up here from time to time as long as we cherish each other's memory."

"Oh I'll always remember you and love you," cried Rebecca.

"And I shall love you too," said Pinky, "but I think, from the look in your dog friend's eye, that you had better be moving along. People don't come here on special trips for nothing you know. They do not lay on sight-seeing tours. This is not like a zoo. If you have been allowed here I've no doubt there's a special job for you to do."

And so saying, she hopped out of Rebecca's lap and re-joined the romping and rousting about of all the little animals on the centre of the lawn.

"Is it true, what she said?" asked Richard.

"Yes, I was coming to that," replied Canis, "but we were diverted by the search for the hamster, and I thought we had better get that out of the way first, so you could concentrate your minds on what is to come."

"And what exactly is to come?" asked Richard, who did not entirely like the sound of that.

"Don't ask me," said Canis. "I only open and guard the ways. I don't say why you should tread them. You've been summoned by my master, that's all I know."

"Where do we go to find out?" asked Richard.

"That will be the Star Maiden," said Canis.

"Oh, she sounds lovely," said Rebecca.

"Yes, but sometimes a bit remote in her manner," replied Canis, "though I suppose that is to be expected as she has her mind not just on this world, but stretched out through time and space, into umpteen other worlds, planets, stars and constellations too. Come on. We shall see her where land and water meet."

"That's where we first saw the Moon isn't it?" asked Richard.

"Right," replied Canis, "but don't go back down the stairs, because this lady works on a higher level. So we take a sighting on where land and water meet by..." and he looked down intently at the ground on which they stood, and as they looked they saw it become transparent, so that they could see the land and the shoreline and the sea far beneath them.

"We need to move just a bit," said Canis. "Come on, follow me!" And he started running towards where the sea met the shoreline far below.

Chapter 5: The Star Maiden

THE children ran after him, until suddenly he pulled up. Then, raising their eyes from looking through the ground beneath them, they found they had halted on the shore of a calm clear lake on their own level, with rushes and water plants at its margin.

They stood on the grassy bank and looked out over the water.

"Where is the star lady?" asked Rebecca.

"Look into the water," said Canis.

The children did so, and to their surprise they saw stars forming in and upon the still water. It was just as if the night sky were being reflected in the water of the lake, but above them the sky was the bright blue of the day.

And then they began to notice that the stars seemed to form a pattern. It was like one of those star maps you sometimes see, with lines drawn on to represent the shape of the different constellations. Only whilst on those kind of star maps the drawings often do not seem to relate very closely to the actual pattern of the stars, in this case there were no lines drawn, but the actual pattern of the stars in the water very clearly showed the outline of a maiden kneeling. And she was holding two vases of water which she poured out, one into the waters of the lake itself, and the other, because the figure was so close to the shoreline, looked as if it were pouring water onto the land by the lake side.

Also reflected in the water, it seemed, despite the clear blue sky above, was a ring of bright stars all around the maiden's head. Rebecca counted seven of them, and also a very big shining star that was immediately over her head, bigger and brighter than any star they had ever seen.

There were parts of a landscape to be seen behind her, outlined in the stars, of low rolling hills. And especially noticeable was a tree with clusters of star blossoms and leaves and fruit all at once, and star birds within it too, and shining butterflies, outlined in the different silvery blue, green, red, purple and yellow colours of starlight when you really look at it carefully.

"Oh what a lovely country there is laid out in the lake," sighed Rebecca. "Can we go in there?"

"Is it under the water or in the skies over the water?" asked

A tree with clusters of star blossoms

Richard. "And why can't we see it in the sky above?"

"It is neither under nor over the water," said a deep fluty voice behind them, and turning with a start, they saw a large white swan standing on the bank behind them regarding them with a hard round eye.

Rebecca edged back a bit because it was a very large swan and she had heard that swans can be very dangerous if you upset them, pecking with their strong bills and beating with their great wings. But the gaze of the swan seemed friendly and it walked past them and with a light splash slid onto the waters of the lake. The outgoing circle of ripples from it caused the pattern of stars in the water to bob up and down for a little, but as the waters stilled there were the star images in the lake, plainly to be seen, of the tree and birds and butterflies and the maiden pouring water from her vases.

"Neither under nor over the water," repeated the swan, sitting comfortably in the water before them, at the feet of the image of the star maiden, "but *on* the water. That's where reflections are."

"But I cannot see the real stars that the reflections ought to be coming from," said Richard. "Why can't we see them?"

"Because you do not have eyes that are able to do so," said the swan. "If you could see properly you would see them but your eyes are blinded by the sun. And that is quite a good thing, is it not?" she continued, "because you learn better by seeing less. There is less to confuse the simple mind."

"I don't think we've got simple minds," said Richard hotly. "Anyway, we could see all those stars at night anyway, when the sun goes down."

"Here, my simple minded one," said the swan, "the sun never goes down any more than it does in your own outside world. You forget you live on a spinning ball that makes it *look* as if the sun goes up and down and round the sky. It does not do so really. Besides which," she continued, "have you ever seen *these* stars in the sky?"

Richard looked discomforted. "Well no," he said. "I suppose we do have different constellations at home. Why are the stars different here?"

"Why do you think they are different, my little simpleton?" asked the swan. "They may well be the same stars you are used to seeing at night, from your bedroom window at home, but seen from a different place, they make a different pattern in the sky. So you see my dears, you find yourselves seeming to be in a different universe according to where you are standing. Thus where you stand, and what you see, is very important – and do not let anyone tell you differently. We are all of us in the centre of our own particular universe."

"That sounds stupid," said Richard, who was beginning to get impatient with the names the swan was calling him. "They are the same stars that we all see, from *wherever* we are standing."

"I did not say we did not *share* things," said the swan. "But we each have our very own point of view, which no one else has in the whole wide worlds. So guard it my dears. There are many who, blinder even than yourselves, but with the confidence of even greater ignorance, will tell you that your own point of view does not matter, because it is simply one of many."

"I say, I wish you'd stop calling us ignorant and blind and stupid and things," said Richard. "It isn't very polite you know."

"It was you who used the word 'stupid'," replied the swan, "and that would have been impolite, but I only said you were simple and ignorant. There is nothing wrong with being simple or ignorant. It can always be remedied by seeking more experience and knowledge."

"We get told off for being ignorant of something at school," said Rebecca.

"What an odd school, if that is so," said the swan. "If the pupils were not ignorant the school would have no reason to exist. However, I trust that you have been brought to the starry lake to learn. Then you may go from here no longer being ignorant."

"How do we learn from the lake?" asked Rebecca. "Do you give all the lessons?"

"Oh no, you learn by exploring," said the swan. "It takes rather longer than listening to me, or reading from a book, but the lessons you learn you will always remember. You have to go among the stars."

"But how do we do that?" asked Richard.

"Where did I say the stars were?" asked the swan.

"Er, um..." stammered Richard.

"You see you have forgotten what I told you already," said the swan, "but never mind, you have only to use your eyes."

"Up in the sky?" said Richard, but he knew as he said it that this was not the right answer.

"Can you see any stars in the sky?" the swan asked coldly, cocking its eye heavenwards.

"On the water?" asked Rebecca.

"Of course!" said the swan. "There they are laid before you like a liquid magic carpet. You have only to use the eyes God gave you."

"Can we walk across it like a magic carpet?" asked Rebecca. "To see the stars in the centre?"

"Do you think you can walk on the water?" asked the swan.

"No, I don't think so," faltered Rebecca.

"Well, if you don't believe you can, I do not expect you will be able to," said the swan. "I know you are used to odd conditions in your world and so you think you are more limited than you really are, but if your faith is crippled then so will you be too. Wouldn't you like to try?"

Richard shook his head. He did not want to risk being made to look foolish. Rebecca hesitantly stepped forward and onto the surface of the lake. She teetered a couple of steps and then turned and staggered out with a splash.

"That was funny," she cried. "Just for a moment I really did think I was walking on the water."

"But not for very long," said the swan. "A pity, you have become so accustomed to the local laws in your own little part of the universe that you think they are universal. Anyone can walk on water here, once they get used to it and make up their minds that they can. But I forget, you are only visitors and have not had long to get used to real life. But never mind, there are other ways and means. Wait here a little."

And so saying, the swan turned, and instead of swimming away, plunged down into the water. As they watched they saw her, now an outline of stars within the picture, receding into the distance toward the centre of the lake.

"I don't know," said Richard. "Is it under the water, or on the water, or over the water?"

"It doesn't matter very much really," chipped in Canis, who had been quietly sitting behind them all this time. "As long as you believe in what you see, the way it comes to you is not important. The important thing is what you do about it."

"I think that star, the big one in the lake, is getting bigger," said Rebecca.

"It can't be," said Richard, but they watched it.

Slowly the great star that was above the maiden's head began to grow in size and brightness, and to such an extent that the other stars in the water became quite pale by comparison. Then, as the big star became like a glowing ball just beneath the surface of the waters, they became aware of nothing else as it moved towards them, until, with a splash, it rose out of the water, and they saw, bobbing on the ripples it had made on the surface of the lake, that it had become a little boat.

It was white in colour and shaped in the form of a swan. Its prow was built up high like a swan's neck and it had a beautifully sculpted swan's head at its top. The rest of the boat curved round like a swan's body but with the normal shape of the wings removed, to reveal the bottom of the boat beneath a planked seat. It swept round to a stern that was similar in shape to the tail feathers of a swan, and at the back of the boat there was perched a tall figure in blue and silver draperies, and with wings.

Chapter 6: The Swan Boat

"COME along then. Get into the boat." To their surprise it was the swan's head figurehead of the boat that spoke. "Haven't you seen an angel before?"

"Not close up to," said Richard, remembering the huge one they had met at the top of the golden stairs. "I thought they were bigger."

"They take on whatever size they wish according to the job in hand," replied the swan's head. "For big jobs like announcing the ending of a world they will naturally take on a gigantic size to impress the unbelieving, but for messages and favours to individuals they will obviously take on less grand proportions. Of course, if need be they can become so small that a thousand of them could dance on the point of a needle."

The boat was close up against the bank, and hustled by Canis, who behaved rather like a sheepdog, pushing at the back of their legs and preventing them from going anywhere else, they stepped into the boat. It was just the right size to take the two of them sitting side by side, looking back towards the angel, with Canis at their feet.

The angel had a nice friendly, warm feel now that they were so close up to it. It smiled at them serenely and they saw that it was holding two cups, just as had the image of the star maiden in the lake.

Smiling knowingly, and with great satisfaction when it saw that the children had noticed this, the angel raised one cup on high and suddenly tipped it so that the contents poured out. The children gasped. It was like a great firework display. From the cup there fell a stream of coloured lights and sparks and flaming shapes, some whirling like catherine wheels, some shooting off brilliant points of light like sparklers, some spouting forth golden rain, and in every shape and colour you could think of. The angel expertly caught the flow of fiery liquid shapes in the other cup and held it forth for them to look at. When they looked into the rim of the cup it was like looking out of a hole let into a huge expanse of sky. And there, as far as the eye could see, were slowly spinning balls of different sizes and colours, like so many marbles floating in space, and some of them orbiting round each other.

"Oh, how wonderful!" cried Rebecca.

"It's like the making of whole worlds and suns and planets," cried Richard.

"Yes," answered the swan's head, from behind them, "now what size do you think the angel is, or indeed that you are? Or those worlds are?"

"Either we are very big or they are very small," said Richard. "But they look to be as huge as whole worlds. In which case we must be enormous."

"Everything is relative when it comes to size," said the swan's head. "It largely depends on what you are used to. Remember that, next time you kick over an ant's nest at home. You might have destroyed something as great to its inhabitants as the Roman Empire or the Tower of Babylon."

But further conversation was ended by the breathtaking sight of the angel extending its brilliantly coloured wings, and after an expert manoeuvre to turn them round, they were propelled across the lake by the angel gently fanning its wings.

"Where are we going?" asked Rebecca.

"Look over the side," said Canis.

And when they did so they were struck by more wonders. For it no longer seemed that they were proceeding over the surface of a lake with reflections of stars in the waters. Now it appeared that the stars were real, and that they were proceeding through the bright indigo darkness (that is the only way to describe it, strange as it may sound) of space.

Whether or not they had descended under the surface of the water, or what else might have happened, they now found indeed that the stars were all about them, on every side and above them too, as well as below the boat.

"Do you study astronomy at your school?" asked the head of the swan.

"No," said Richard, "it isn't a main subject."

"What a very odd school," said the swan. "It is the most important subject there is. Next to music of course."

"Why music?" asked Richard. "Not many people do that either."

"Use your ears," said the swan's head cuttingly. "It is music that guides the stars in their courses. Understand music and you understand the stars."

They listened, and sure enough, there was coming from the stars

They were propelled across the lake by the angel fanning its wings above them a beautiful singing, like a great harmonious choir, that had all kinds of other sounds in it as well, as if from instruments not known, or yet to be invented, on Earth.

"Of course," continued the swan's head, "One can come to an appreciation of music and the stars by the study of number."

"Ugh!" said Richard. "We do maths all right. That's horrible."

"What a strange way they must teach you," remarked the swan's head, "to make the true and the good seem horrid. I can only suppose they confuse divine astronomy with mechanics, and heavenly music with noise."

"We just study what we are told to," said Richard.

"Until you are as blind and deaf to all that is real and good as those who teach you, I suppose," said the swan's head. "Well there will be no excuse for you after you have seen all this. It will be your task to put them right when you return."

"I don't think they will listen to us," said Richard.

"The greater misfortune for them, then," said the swan's head, "but one must not lose heart. There must be some hope for that strange world you inhabit, otherwise they would not have sent you."

"Nobody really sent us. We just wandered in," said Richard.

"Do not be so sure," said the swan's head. "Everything has a reason and a purpose. And those things which seem accidental are often those which are most planned."

"I suppose it was because of granny that we are here," said Rebecca.

"Ah, obviously a wise woman," said the swan's head.

"I don't think many people would think she was wise," said Richard.

"In a foolish world, that is not surprising," said the swan's head.

"She did not have much schooling."

"That, no doubt, is why she is so wise."

But now the conversation was interrupted by a magnificent sight that appeared on the horizon – if you can imagine the space between the stars having an horizon.

A great golden glow was appearing, and they turned in their seats to watch it. So great did the golden glow become that it began to blot out the stars and light up the airy waters about the boat so they seemed to be proceeding upon a mirror of golden glass. And then they realised that their craft had stopped.

They turned and saw that the angel had ceased to propel them and was smiling at them gently, and in that smile was a blessing and also, although no words were expressed, the clear intention that they alight from the boat.

"As you have noticed," said the swan's head, as they rose from their seats, "angels are telepathic. They can read your thoughts and put their own into your heads, and can do that so gently that you may quite easily think the thoughts are not theirs but your own."

They saw that the boat had beached upon the edge of golden yellow sands, which seemed to stretch for miles ahead as far as the eye could see. The whole scene was lit by bright golden light which seemed to have no source.

"Where is the light coming from?" asked Richard, "I can see no sun in the sky."

"You do not need a sun to give you light," said the swan. "Light was created before there was any sun or moon or even fire on Earth, let alone gas, matches or electric light bulbs."

"I don't see how it could have been," said Richard.

"Well if you do as you are instructed you may learn to see," replied the swan, "provided you do not remain blinded by your own opinions. Now listen carefully."

"You are coming to a dangerous part of your journey. This is a wide desert near the edge of the universe. And near the edge of the universe one finds all kinds of less desirable sorts of things. Those who cannot bear to live near the centre, where most of the angels dwell. That is why they choose to live in a desert wilderness, because they themselves inside are like wild and barren deserts. We always find outside us what is really within."

"You may be tempted to stray from the narrow path by which your friend the dog will lead you across the wilderness. And you must resist the blandishments of those who would try to lead you astray, or who may try to frighten or threaten you. Take no notice of alien powers. You have all the strength and protection you need if you remember to trust my words. And now farewell."

And as the two children stood with Canis, on the edge of the desert strand, looking at the swan boat, the angel reared up to a huge height and gazed down upon them, laughing with joy as it once again poured streams of coloured fire and light from one cup to another. Then it up-turned the lower cup so that it poured into the

Perched on the swan's back was the star maiden, shining like silver

swan boat. There was a sizzling sound and the boat reared up out of the water, in the form of a great swan, which beating its massive wings, soared above them, up and away, back over the way they had come. And they saw, perched upon its back, between the beating pinions, the figure of the Star Maiden, shining like silver. And as the swan and the maiden disappeared into the distance, to become no more than a tiny point of radiance like a bright silver star, the form of the angel slowly disappeared, dissolving before their eyes until nothing was to be seen. But then a thought came into their heads. "Because you cannot see a friend it does not mean you are alone."

Chapter 7: The Desert Reapers

"WHAT do we do now?" asked Richard, turning to Canis. "I don't think I like this journey any more," said Rebecca. "I want to go home."

"It is almost as bad to turn back now as it is to try and go forward," said Canis. "You might as well go through with it."

"But where are we going?"

"Like I told you in the beginning, to find your Own True Goodnesses."

"Can't we do without them?" said Rebecca.

"Lots of people try," said the dog, "and a fine mess it gets them into, and everyone else besides. Come along, it's no use arguing about it. Follow me." And the dog began padding along. It was rather like a footpath that had been hardly ever used, in a landscape that was all footpath in appearance, flat and hard packed. Richard followed behind him.

"I shan't!" shouted Rebecca, and stood her ground by the edge of the lake.

"Oh dear," said Canis, in a low voice to Richard, "this does not look so good. If she feels like this now, what kind of fuss is she going to make later?"

"She may not be so bad then," said Richard. "She often does this when we are about to go on a family outing, but when she gets there she quite enjoys herself."

"What is she like about going to the dentist?"

"The same," said Richard. "A terrible fuss about going and then, well fairly all right when she's there."

"Yes, plenty of common sense but too much imagination," said the dog. "Or perhaps I should say," he continued, "she uses her imagination in the wrong way. Because you can hardly have too much of a good thing."

"What shall we do?" asked Richard, as Rebecca sat down hard upon the ground with her back to them in the most ferocious of sulks.

"Get her to use her vivid imagination in the right way," the dog replied. He called to Rebecca. "Very well, stay if you like. But keep a sharp look out for ripples in the water; for the crocodiles come to feed around here before dusk. And watch out too for the sand spiders that burrow under the ground and come up and nip you where you are sitting. We will go on to the Tower of Delights. Do you want anything brought back for you? Sweets, ice cream, jellies? Though if we cannot get back to you before dark we will have to wait until dawn before we return, because of the desert bats that get caught in your hair. If you see any swooping toward you just pull your skirt over your head."

"Wait a minute, I'm coming!" shouted Rebecca, and raced to join them, and the three of them trudged on over the desert pathway, the dog leading the way and the children following. Richard with his wand and Rebecca with her jewelled disk.

"All these things you said," said Richard, a little later, as they trudged across the desert, "they weren't true were they?"

"No," said Canis. "Not exactly."

"You fibbed!" cried Rebecca, who overheard them. "You told me lies for nothing, just to yet your own way!"

"Not to get my own way," said Canis, "but to get you on your right way. There is a difference. And though I made it up about the crocodiles, bats and spiders, there are far worse things that might have happened to you had you stayed there on your own."

"What kind of things?" demanded Rebecca.

"Things I cannot describe," said the dog.

"Why not?"

"Because I don't know how they may take shape until they happen."

"Sounds silly to me!" snorted Rebecca.

"Not so daft as staying on your own, sulking!" snapped Richard.

"You should have stayed with me. You are supposed to look after me when we are out alone. Mum said!"

"But I see we are getting into the Dangerous Wastes," interrupted Canis, "and dangerous things are about us, because they are making you quarrel."

"I'm not quarrelling!" said Rebecca.

"You are!" said Richard.

"I'm not!" she shouted.

"Children," commanded the dog, sitting on his hind legs before them. "Listen to me. Think of my Master. Put your left hand on your heart, and raise your wand and your jewelled disk into the air above your head."

"Whatever for?"

"Please do as I say," the dog repeated urgently. "It's important. Come on, let's do it together. One, two, three – now!"

The children did as he had bidden, and as they did so, it is difficult to describe, but there was a sudden feeling of a very rapid wind departing from them suddenly. And as it did so, a certain darkness they had not observed, lifted from them. Somehow, things seemed lighter and brighter than they had before.

"What was that?" asked Rebecca.

"Why are we quarrelling?" asked Richard.

"Aren't we sillies," said Rebecca.

"We are," said the dog. "But we will come to no great harm as long as we are not too proud to realise we are. We have just been over-shadowed. Did you not feel the darkness leave us?"

"Yes," they cried. "What was it?"

"I do not know exactly," said Canis, "these things go silently and by stealth, declining to show their faces. But it was probably a demon of the desert, or of the Dark Tower."

"Demons?" cried Rebecca. "They are horrible to look at aren't they?"

"Don't make that mistake," said Canis. "If they show a face, it may be horrible if they want to frighten you. But that is no more than like a mask you might buy at a toy shop. They can be more dangerous if they put on a beautiful and friendly looking face, because that is still a mask, and designed to deceive you, so really it is worse than a horrible face."

"What are they really like then?" asked Richard.

"No one really knows," said Canis. "I think they are close to being nothingness – like sulks or bad tempers or bad thoughts, that will take on any shape that most suits their unhappy state. But you have felt what they are like, when you started to quarrel. You remember the swan told you that angels' thoughts can come into your heads. Well demons' thoughts can do likewise. In one case you will be true and good, in the other you may be nasty and quarrelsome or full of spite and lies."

"How horrible," said Rebecca.

"I don't like the idea of all that," said Richard. "How can we know when we are having our own thoughts and feelings or not?"

"You can always tell," said Canis, "if you know these things can happen. Your free will is your own, it is just the pictures or thoughts that come into your head that may be someone else's. And it is what you do about them that counts."

"It sounds all very sneaky to me," said Rebecca.

"That is why the good angels will not try to come into your head too much," said the dog. "Because they want you to be good without their pushing you into it. So they will come to you in this way only if you are in great danger."

"Oh, is that fair?" asked Rebecca.

"It does give a certain advantage to the demons," said Canis, "because they are very willing to buzz in and bend people to their evil ways. And that is why the world in which you live seems more bad than good."

"Ah, I see," said Richard, "but maybe that is not so bad as it seems, because when people are being wicked in the world it may not be their own wickedness they are acting out, but one of the demons'. And afterwards they will go back to being good."

"That is nearly so," said Canis. "But they are always slightly worse for doing so. Slightly easier to be open to bad demons again. And so they can get worse and worse and worse. It may be not *their* badness they bring into the world, but it will not do them much good for having helped to bring it. That is when the good angels try to intervene, when they see that people are losing the strength to do their own good."

"It's funny, I've heard about everyone having a good angel and a bad angel," said Richard, "but I thought it was all a load of nonsense."

"That is just what the bad angel would like you to believe," said Canis.

"Oh look!" cried Rebecca suddenly. "What is that in the distance? Is that what they call an oasis?"

"If it is a spot in the desert where water wells up and brings life to all around it, it is an oasis," said Canis. "If it isn't, it's a mirage, and will disappear as we approach it."

"Oh it's beautiful!" cried Rebecca. "I hope it doesn't disappear."

"There are some mirages that don't, in this desert anyway," said Canis. "And they can be the worst kind."

"Is this one?" asked Richard.

"You never know," said Canis. "Until you get inside them."

The place they saw in the distance was indeed beautiful. It was a great ivory tower, each window gay with colours, and at its top was a shining golden dome, capped, onion like, with a high point. The tower rose out of the desert emptiness like a giant pillar or a lighthouse, and about its foot were delightful shady trees and gardens laid out all around the rocky promontory upon which the tower was based.

"I think there's someone waving to us," said Rebecca.

"You must have good eyesight, or they have!" said Richard.

"Don't be horrible," said Rebecca. "You know what Canis just said about that. Think nice thoughts not nasty ones."

And she started forward toward the tower, followed by the others.

As they approached, the sun began to go down, or that is what they would have assumed, had there been any sun to be seen in the sky. But anyway, the sky gradually grew darker and the air colder as they approached the tower, which is always what happens at evening time, and they had been travelling long enough, it seemed to them, that night should shortly fall.

The tower appeared yet more beautiful in the twilight. A tall, slender, graceful, purple silhouette against the crimson coloured sky beyond it, that was giving all the appearance of a sunset, even if there was no sun. And gradually, welcoming lights began to shine in the high windows of the tower, and in the gardens at its base. Fires also seemed to be lit somewhere, and the savour of herbs and spices and appetising cooking smells drifted towards them across the desert air.

"Come on, hurry," said Rebecca, "I'm starving!"

"Wait a bit. I'm not so sure," Richard replied.

"What's the matter?" Rebecca cried. "It's usually you that's moaning at me for dragging behind."

"It looks a bit too good to be true, that's all," said Richard.

"Oh don't be such a scaredy cat," said Rebecca.

"I'm not scared, I'm just being sensible," said Richard. "What do you think Canis?"

But as he spoke they heard a noise. It was like a steady drumming sound in the far distance behind them. Although it was not loud it was powerful, and in fact the ground began to shake beneath their feet as the noise gradually approached.

Each was clad in robes of black that streamed in ragged tatters

"Whatever is that?" asked Richard.

As he spoke they heard a high pitched kind of singing, like a whistling noise, quite soft, but very eerie. And then Rebecca gave a cry of alarm, and pointed to the ground. Beneath their feet and all around them, cracks were beginning to appear. The sand was running down into some of them. And the cracks spread out in a regular pattern like the tracing of a web.

"Is it the sand spiders you teased me about?" said Rebecca. "You said there was no such thing!"

"This is worse," said Canis. "It is, I think, the Desert Reapers!"

"Who are they?"

"They reap whatever they find in the desert," said Canis. "And if they catch up with us it is unlikely we will ever leave."

"What happens to people they catch?" asked Richard.

And as if to answer him, the ground beneath their feet shook more violently and a large crack opened beside them. In it they could see livid red earth and, to their horror, the dry bones of what looked as if it once had been a human arm. With a crackling noise other fissures opened in the ground about them and in all of them they saw, just under the surface, nothing but dry bones.

"I'm not staying here!" cried Rebecca.

"Nor me," shouted Richard. "Let's make for the tower!"

And the two children and the dog ran towards the tower outlined against the darkening sky. It was, as they ran, like a bizarre game of hop scotch as they strove not to put their feet in any of the cracks that were opening up all round them. But at least it kept their minds off the drumming noise behind, which had become louder and louder, a dull throbbing flat beat inside the brain. And the whistling noise too had become a high pitched shrieking that made the hair stand up on the back of the head and brought them out in goose pimples.

It seemed as if something was chasing them, and as they threw themselves into the first welcoming trees about the tower, it was almost upon them. They turned at bay to face it, and saw that the drumming noise had been the beat of the feet of a group of galloping horses. A dozen or more great black horses raced towards them as if to run them down but sheered off at the last second, unwilling, it seemed, to enter the grove of trees and bushes. And as the horses wheeled past them at full gallop, whinnying fiercely, showing long yellow teeth and the whites of rolling eyes, the children saw with horror the riders on their backs. Each was clad in robes of flowing black that streamed in ragged tatters behind. They carried long scythes which they whirled beside their charging steeds to cut down anything that came their way. And from beneath each dark cowl of this hooded band there peered not a face, but a bare skull, with grinning teeth and saucer like vacant sockets for the eyes, lit up with a horrid luminous green. And the children saw, from the bony hands that gripped the scythes, and the bony feet in the stirrups, that each one of them was a skeleton.

They wheeled back into the surrounding darkness, and the ground gradually ceased to shiver and crack, and the sound of the hoof beats and swinging scythe blades receded into the night. The children suddenly realised that they were very cold.

"Come on," said Rebecca, her lip trembling a bit. "Let's ask for shelter in the tower."

"It can't be worse than here," said Richard.

"I would not be too sure of that," growled Canis to himself.

However, if Richard heard him, he chose to take no notice, for the tower, with its bright lights and appetising smells, certainly appeared more inviting than the cold dark desert with its bones and fissures underfoot, and galloping bands of murderous skeletons.

Chapter 8: Into the Dark Tower

THEY made their way toward the tower and mounted the winding row of steps that spiralled round its base of grey rock. They approached the wooden door and could now hear sounds of music and great festivity going on within. Beside the door was an iron ring on the end of a chain, with the word "Ring" inscribed on it.

"Do you think that is what it is, or what we have to do?" asked Rebecca.

"Both, I should think," said Richard, and boldly seizing the ring, he pulled it. There came a jangling nose above them from within the tower walls.

"Now we've done it!" said Rebecca.

There was a pause while they wondered nervously who or what might answer the door. But they did not have long to wait, for the door was thrown open and in the light that streamed out from it there stood a tall and dazzlingly beautiful lady. She wore a long jewelled dress of red and gold.

"Come in my dears!" she cried, as soon as she saw them. "Whatever are you doing out in the cold? You must come inside at once and be looked after. Oh my poor dears!" And she hustled them inside and closed the door against the cold night air.

They found themselves in a narrow hallway, which was hung in rich red velvet on the walls, with golden facings. The hall swung up immediately into a curving staircase, carpeted in the same rich red, for the tower was quite narrow, indeed rather like a lighthouse. They were also struck by the warmth of the place. After the cold night air it seemed almost oppressive and made it hard to breathe. The air was scented too, with a sugary smell, like hot fudge toffee. At a distance from the tower this had seemed very enticing and inviting, but close to, in the thick of it, it seemed more sickly and slightly suffocating.

A tall man appeared and stood behind the lady. He too was richly dressed, in a tight fitting coat of black, with silver and pearl buttons, and a wide starched collar that stuck out like wings on either side, and which was so high that he had to hold his head forward and up in what must have been a most uncomfortable way, although he did not seem to mind it.

"Are these the little visitors we have been expecting?" he asked in a dry cracked voice, peering at them through little spectacles upon a long jewelled holder.

"They are, my treasure," said the lady. "Let us take them to the Receiving Room."

The man smiled at them in an oddly eager way, and did not take his eyes off them, but beckoning continually, shuffled backwards and sideways up the stairs, rather like a crab, or perhaps a spider.

"Come along my dears," said the tall lady. "We have a very special welcome for you."

She advanced upon them with her skirts held wide like a net, sweeping them on before her. And so they climbed the spiral stair, towards the sound of much shouting and singing and dancing and jollity.

"I don't much like the look of them," muttered Richard to Rebecca.

"Whatever we do, keep close together," growled Canis.

The tall man stopped, stooping outside a tall narrow door hung with rich curtains. The noise from behind it was intense, as if a combined circus, fairground, amusement arcade and hectic party were in progress, all at once. He swung the curtains back upon their rod, and instantly – there was silence!

The children were ushered into a strange scene. The room was full of people; but everyone had stopped stock still and silent at their entry, and was staring fixedly at them. It was as if each one of them had suddenly turned into a statue. But they were living and breathing all right. Their hot flushed faces were plainly not made of stone, and they breathed heavily from their exertions of barely a second before.

The man and woman, who stood at least head and shoulders above any who were in the room, walked forward with Canis and the children, into a clear space in the centre.

The children looked around uneasily at the circle of heavily breathing, staring faces around them.

Obviously a riotous party had been taking place. There was jam, jelly, bits of cake, half-eaten sandwiches all over the floor, trodden into the carpet, dripping from the walls. Tables round the edge of the room had their cloths half pulled off, with their contents spilled onto the floor. All the faces that surrounded them had jam and

"Come along my dears, we have a very special welcome for you."

cream spread over them, especially around their mouths, but even in their hair and ears. How this had come about was obvious from the sight of two or three of them who, when they had entered, were in the act of plunging their faces into great bowls of jelly, trifle and blancmange.

"Children dear," said the tall woman to the gaping company, "I want you all to meet two little visitors, who have come to join our party."

The children in the room still stood and mutely stared.

"We are going to be especially nice to them," the lady went on, whilst the man rubbed his hands together as if washing them with invisible soap, nodding and bowing with an ingratiating smile upon his face, "because they have brought us very special gifts."

"Have we?" said Richard in surprise.

"The little boy has brought us a magic wand. It is only a pretend one of course but it has a pretty little flower at its tip."

Richard clutched the wand firmly in his hand and glanced at Canis, who was looking very fierce.

"And the little girl has brought a pretty little ornament." She smiled sweetly and held out her hand to Rebecca.

"No I have not!" cried Rebecca, clasping her talisman closely to her chest.

"Now don't be silly my dear," said the woman, "I know it's a pretty little trinket but it really is too large and heavy for you to wear isn't it. And wouldn't it go nicely about my neck?"

"These treasures were given to us!" cried Rebecca.

"I know, I know," smiled the tall woman, "but not to keep!"

"To exchange, to exchange," said the man, coming forward and trying to take Richard's wand.

"In exchange for what?" cried Richard.

"For coming here, joining our happy company!" said the woman.

"It doesn't look very happy to me," said Richard.

"Oh how silly! What a quaint idea," said the woman. "Here everyone can do as they like!"

"They look like a lot of greedy hooligans to me," said Richard, "who will soon be very sick!"

"What a nasty moralising mind you have," said the lady, fighting to retain her ingratiating smile. "Just like a spoil-sport grown-up!"

"Can we do as we like if we stay here?" asked Rebecca.

"Of course, my dear," said the lady, turning and beaming down upon her. "This is the Tower of Free Delights. I am its Queen and there is its King."

The tall man bowed and smiled.

"I never heard of a tower having a King and a Queen," said Richard.

"We can call ourselves what we like," said the woman, "without permission from you! This is a place where we do as we choose."

"Well I choose to keep my special jewel," said Rebecca.

"And I choose to take it from you, you cheeky little brat!" snarled the Queen.

"Now, now, let us not be hasty," cried the King, intervening between them. "I am sure it is all a misunderstanding. You just don't quite understand our rules. Not that we have any of course."

"How can you have rules and not have them?" asked Rebecca.

"Well I suppose our lack of rules has certain consequences that we find work out in practice and might be termed a natural law. The only real rule is that you may take whatever takes your fancy. Nothing wrong about that. But of course that only applies if what you fancy is not wanted by someone bigger or stronger than yourself."

"And you want our wand and jewel?" said Richard.

"Yes, and we are bigger and stronger than you," said the Queen.

"So it makes good sense to hand them over," said the King.

"Well we are not going to!" said Richard and Rebecca together.

"Very well," said the King and Queen, and advanced menacingly upon the two children. But they had not reckoned with Canis, who stood before them, the hair on the back of his neck risen up into spikes, his nose quivering into a ferocious snarl, baring his long terrible teeth.

"Call that dog off!" said the Queen, retreating before him.

"That animal has no business to be up here," said the King.

"I thought you had no rules," said Richard.

"Inferior creatures should be kept in the basement," said the King. "That stands to reason."

"Who is inferior?" snarled Canis, advancing slowly towards him.

"Oh how horrible, the wretched thing talked!" cried the King.

"It's not an ordinary cur, it belongs to that grinning Fool!" cried the Queen. "We should never have let it in."

"You opened the door!" snapped the King.

"Don't criticise me!" shouted the Queen.

"I told you not to!" continued the King. "But you took no notice."

"I can do as I like!" the Queen cried.

"You said we could kill it and make meat pies of it," cried the King. "Very clever!"

Canis gave a snarl of rage and made a sudden rush at the Queen.

"Help! Help!" she cried. "Call the mongrel off!" and jumped onto a table, treading into a bowl of custard as she did so.

"Yes my good dog, you seize her!" said the King. "She is the one who plotted to harm you. I quite like dogs myself."

Canis crouched menacingly before them. "You are both evil liars," he said. "Dogs are faithful and true. And that is something you would never understand."

"You will understand a good beating, which is what you will get!" cried the Queen, from her point of safety. "We will teach you to snarl at your betters. You will be tied to a kennel and given no food and water to teach you a lesson."

"You will have to catch him first," said Richard, "and you won't do that while we are around."

"Brave words," snarled the Queen. "But the strength still lies with us. You are prisoners in our Tower."

"Children!" she cried to the host of others that still stood stock still. "They are horrid goodies! Scroff them!"

The children immediately took on life and movement. With a wicked bully gleam in every eye they slowly advanced in a circle that completely surrounded the gallant three. There seemed no way that one dog and two children could defend themselves against a roomful of greedy and spiteful bullies.

"You don't have to do what she says," shouted Richard. "She said that you can do as you like!"

"Oh but they like giving someone a good scroffing," said the King. "Next to stuffing yourself with goodies, what is better than being in a gang and making goodies cry?"

"Stay together!" snapped Canis, to Richard and Rebecca. "Now use your weapons."

"Our weapons?" said Rebecca.

"Touch the pentacle with the wand," said Canis.

Richard and Rebecca did so, and as the rose at the end of the wand touched the jewelled star design on the golden disc, a warm rosy glow arose that complete enclosed them like a radiant cloud.

"Begone all phantasms!" cried the dog. "Show yourselves as you really are!"

Chapter 9: The Great Beast

THERE came a great rumbling and crumbling, that grew louder and louder, until there seemed to be a great explosion and a sensation of falling objects all around them. Then when all was silent Canis said, "Very well, you can break the contact. All is revealed now."

And as the children separated the wand from the disc, the rosy cloud about them dissolved, and they found themselves standing in a dusty pile of crumbled stone and rubble. It was as if they were in the midst of a decayed ancient city. One that had been overcome by a great catastrophe of fire or flood or earthquake and had been left for the wild beasts and the elements for countless years.

But they were not alone. They stood in what seemed to be the remains of a courtyard or open room.

The remains of broken pillars stood all around, mossy boulders and crumbled masonry scattered on the ground before them. And on the far side of the clearing stood a massive block of grey stone and plaster. It was rather like a stage in some broken down old theatre. And upon this block or stage was sitting, cross legged, a huge revolting creature.

It could well have been very frightening because of its great size. Its head was like a goat, with long curling horns, and although it had the body of a man, its legs had scales, which turned into bedraggled feathers and clawed feet like a bird. And at its feet, with chains around their necks that fastened them to the block below, were the King and Queen of the tower – one on each side. Although now, instead of seeming grand and powerful and dangerous, beside the great beast they were small, and powerless and pitiful.

"Now see what you have done!" screamed the Queen at them, but her voice was a weak thin shriek that was almost lost in the air. "You wicked naughty children!"

"We have shown you for what you are," replied Canis.

"You will be sorry for this!" shouted the King, only it came as a wheezing high pitched croak. "We shall set our pet upon you!" And he turned towards the towering figure above him and pointing to the children with a skinny hand cried, "Go get them! Devour them, Majesty!"

But the great figure, far from doing as it was bidden, cried out in a loud and petulant voice: "Shan't! Shan't! Shan't!"

And its voice was not that of a giant, or what you might expect from a monster, but was a chorus of high pitched voices, that were just the same as the raised voices of the greedy bully children that Richard, Rebecca and Canis had met in the room.

"I do what I li....ke! I do what I li....ke" the creature chanted in a sing-song mocking voice, and as it did so it struck the pretend King repeatedly with a great balloon on a stick that it held in one hand. It was not hard enough to injure anybody but it was big and bouncy enough to bowl him over and knock the wind out of him. It was also very dirty and slimy from where it had been lying in the mud around the ruined slab to which the couple were chained.

"Sacred Imperial Majesty!" cried the Queen.

"What do you want, gobbledy guts?" sneered the monster, looking down at her with a baleful eye.

"Most Wise and Powerful One," cried the Queen, "may I respectfully suggest that *there* are our enemies!" and she pointed at the children and the dog. "*We* are your faithful servants!"

"Slaves, you mean! Slaves!" cried the monster, in all its dozens of voices, giving the Queen a blow with the greasy balloon.

She sat down straddle legged at the force of the blow, looking far from queenly, but still able to continue.

"Yes, slaves, Oh Omnipotent One, anything you say!" she cried. "But look at the lovely toys they have. We wanted to give them to you. But they don't believe in you. They don't respect you. They are stuck up little pigs who think they are too good for us."

"Ugh?" the monster grunted, puzzled, and looking round. The children realised that it was probably very short sighted. Then it caught sight of them, and hissed and growled and muttered to itself with its many voices. They felt it was probably also fairly slow witted. Then it focused its gaze and attention on them.

"Baubles!" it said. "Toys! Pretties! Me, me, me! Me want! Give to me!"

And it stood up, towering high above them.

"No you don't!" cried the children, realising that it was after the wand and the jewel that they carried.

"Kill them, Majesty! Squash them!" cried the Queen.

The Great Beast suddenly opened creaking jet wings

"Seize them in your Mighty Claws oh Master!" chanted the King, from where he lay flat out in the mud.

To the horror of the children, the great beast suddenly opened creaking jet-black wings that had been concealed behind its back, and beating these wings with a great shattering clatter it rose into the air above them, its claws extended downwards to grab either their treasures or themselves.

"Oh what shall we do?" cried Rebecca.

"Only one thing to do with things like this," said Canis. "Go straight at them. Come on!"

And he rushed straight towards the hovering monster and between its legs, straight at the block upon which it had been standing, and into a dark and narrow little door that had been between the monster's feet, between the chained king and queen.

The children were momentarily conscious of the stench of the monster, like goats and bats and chicken coops that have not been properly cleaned out, and then they were scampering over sticky mud that was like a quagmire between the sitting queen and the prone king, and were squeezing through narrow rock walls in single file behind Canis.

"Oh I don't like this," said Rebecca. "It's so narrow and close."

"It's better for you than for me, you're smaller," said Richard, squeezing along behind. "But at least that great old bat thing will be too big to chase us in."

"What was it?" asked Rebecca.

"A walking bad dream," said Canis. "And only real if you are afraid of it. You heard its many voices. It has many names. Perhaps the best one is Legion."

"I suppose it can't change its shape and follow us, can it?" asked Richard anxiously. "It seems that anything can happen here."

"Anything can *not* happen here," said Canis. "There are laws of living here just as there are in your outer world. It is just that here the laws are different. And it is true that shape-shifting is something that we can do here that you can't do easily there. That means we can often look like different things – just as the monster earlier appeared like the children in the tower. Of course it could appear in different ways in your world too, though not in actual shapes, but getting people to do evil things. You remember what I said about demons and dark angels?"

"Well what is to stop it turning into a long thin slippery worm and following us in here?" asked Rebecca. "Couldn't it do that?"

"It could indeed," said Canis, "turn into such a shape. And it would be very easy for it to take on one like that, for it is true to its slippery, slidy, slimy nature. But it cannot follow us in here."

"Why not?" asked Richard.

"Because this is the place it is trying to guard. That it is trying to prevent people from finding. That is why it sets itself up as a frightening horror. It wants you to go back to death and the desert, or else become its slaves in the tower. But down here it cannot and dare not go – which is one reason why it wants to stop everyone and everything else. It is only a great greedy spoilsport, when all is said and done, that wants to stop others having the pleasure it is too greedy and selfish and nasty to be able to get near and enjoy itself."

Chapter 10: The Journey to the Centre

AS they talked the narrow crevice had been getting wider and they found after a little while that it was fairly comfortable to walk. The path sloped quite steeply downwards but although it was not steep enough to be called a staircase, natural shelves in the rock beneath their feet made their descent easier; and the path seemed to be ever curving so that you could never see very far in front or very far behind. This gave them the chance to examine the walls and narrow ceiling and floor of the passageway. They found to their surprise and delight that the rose at the end of Richard's wand and the jewels in Rebecca's talisman gave off a cool clear light which enabled them to see where they were going without stumbling. They saw that they were going through solid rock, which changed in colour and texture from time to time as if they were descending through different levels of it piled one below the other. Sometimes veins of other brightly coloured rocks ran through the duller rock of the floor, walls and ceiling. Sometimes there were isolated pockets of crystalline rocks, that seemed like strange flowers or gems embedded in the surrounding rock. Then to their excitement they realised that some of these were in fact gems.

"This is like a gigantic treasure box," said Richard, gazing around at what appeared to be emeralds, rubies, sapphires, diamonds gleaming in greens, and reds and blues and starlight crystal fire about them – in clusters, or single, like stars in the night sky. And like the stars in the night sky, as they got deeper and deeper, so did the gems glitter and glisten with their own light – not simply reflecting the light that the children carried. And so, not only did they shine in this way but little living flames could be seen flickering about them and the way became light enough from its own light bearing properties for them not to need the light from the wand and the talisman at all.

Even the very walls of roof and floor of the cave began to glow with its own quiet light and then to become almost transparent, as if it were, although still solid as rock, like a mountain mist, swirling and thickening and clearing unexpectedly, making strange shapes.

Then they began to think they could see movement in the rock all about them, like figures moving through the mist, all going in the same direction as they were themselves.

"Canis," cried Rebecca, "I think I can see through the rocks."

"That is because they are purer down here," replied Canis.

"And I can see people, little people," she cried excitedly.

"They are the gnomes who live in the rocks and fashion the gems," said Canis. "Have no fear, they will not harm us."

And sure enough, on either side of them as they travelled on they began to see little men with long beards and pointed caps and bells on their pointed shoes, marching along beside them beyond the walls of the rock. Most of them carried sacks on their backs or tools one might see in a blacksmith's shop. Hammers, tongs, even little anvils.

"I think it is beginning to get warmer," said Richard.

"That is because we are nearing the centre," said Canis.

"The centre of the world?" asked Rebecca, wide eyed.

"Not exactly," replied Canis. "There are worlds within worlds and who knows where the real centre is. But as near the centre as you are likely to be able or to want to go."

And then they began to hear a dull low roaring noise, and also a clinking of what sounded like hundreds of tiny hammers. And they realised that the path was now not sloping downward so steeply. That in fact it had levelled out and the walls of the rock had become so clear that it was as if they could see through clear pink mist at a wide circular clearing in which sat, as far as the eye could see, hundreds of little gnomes. Each was sitting cross legged, with a little golden anvil before him, beating away with hammer and tongs, fashioning the most beautiful gems and jewels that ever the eye had seen.

"Oh if only that greedy king and queen could see this," sighed Rebecca.

"They dimly know it is here," said Canis. "But like the monstrous beast they worship they also know that, much as they tried, they could not reach these treasures. They are too pure for them. Even if they could, by some impossible chance, lay their hands for a second upon them, the treasures would fade into the appearance of old leaves, or dust and ashes in their grasping hands. They are allowed to have and to hold certain low quality gems and metals in their world, as an act of mercy, but it is their own debasing greed that stops them from valuing anything much better than dirt. And the really precious things seem to them to have no value."

Each gnome sat at an anvil, fashioning beautiful gems

They walked slowly through the ranks of labouring gnomes, admiring the beautiful objects they were fashioning. And then they realised that the little folk were in fact seated in circles around a central rim from which shone an incandescent light. At the same time, as they approached they became aware of a sensation of movement. That they were slowly revolving around this centre, as if on a great carousel.

"Why do we feel as if we are going round?" asked Richard.

"Because we *are* going round," said Canis. "Everything that exists is always going round. That is called the Great Dance, and all little atoms and great worlds do it. You do not notice it of course because you are usually so far from the centre. But as you get near a centre so you begin to realise you are spinning and to feel the movement. The centre of course, any centre, for there are many centres besides the One Great Centre, is still."

"What is the One Great Centre?" asked Rebecca. "Is this it? Can we go and see it?"

"No, this is not the One Great Centre," said Canis, "but it is quite an important one. And if you go to one centre, you are not far off *all* centres, for they *all* have the quality of stillness – what some people who understand such things would call Eternity. As to whether you will see the One Great Centre, that depends on you, and whether you really want to."

"Oh I'd jolly well like to see it," said Richard.

"Just curiosity may not be enough," said Canis. "That is not wanting hard enough to be there."

"Is it far?" asked Rebecca.

"Very far and very near," replied Canis. "If you don't know how to look for it, it is a universe away. If you do know how to look, it is very near."

"How near? How near?" cried Rebecca.

"We have a centre very near us now," said Canis, "and, as I said, looking into one centre is like looking into any one of them or into all. And we have, each one of us, a centre in ourselves. It is called the heart."

"Oh look, look!" cried Richard, starting forward toward the white shaft of light that powered up from the ground before them.

"Be careful!" called Rebecca. "It's a great high cliff."

And sure enough, they found themselves, as they went forward to stand with Richard, at the brink of a most enormously high precipice, or a circular well that plunged into untold depths below them, but from which was coming a kind of light so bright that, like the sun, it was almost impossible to gaze upon it.

"What can you see?" asked Canis.

"Nothing!" gasped Richard. "It's far too bright down there. Is it a volcano?"

"Not exactly," said Canis. "A volcano is a much hotter noisier thing you find only at the edge of the worlds. But you might perhaps call it a volcano of light. Or you could prefer to think of it as a fountain."

"A light fountain!" breathed Rebecca, in awe, gazing at the jets of coloured light that could just be discerned in the overall brightness. Her eyes followed the pulsing jets downward, into the depths of the light well.

"I think I can see something down there. Or someone!" she cried. "Look!"

Richard stared into the incandescent light along with her, and as their eyes slowly got used to the brightness, so did they begin to see movement, and shapes down there.

"It's a great wheel isn't it?" breathed Rebecca. "And another wheel within that , going another way. And another one still! Wheels within wheels!"

And indeed, as they gazed they began to discern the outline of what looked like a giant gyroscope. That is, a circular wheel turning between two rings that hold it as in a simple cage. There are children's toys made like them, like spinning tops that will stand secure and still, kept so by the speed and force of their spinning.

Only in this case all the rings were in motion. And in a slow stately movement like the turning of the Earth or of the stars. And as well as being three rings, there were also disks, for the material of which they were made went from the rim to the centre of each disk, and so the three disks turned and interpenetrated each other all the time, and when they did so they caused currents of light to form at their points of interchange, so that they were looking down not only onto a great slowly turning sphere of light, but within that sphere of revolving rings, great rays of light were traced out in a pattern that made huge figures of eight that each had their centre in the centre of the sphere. Richard counted six of these, great double lobes of solid

figures of eight, each one in a different colour. And as well as this the sphere was forming bands within itself, also of different colours, and Rebecca counted seven of these, spheres within spheres, all inside the great spinning sphere made up of three turning rings.

Altogether they gazed upon the most magnificent many-coloured jewel that it is possible for you to imagine, its colours ever changing.

"Isn't it beautiful," said Rebecca, as they stood and watched it, accompanied by the silvery clanging of the hammers of the dwarfs all about them.

"Would you like to see it closer?" asked a gruff but kindly voice beside them.

They looked round to see one of the gnomes, who seemed to be a chief or senior one. He had a very long grey beard that reached almost to his toes, and a brown leathery face wrinkled into a broad grave smile.

"Yes please," said Richard.

Chapter 11: The Wheels of Fortune

"VERY well," said the gnome. "These are the Wheels of Fortune and I will summon the Lady who spins them to tell her that you are here." And he took a horn from his side and gave three mighty blasts that echoed and re-echoed before them. And as the last note died away, as if formed from the vibration of the notes in the air, there appeared before them, standing it seemed in thin air over the abyss, a fair lady dressed in sky blue, with long golden hair.

She smiled at them and beckoned them to approach her, and as she did so a pathway of brilliant light formed before their feet, and taking their courage in both hands, and not looking down at the horrendous depths below them, they stepped out onto the narrow bridge towards the lady, whose radiant loving smile of welcome dispelled their fears.

There the three, the children and the dog, stood at the centre before her, looking up, for she was twice the size of an ordinary life sized human being, and also twice as beautiful.

"Have you come to look at my beautiful spinning wheels?" she said. "Or do you wish to pass through the Gates of Space and Time?"

"We've been told by our friends," said Rebecca, "that we ought to look for the One Great Centre and maybe there we will find our real Names and our real True Goodnesses."

"And then we will want to come back," said Richard, "to take them back to our world."

"It seems you had better see both," smiled the lady, "the Spinning Rings *and* the Gateway at their Centre. Come, we will proceed to the great Gate, but although I could take you there in the twinkling of an eye – or in a slower way that would show you much but take millions of years – we will proceed at a gentle pace through a secret central path that will not long delay you."

And so saying, she turned them round so that she stood behind them, and wrapped her long gown protectively at each side of them, her hand on their outer shoulders as they stood either side of Canis. And as she did so they felt themselves begin slowly to descend.

They descended between cylindrical walls of bright white light, and then there was a slight, almost undetectable, bump, and a feeling of gentle vibration to the disk of light on which they stood.

"We enter the North Pole of my spheres," said the lady. "All will change now."

And so it did, as they descended, so the vibrating feeling enclosed their heads and they could no longer see the white light walls of the well, but found themselves enclosed by a sphere beyond which they could not see.

"No-one on the inside of my circles can see there is a beyond," said the lady, "but you know differently, don't you."

"Isn't it a bit like a trap?" asked Richard.

"No more than the walls of your house," said the lady. "Would you like all your walls to be of glass?"

"No, I don't think so," said Richard. "But there are doors and windows."

"So there are here," said the lady, "but they can only be found in the middle of things."

"How funny," said Rebecca. "At home we have doors and windows on the outside."

"That is because, I expect, you live in a topsy turvy world," said the lady, "where everything is backwards."

"It seems all right to us," said Rebecca.

"That is because you are used to it," said the lady, "but in the end you might prefer it our way, when you have seen our way of living too."

But they spoke no more because of the wonder they found all about them. As they descended through the top of the revolving spheres they found that not only were they in a world of rainbow colours but in a world of sound as well, and also scents and tastes and feelings. It was like being taken inside a piece of music. The nearest way to describe it would be like standing in the middle of an orchestra in a great concert, with massed bands and choirs there as well, or in a great organ that was able to reproduce any sound you could think of, and many more you could not. And that each sound had a colour and a shape so that you not only heard it but saw it as well. And there was no discordant noise or ugly shapes. But all was melody and rich harmonies. And melodies appeared like strings of beautiful coloured shapes like necklaces of gems of light, and harmonies appeared like deep pools of harmonious colours into which the eye as well as the ear could sink in delight. Whilst at the same time, difficult though it be to describe in terms of the limited sense of taste and smell and

They descended through the top of the revolving spheres

touch we have in our world, along with the sights and the sounds there came strings of sensations like melodies of sense and depths of wondrous feelings like harmonies of experience.

"Oh it's wonderful," sighed Rebecca. "Is this what they call heaven?"

"There are heavens within heavens," said the lady, "and this is the heaven of the spheres. All the sounds and sights you see and hear are angels making patterns."

"I cannot see any angels," said Rebecca.

"But you are in the midst of them," laughed the lady. "Because you cannot see people with wings dressed up in drapery do not think there are no angels here. They are what they create. Each of the sounds and colours is an angel singing."

"Heaven always sounded a very boring place," said Richard. "when they described it as a place where people with wings sat on clouds twanging harps. But this is not so very different is it? And I feel I would like to stay here for ever."

"So you may, if you wish, some day," said the lady. "But this is the place of patterns, and you, as a little human from outer Earth, have a job to do first."

"What's that?" asked Richard.

"You have to copy these patterns in the life you lead. And then your little world will be heavenly like this too."

"That sounds impossible," said Richard.

"That is what the caterpillar said when it looked at a butterfly," said the lady, "but one day it found it had become one."

"But it's all so complicated – and different," said Rebecca. "How can we trail sounds and colours round at home? I cannot even play the scale very well on my recorder."

"The difficulty is not that it is complex," said the lady, "but that it is so simple."

"How do you mean?" said Richard.

"So simple that nobody thinks it possible," said the lady, "particularly the ones who think that they are clever."

"What do we have to do?" asked Rebecca.

"The same as the angels," said the lady. "They do not think of the great harmonies they weave. They simply sing for joy straight from the heart, and being full of love and joy all the rest follows. It's really very simple."

"It seems too simple to work," said Richard.

"It does here," said the lady, "as you can see and hear."

And they continued their journey into the centre of the spheres. And as they proceeded so they saw there was a vast natural pattern forming. That what seemed complex and difficult to understand at the outer edge began to seem part of a grand simple whole as they progressed toward the centre.

For a start they saw that they were descending through great bands of light. That although there was every conceivable colour about them, so at each stage one colour seemed to predominate. Thus on the outermost edge crimson seemed the dominant colour, as though all the other colours were threads of light woven onto a coloured fabric of light that was shot with all the shades of red – and living colours too, like gazing into a fire.

Then one by one they realised they were going through the colours of the rainbow. First orange, where all seemed rich with gold, then yellow, green, blue as they proceeded to the deep indigo and purple of the centre.

"Do you think there will be a pot of gold when we get to the centre of the rainbow?" whispered Richard.

"There could be," smiled the lady.

And as they approached the deep rich centre of the spheres, where all the melodies and harmonies seemed like the triumphant pomp and circumstance of royalty and kingship and majesty, they looked outward through the spheres and saw that from the deep centre there radiated great bands of light, and now they could see the intelligent design behind the mass of sound and colour, and it was almost as if they could see choirs or bands of angels measure out a stately dance, yet each one of them dancing individual steps that were his or hers only. Perfect freedom in a perfect pattern.

"I can see our trouble," said Richard. "We cannot get our freedom to do what we like to make such a marvellous pattern."

"You are learning wisdom," said the lady, "but wisdom comes easier near the centre."

"We all want to be a centre with other people being the pattern. And they want us to be a part of a pattern round their centre. And we can never agree."

"And it's no use arguing about it, is it?" said the lady.

"No," said Richard, "the answer lies in Love."

And as he said this the children found themselves at the very centre; and thus not only at the centre of all the seven rainbow bands, but at a junction of twelve great corridors of light and echoing sound that swung off through the spheres, and each of which had its own dominant shade of colour, and different range of harmonies.

"I suppose each one is like the twelve notes on a piano," said Rebecca. "There are seven notes in a scale, like the colours of the rainbow, but they are chosen from twelve different notes on a keyboard."

"And look down the corridors," said Richard. "I can see huge figures appearing."

And sure enough, if they gazed in turn down each great corridor they were conscious of a mighty shape appearing at the point as far as the eye could see. Many of them seemed to be animals. They noticed a great golden lion in one, a huge crimson coloured bull in another, and in another a curly horned ram. And some were people, a man pouring water from a pot, and a pair of twins.

"I know what they are!" cried Richard. "Aren't they the signs of the Zodiac?"

"Oh yes, Granny looks them up in the newspaper every day," said Rebecca. "Dad says she's silly to do so. And she reads all our fortunes from them. Not that they ever come true do they?"

"Not much in newspapers is true," said Richard.

"Are they all there?" asked Rebecca. "What is the rhyme she taught us? The ram, the bull, the heavenly twins … "

"Yes they are all there."

"And next the crab, the lion shines – oh, isn't he gorgeous!" and she stopped to gaze at the great golden lion who stood in the distance of a long golden corridor, with a bright blazing star at his heart.

"The virgin and the scales..." continued Richard.

"The scorpion, archer, and sea-goat..."

"The man who holds the watering pot..."

"The fish with the glittering tails."

And sure enough, as they recounted them all in the rhyme, they turned and saw first a fair maiden made out of stars with a great balance, like used to be seen in grocers' shops, with two swinging pans at each end of a long balance arm. They saw the scorpion, huge like the lobsters or crawfish they had earlier seen. A centaur, half man and half horse with an arrow drawn tightly in a bow held before him. Then a goat with wide spreading horns. A strong fair man pouring water from a pot on his shoulder. And two brilliantly glittering fish, their scales like starlight.

"What are they?" asked Rebecca. "Are they real?"

"They are pictures on windows," said the lady.

"I thought all the windows were on the inside?" said Richard. "We are looking out."

"Windows are also for looking into," said the lady, "and we are on the inside of things. What you see out there are reflections of pictures on the outside of twelve different windows. But they all look into the same thing at the centre."

"I can't see any windows," said Rebecca.

"That's because they are such perfect windows," said the lady. "And windows are for looking through, not looking at."

"And what would people see who looked in through any one of those windows?" asked Richard.

"Turn round and you will see," said the lady.

Chapter 12: Through the Mirror Door

THEY turned and gasped, for there on the floor before them was a shining round mirror, so bright and clear that it was impossible to see the glass. And in it was the image of a man who was upside down.

That is, his head was closest to the floor at their feet, so in a sense he must have been the same way up as them. But past his head they could see that he was hanging. Hanging by his feet from a wooden frame that straddled a deep precipitous chasm.

Whether it was a kind of distorting mirror they were not sure, like one of those they have in fun fairs, but it seemed as if the man was very long and tall, that his feet were miles and miles away, so small and distant were they. But his head and smiling face were right at their feet and a golden glow seemed to emanate from it and from out of the mirror towards them and it was like standing in the warmth of a radiating fire.

"Whatever is that?" cried Richard.

"It is the mirror centre," said the lady.

"Another window?"

"No, a door," she replied.

"It doesn't look much like a door," said Richard. "But then I suppose you will say a door is a thing for going through and not just for looking at."

"There are many kinds of door," said the lady, "and some are for going through, and others are best kept shut to keep things out. But where there's a door there is always a choice. So it is for you to choose whether you wish to go through."

"It's very strange," said Rebecca.

"Yes, how can you have a mirror that reflects something that isn't there?"

"It reflects something that very much is there," said the lady. "But you must remember we are at a centre of things, and so a mirror image will be in the same place as that which it reflects."

They stared down at the huge figure in the floor before them. They saw that he had vari-coloured clothes, and that his hands were held behind his back. He gazed back at them, smiling at their astonishment.

"He's very big," said Rebecca. "And I don't like the way he is hanging there by one foot. It looks very dangerous."

"I've got an idea I've seen his face before," said Richard. "But it is very difficult to recognise someone when they are upside down."

"It may be you that is upside down," said the lady, "but he seems to recognise you. Do you want to go through the door to him?"

"How do you go through it?" asked Rebecca.

"Just wish," said the lady.

"All right, I'm game," said Rebecca. "He looks very friendly."

"If we have come this far," said Richard, "we might as well carry on as try to go back."

"I don't think that is really good enough for a wish," said the lady.

Richard paused, and gazed at the hanging man's face.

"Oh," he said at last, "I feel he's a friend. Someone we can trust. Yes, I wish we were through the door."

"So do we," said Rebecca and Canis.

And as they said so they were amazed to see the hanging man's arms come from behind his back and up and out through the mirror floor. At the same time showers of golden coins fell round and about them, but they had no time to pick them up for they found themselves seized in strong protective arms and pulled through the mirror. There was a confusing topsy turvy dizzy moment when they knew not whether they were up or down as they passed through the mirror surface, and then they were plainly in the mirror with the man, hanging upside down in a terrifying abyss whose depths seemed bottomless. But they had no time to feel frightened, for doubling himself up from the waist, the man, still holding them in his arms, placed them at the top of the chasm, on firm ground, and with masterly agility unhooked his foot from the hanging loop of rope and leaped over the yawning gap to stand before them.

They now saw, however, that he was of normal human size.

"Are you the Fool?" said Richard, for although he seemed to be similar, there was a radiance about his face that made it difficult to look upon, and recognise him.

But there was no doubt from the actions of Canis the dog, who threw himself upon his master with a paroxysm of twisting and curling and tail wagging and turning round and round and jumping up and down.

Seized in strong protective arms and pulled through the mirror

"What's in a name?" said the Fool, smiling down at them.

"A lot, you told us," said Rebecca. "Because that's why we've come all this way. To find out our True Names."

"True enough," said the Fool. "And when you get there you will discover mine."

"You mean we aren't at the end of our journey yet?"

"Some would say you've only just begun," said the Fool. "But now that you are here I can tell you what to do."

At this, Canis ceased his cavorting and came and sat by the children, his head on one side and his ears cocked, looking up at his master attentively.

"Beyond you is a hill," said the Fool. "You will find those who will guide you at the top of that."

They turned, and saw, over rolling green countryside, a round green hill, prominent in the middle distance.

They turned again to ask him more, but found that he had disappeared. Of him and of the gaping chasm and scaffold over its depths there was now no sign.

There was no sign of life in the deserted landscape either, but the countryside had a kind of friendly feel, for all countryside does have feelings, but when we go through it we often think the feelings are our own.

They proceeded quickly toward the hill but it seemed to take them an awfully long time, perhaps because of the quality of stillness about the place. It seemed as if they were making their way to that round green hill for ever but still it seemed as far from them. But eventually their persistence was rewarded and they saw that after only two or three more undulations of the rolling downs they would be at its foot.

And as they grew closer their interest was attracted by what appeared to be white marks on the side of it. At first they could not make out what these were, but suddenly it became apparent.

"Look," cried Rebecca, "I can see what it is, carved in the side of the hillside. It's a great white lion."

And so it proved to be, just like the hill figures that are carved in the turf on some chalk hills in England, usually of horses or of giants. But this one was unmistakably a lion, with long curling tail and huge shaggy mane.

And they saw too, again like many hilltops at home, that there was a ring of standing stones.

"Oh come on, let's hurry," said Richard, who was very interested in history, especially of ancient times. "This is a super place."

They broke into a trot until they were puffed out and were obliged to walk again. But soon they found themselves at the foot of the hill.

It did not seem so little now they were at the foot of it. Certainly it was perfectly round, but whilst this looked very pretty from a distance, when they arrived at the foot they found that this meant that the sides at the bottom were almost sheer. And from this point you could see nothing of the lion carving or of the standing stones at the top.

"Come on," said Richard. "There's nothing else for it but sheer grit and determination. Fortunately the grass is quite long, we can hang on to it to climb."

And so they did.

Chapter 13: Up the Lion Hill

THE grass was quite slippery to stand on or to hold, but it grew in great tussocks, which they found they could use like stepping stones. And so they scrambled on and up, sometimes giving each other a heave over the difficult bits. It was easier for Canis, with his four legs and his body closer to the ground, but the children managed quite well for on such a steep climb they too were using their arms like legs and their bodies came naturally close to the ground. It was all right as long as you didn't try to stand up. Then you felt dizzy and wobbly and insecure.

But after a time the going grew easier as they rounded the vertical curve of the hill and soon, to their excitement, they began to see the lower markings of the lion cut into the turf, the end of the tail, and the feet, although it was difficult to see that it was in fact a lion now they were so close to it.

Gradually the rest of the carved figure came into view and they found themselves standing along the underbelly of the huge figure. The grass was cut away in a huge curve to either side of them, and before them was the bare chalk of the figure.

"Do you think we ought to walk over it?" asked Rebecca.

"I don't know if we can," said Richard. The chalk looked very white and very polished and very slippery.

"Even if we can I don't think we ought," said Rebecca.

"It's a long way round," said Richard.

"That doesn't matter," said Rebecca. "The carved out lion seems very special, and I don't think we should walk on it."

So they made their way sideways beneath the white carved figure. The going was not so hard, for they were no longer climbing, but they had to take care not to slip, for once anyone began to tumble they would have a nasty fall, especially if they rolled all the way to the bottom.

And then they came to the beginning of the front legs.

"Oh dear," said Rebecca, "I did not think of this. We shall have to go back down again, the whole length of its front leg and then up its other one, and then all round its head, and that is huge."

"Well there's nothing else for it if we are not going to climb over the figure."

"Do you think we should?" asked Rebecca.

"No, I don't," said Richard.

"Well let's get on," said Rebecca, and with a sigh they began to descend the leg of the lion, realising that when they had done so, puffed as they were, they would have all the distance to climb up again.

"There is another way, you know," said a voice.

They looked round in astonishment, wondering where it could be coming from. And then saw, high above them, the head of a maiden. Her head was all they could see because of the curve of the hill.

"You are wise not to tread on the lion," she called in a gentle but commanding voice, "for this is holy ground. But if you show due respect for that which is beneath your feet, you may be allowed the short way up."

"What is that?" called Richard.

"Remove your shoes," called the maiden. "Then you may come up straight to where I am."

The children sat on two tussocks and began to remove their shoes. They were not, of course, dressed in their ordinary clothes but in the clothes they had taken on to begin their journey, and the soft shoes they wore were easily carried. They then started up across the chalk of the carved lion. And although it had seemed as if it might be as slippery as ice, to their bare feet it was warm and gave a reassuring firm foothold. Canis padded up beside them.

"It's all right for you," said Rebecca, "you don't have any shoes to take off."

"Perhaps that's because I am holier than you," said Canis, with a one-sided mischievous smile, that made both the children laugh. "Wearing shoes and clothes doesn't make people any better you know. Though often they think it does."

And together they climbed up the decreasing slope to the top of the lion's back and found themselves face to face with the maiden who had called to them.

She was very beautiful, with long yellow hair with many coloured flowers plaited in a wreath to make a little ringlet crown. Her dress was patterned with flowers, and she had more flowers in chains all around her neck and waist and spilling onto the ground about her feet and onto the chalk face of the lion. And they saw too that the grass of the upland above the lion was no longer lush dark green tussocks of coarse bladed grass but rich short turf covered with vari-coloured little flowers, not only buttercups and daisies but all imaginable kinds of little rock plants.

"How different the grass is up here," said Rebecca.

"It is like the fur on the body of a lion," said the maiden. "Long and shaggy around its legs and body but short and soft and smooth on the top of its head."

"Is this hill like a lion then?" asked Rebecca.

"The chalk figure is not just a decoration," said the maiden. "It shows what it is."

"How can a hill be a lion?" asked Richard.

"Why shouldn't it be?' asked the maiden. "Don't you believe me? Here, see its hot breath."

And she waved the end of her long skirt over a patch of ground in front of her, in which there was a fissure in the soil, like the cracks that appear on a long dry summer. And as she did so, "Huff! Huff! Huff!" there were three great rumbling snorts, and from the cracks in the ground three puffs of smoke came out, accompanied by a shower of sparks.

"Lion's breath?" cried Rebecca. "It seems hot enough to be a dragon!"

"Some people do call it a dragon," said the maiden airily, "but I think of it just as a friendly old lion."

"I didn't know lions were friendly," said Richard.

"Perhaps that is because you have never really got to know one," said the maiden. "Most things are friendlier than you think."

"The ones I've seen at the zoo didn't seem very friendly," said Richard. "Or at the circus."

"Nor would we be, I expect, if people shut us up in cages and made us do stupid tricks," said Rebecca.

"I still wouldn't care to meet one on the street," said Richard.

"Although things are friendly when you approach them properly, that does not mean that they are not wild," said the maiden. "This one could burn us all to a cinder, or shake us off his back, or swallow us all up, if he had a mind to. He's very strong."

And she swirled her dress about in a few wild steps of dance, the strings of flowers whirling into spiralling shapes about her. And as the did so, between her bare feet the ground shook beneath her, and trembled, and shot forth jets of smoke and fire.

"Dance on the back of the lion," she sang.

"Aren't you frightened?" quavered Rebecca.

"Why should I be?" laughed the dancing maiden.

"It's like standing on a volcano," said Richard.

"Well that's what we do, all of our lives," said the maiden, stamping her feet rhythmically so that a pattern of puffs of different coloured smoke hung in the air about them. "The middle of your world is hot is it not? But you don't let that worry you."

"Yes, I suppose so," said Richard. "It is only when the molten lava breaks through in volcanic eruptions, or the crust of the world shifts about to cause an earthquake that we ever think of it."

"You see, you take it for granted," cried the maiden. "Come along, dance with me. Otherwise the lion may think you don't like him."

She laughed as she said this so they knew she was teasing, but the infectious gaiety she had as she whirled about them, and the drumming of her bare feet on the turf, drew them into imitating her dance, whirling and spinning and spiralling. And the maiden was dancing so rapidly now that the whirling of her skirts and the ropes of flowers she had, became blurred to their sight, so it appeared as if she herself were somehow made entirely of flowers.

"The grass and the flowers and the trees and the moss and all things that grow, dance on the back of the lion," she sang. "Let us dance the dance of the life of the lion."

And so they proceeded in wild spiral dance, the two children and the dog, he prancing up and down on his hind legs, now on all fours like bouncing ball, spinning round and round at the same time chasing his tail. And as they did so, led by the dancing flower maiden, they did not realise that they were gradually approaching the stone circle that stood on the top of the hill.

Chapter 14: Shot from the Gates of Time

IN fact it was not until they found themselves under a trilithon gate, two huge grey upright stones with another massively balanced across them, that their dance was stopped by a deep shout of "Who comes?" And in that instant they stopped stock still, as the maiden danced off back down the hill again, waving a joyous farewell with the swirling garlands about her head. The children and the dog, under the shadow of the great stones, where all appeared to stand stock still, looked up at a tall figure who stood between them, gazing down sternly upon them.

He was as lean as he was tall, and had a long white beard, a robe of white, and long white hair about a bald patch on the top. In one hand he held a long thick staff, intricately carved with twining serpents, and in his other hand he held aloft a flickering lantern.

"Who comes to the Temple of the Stones of the Eternal?" he asked again.

"I'm Richard."

"I'm Rebecca."

"And this is Canis the dog," they said.

"Thank you, but I can speak for myself," said Canis.

"Give me first the password," demanded the tall man.

"Oh, um."

"I'm afraid we don't know."

"That which is reflected, is as that which is upright," said Canis the dog. "Now may we come in?"

"Enter, O Little Ones of the Flickering Light of Time," said the old man, standing aside.

And as each one of them crossed the threshold of the grey stones he bent down and scrutinised them most carefully, holding his lantern down to illuminate their faces. As he did so they saw that the candle inside was minutely divided with marks to record the passing of the hours and minutes and seconds as it burned down.

"Is that a clock candle in your lantern?" asked Rebecca. "We heard in our history lesson that King Alfred invented them."

"The light within is time itself," replied the old man, walking gravely before them, "which ever burns itself away."

"What will happen when it is all burned away?" asked Richard.

"Then the light of time will be no more," said the old man, "and will give way to the brighter light of eternity."

"I thought eternity meant just a long time," said Rebecca.

"It means the freedom from time," answered the old man.

And as he spoke he led them through a maze of standing stones. Although they seemed to be in some sort of complex order, there were so many of them that it was like the mechanism of some kind of enormous stone clock. But in the centre was a clear circular space, in the middle of a pattern of dark blue coloured stones, and in the very midst of all a low rounded stone, with a smooth flat top of light pinkish grey. And upon that a smaller stone, of pure white, cut into the shape of a perfect cube. Although when they talked about it afterwards they found they each remembered it differently. And they remembered it differently themselves on different times when they remembered it. Sometimes it was as a cube, sometimes as a pyramid. Sometimes like a diamond shape, and other times more complicated than that, with lots of little sides, that sometimes they remembered as triangles and at other times as five sided faces.

"Wouldn't everything just stop," asked Richard, "if there wasn't any time?"

"Of course not," replied the man. "It flows in other directions."

"I cannot think of any other directions," said Richard.

"That is because your mind is limited by the flow of time you are in," said the man.

"What kind of place is it that has no time?" asked Rebecca.

"It is called the Land of the Ever Young," said the old man.

"Do you come from it?" asked Rebecca. "Because to me, if you don't mind me saying so, you look very old."

"I am the steward at its gate," said the old man. "On the outside I look very old and on the inside I look very young."

"Why is that?" asked Richard.

"Because it is also the Land of Great Wisdom," said the old man. "And on the outside, in the realms of time, wisdom is thought to come with great age."

"I don't think it does," said Richard.

"That is because you are young in earthly years," said the sage. "You still have the folly of youth. But do not fret," he continued, "I too am in your condition. When it comes to true wisdom I too am like a stripling boy and find it hard to understand."

Hovering in the air before them was a young boy

"It seems impossible to me," said Richard. "How do you get wisdom?"

"By experience," said the old man.

"That, I suppose, takes a lot of time," said Rebecca.

"It can do," said the old man. "But it need not. If you had enough love, it would take no time at all."

And as he said this he raised his serpent staff high above the white stone, and in the lantern light the serpent carved upon it seemed to wriggle and to hiss, and two wings grew out from either side of the top of the staff and beat rapidly, and the top, which was like a pine cone, glowed as if it were very hot.

"Let us open the Gates of Time," he cried, "and let Eternal Love come in."

And he suddenly thrust the bottom of the staff, which was sharpened to a point, a point that wriggled and squirmed like a sting, and struck the white stone with it, and as he did so the stone took on the appearance of an egg, and his staff cracked and smashed a hole into its shell, and it fell into a thousand fragments onto the stone beneath, its yoke wetting the stone and pouring away into the ground. But from it, hovering in the air before them was a young boy, younger even than Rebecca. He seemed no more than four or five years old, and he glowed, brighter than the old man's lantern, with a warm ruddy kind of colour. It was as if he came from the midst of invisible flames. And he hovered on bright wings before them in the air, holding a bow and arrow.

"Oh," cried Rebecca, startled. "How lovely. Are you a fairy?"

The hovering child made no answer but smiled at them and stretching the bow string tight turned and sent an arrow high into the air. And as it went it was like an ascending rocket and left behind a rainbow trail of sparks and coloured vapour.

"Quickly, quickly! Over the rainbow bridge!" cried the old man. And he hustled them up onto the central stone where a cloud of coloured vapour from the arrow had descended and they found it was like solid ground they could stand on.

"On you go!" cried the old man. "Out of the stones of time!"

And Canis led the way, racing up the rainbow path, followed by the children, hurrying and scurrying after. It was like climbing the green hill all over again, except that this time it was like going up a narrow bridge rising high into the sky. Looking down they could

They whizzed down the rainbow path of the arrow

see the rolling countryside far behind them, the green hill with the carved lion upon it, with the flower maiden still dancing round it, puffs of smoke and fire coming from beneath her feet. And at the top of the hill, now far, far below them, the circles of stones within stones, in a complex pattern, but looking no bigger than a button, so great was their height. And still the old man's voice urged them on. "Go, go! Out of the circle of the stones of time!" But now his voice was no longer that of an old man, it was a childish treble that called after them – or so it seemed at this height.

Gradually the steepness of the rainbow decreased until they reached the top of its arc.

"Now I think we can slide," called Canis. And he sat down with his front legs between his back ones, and his tail held up behind, and began to slide down the other side of the rainbow. The children jumped into a sitting position behind him and together they all whizzed, at increasing speed, like sliding down a gigantic banister, in the rainbow path of the arrow.

And as they whizzed downwards so they got faster and faster. But their speed had become so great that everything about them was nothing but a blur. And then it all became so fast that they no longer even had the sensation of falling.

"What's happening? Where are we?" cried Rebecca.

"You are in my chariot!" came a clear laughing voice from behind them. "Can't you see my fine horses?"

Chapter 15: Beyond the Mountains of the Stars

AND as they looked around they found they indeed seemed to be sitting on something flat and square and solid, with beautiful patterns on it. It was rather like a magic carpet for it flew swiftly and silently, with the three of them sat upon it. But at the rear side of it there stood a young woman with a flowing dress and golden reins in her hand which stretched over their heads to where they could now see, before them, a team of four beautiful horses, with silvery golden backs, and, what was more, with huge golden wings, held upright over their backs. Although they did not seem to need them to fly, but galloped merrily through the air as if it were their natural element.

"They are beautiful," said Rebecca. "Are they yours?"

"I am the Spirit of Victory," said the maiden, "and these are my four great steeds."

"Why don't they use their wings?" asked Rebecca.

"They have no need to at this height. Here everything floats freely. You only need wings when you are earth-bound or moving very slowly."

"Are we far from the Earth then?" asked Richard.

"You have been shot from there by the arrow of love," said Victory. "You could hardly be farther away."

"And are we going fast?"

"Faster than the speed of light."

"That's impossible," said Richard. "We learn that at school."

"It may be impossible there," said the lady, "but here we break all your rules."

"Isn't that naughty?" asked Rebecca.

"If you love well enough you can do what you like," said the lady.

"Who said so?" asked Richard.

"Isn't it obvious?" said the lady.

"No, I don't think so," said Richard.

"Well perhaps you haven't loved well enough to find out," said the lady.

"I love horses," said Rebecca.

"Well that's a start," laughed the lady. "Do you love centipedes?"

A team of beautiful horses with huge golden wings

"Ugh, no," said Rebecca. "Who could love a nasty creepy crawly centipede?"

"I expect another creepy crawly centipede would," said the lady.

"I say, where are we going?" asked Richard.

"Where does an arrow usually go?"

"I don't know. To a target?"

"Exactly. Why do you ask?"

"Well if we are travelling faster than the speed of light then during the time that we've been talking we must have passed right out of our solar system. That seems impossible."

"When we are travelling as fast as this all kinds of things happen that you might think impossible," said the maiden. "For a start, no one behind can see us. And even with people who are in front of us we approach them so fast that we are past them before they see us coming. And of course once we are past them they cannot see us anyway. Then things get shorter and lighter the faster they go, and we are now so short and light that as far as the slow coaches in the solar system are concerned we don't exist."

"Don't we exist any more?" asked Rebecca.

"Do you feel as if you exist?" asked the lady.

"Yes," replied Rebecca.

"Then I would not worry too much about anyone who thinks you do not," said the lady, "for they only show their blindness."

"But I don't think I like being so far away from home," sniffed Rebecca.

"Oh my dear, don't cry," said the lady. "Who would take you from your home?"

"But if we are travelling so far and so fast we must be millions of miles away."

"Oh if you travel fast enough you are always in the same place. All straight lines join up together somewhere and turn into circles, because everything is curved. And if you go round a circle fast enough you are always in every part at once."

"So where are we?" asked Rebecca.

"Wherever you want to be, or where your heart is. If we slowed down you would find yourselves not so far from home."

"But first we've got some things to do," said Richard.

"Oh yes," said Rebecca. "We can't go back until we have found our True Names and our True Goodnesses."

"Then let us go to where they can be found," said the lady.

"Where is that?" asked Richard.

"In the direction of love's arrow, which is where the horses of victory are taking us. Straight to the heart of the empire. And look below you, for there it is."

And looking down the children saw that the horses pulling the car had begun to circle and that they were gradually spiralling down onto a flat plain that lay just beyond a huge range of mountains.

"Oh look at those mountains," cried Rebecca. "Aren't they a beautiful dark blue? And all lit up, with tiny diamond lights."

"They are the Celestial Mountains, or the Mountains of the Stars," said the lady.

"You mean there are stars in those mountains? And those mountains are like the night sky?"

"Yes," said the lady. "This is where the arrow of love and the chariot of victory brings you. To the land of the Emperor Beyond the Stars."

"I've never heard of such a place," said Richard.

"Seeing is believing," said Rebecca. "Look, is that a palace I can see down there?"

"Yes," said the lady. "And all the people from the palace have come out to welcome us I expect."

"I think there is a space marked out for us," said Rebecca. "Isn't it exciting! It's just like being one of those parachute jumpers who land on a target. Can you see it there beneath us?"

And on the ground as the horses circled round it, getting lower and lower, they saw marked out on the ground a system of circles, one within the other, and coloured like a rainbow.

And all about this central circle were ranged people who had come out to see them. As they got lower still they realised that the great square in which the circle was placed was a central square in the palace. The palace was huge, like four palaces in fact, each ranged on each side of the square, with tall white and golden spires and turrets reaching toward the sky.

"The army is out to meet us," said the lady.

"Do they have an army here?" said Richard.

"There are far frontiers to guard," said the lady. "But here they are ranged up in your honour."

"Have we deserved it?" asked Richard.

"Hard though it may be to believe," interjected Canis, "you only get what you have deserved. Or what you are able to earn."

"I don't think I like the sound of that," said Rebecca.

"Aren't they a wonderful sight," said Richard. "This is better than changing the guard at Buckingham Palace."

For as they descended onto the shimmering rainbow carpet, right at its dead centre, there was a crash of resounding martial music and the surrounding soldiers, as one man, raised their spears and banners in salute to them. And at each side of the square about them were ranged soldiers in different coloured uniforms.

Before them were rank upon rank dressed in gold and yellow. To their right rank upon rank dressed in the reds of fire. Behind them rank upon rank dressed in purple and blue, and to their left rank upon rank in shades of green.

An ensign stood forth from each side of the square and took one of the winged horses from the chariot of victory, throwing upon it a cloth of the appropriate colour, yellow gold, crimson red, dark purple blue, or emerald green.

"Oh may I speak to the horses?" asked Rebecca.

"Of course," said the lady. "We must give them thanks for bringing us here."

And one by one she took Rebecca to speak to them and stroke their noses. And wonderful horses they were too. Each was named after a wind. The one in gold and yellow was called Oriens, the one in red Meridies, the one in blue Occidens, and the one in emerald Septentrio.

"Now you must inspect the guard of honour," said the lady.

And so they did. As the band played, they walked between the ranks with a smart officer behind them.

The ranks of soldiers wore no armour, but were tall shining creatures, with flowing hair and tunics that were meant to give fleetness of foot rather than protection.

"In swiftness there is no need of protection," said the lady of the chariot, to Richard's question. "They are fast to the prevention of wrongs and to upholding of the law, and fast to return again. Besides, no foe dares to stand up to the Emperor's might. All evil is only done by stealth in the lands of night."

The yellow clad angels, for that is what they appeared to be, for they had wings arched behind them, were armed with bows

The soldiers were tall shining creatures clad in
red, blue, yellow and emerald

and arrows, like the Lady of Victory and the child who had so wondrously shot them here from out of the stone circle.

The red ones had long slender spears with flames at the tip. "They are controllers of dragons and giants," said the lady, "which is why they have long spears."

The blue angels had nets and tridents. "They are equipped for seeking the depths of the seas," she said, "for monsters who lurk in the dark depths."

The emerald angels had mirror-like shields. "They are not only for defence," said the lady, "for any attacker will see the reflection of his own wickedness and be stunned by it or even turned to salt or stone."

"Are there all these enemies to be fought against here?" asked Rebecca. "It seems a very dangerous country."

"Oh no," replied the lady of the chariot. "There is no need for them here, except for demonstrating the glory of the Emperor, or to be a guard of honour for distinguished or well loved visitors. No, they are used to keep the law in the troublesome mists and waters and lands of time."

"I have never seen any of them there," said Richard. "I wish we had."

"They are too swift for your seeing," said the lady. "But they keep all the laws that you take for granted. They see that things always stay the same. That your bedroom has not shrunk in the night. That the walls have not turned to water. That the colours of the grass stay the same. That the flowers in the garden do not grow to twice their size, or ten times or not at all. That apple pips do not grow into cucumbers. That your ears have not become pointed. That you grow taller with your age. That ice cream is always cold and never hot. That strawberries do not taste of sawdust one day and fish and chips the next."

"Do all those things need laws?" asked Rebecca.

"Of course," said the lady, "or everything would be a great jumbled muddle."

"Like your bedroom," said Richard.

"Worse even than that," said the lady, "for the muddle would be ever changing of its own accord and life would be impossible."

"It's never very easy anyway," said Rebecca. "It would be nice if sometimes the laws would change. If we really wished it. So that if you fell over, the ground would be soft or bouncy in that place."

"Or if you kicked a ball against a window, the glass would go hard instead of breaking," said Richard.

"The laws could be made less rigid," said the lady, "if you were better at keeping the rules yourselves. But everything needs to be kept the same so that, when you have learned to live in the limits of the laws, you can learn to live happily without them. But that, my dears, is far far harder."

"Oh how can it be harder, not having any rules?" said Rebecca.

"It would be all right if you all wanted the same thing," said the lady, "but as soon as you didn't, where would you be? If one of you wanted it snowing so they could play snowballs, and another wanted sunshine to go for a swim."

"Oh most people would rather have sunshine," said Richard.

"I wouldn't," said Rebecca.

"You would if it was always snowing," said Richard. "Last winter, after it had snowed for a week, you started grizzling because it was too cold."

"And if you went swimming," continued the lady, "and dived in to the water, what would happen if halfway through your dive someone else made the water shallow because they wanted to paddle?"

"We could all have our own swimming places then," said Rebecca.

"Ah," said the lady sadly, "and everyone would be in their own little worlds, doing their own little things, and where would love be then? We need other people to share things with before they are really enjoyable."

"Yes, but Richard never wants to do the same as I do," said Rebecca. "That's why we always quarrel when we play."

"You can choose to want the same as each other," said the lady.

"Why should we?" demanded Rebecca.

"That is why you are in the world. To have the time to find out," said the lady. "But it might be easier if you found some of your Own True Goodness. Then you might prefer to do what the others wanted."

"Doesn't sound much fun," sniffed Rebecca.

"How do you know until you try?" said the lady.

"Anyway, who makes up the rules?" said Richard.

"No one really knows that," said the lady, "but you can always go and ask."

"These don't make them up do they?" said Richard.

"No, they are only angels. They do what they are told."

"How funny," said Rebecca.

"They like to be obedient," said the lady.

"I wouldn't," said Rebecca.

"That's because you are not an angel," said the lady.

"What am I then?" asked Rebecca.

"A human."

"Did I ought to try to be an angel?"

"Oh no," smiled the lady. "You can't become what you are not."

"Mum sometimes says 'Now be an angel'," said Rebecca.

"What she means is be obedient. Do as you are told."

"And don't I need to?"

"Oh sometimes, yes. But you'd be very dull if you always did. No better than a vacuum cleaner or a motor car or some kind of machine."

"Are angels like machines?"

"Oh no, they are like you. They have characters and are very nice. But they always do the same thing, which is whatever they were made to do."

"They've been programmed," said Richard. "Like a computer."

"That's right," said the lady.

"So they couldn't do wrong if they tried?" asked Rebecca.

"They would not know what it was. It would not enter their heads," said the lady.

"But we are different from them," said Richard. "Because we can do right or wrong."

"Exactly," said the lady.

"Oh, we are better than angels!" cried Rebecca.

"Or worse," warned the lady.

"Oh dear, I hadn't thought of that," said Rebecca. "It's very hard being human, isn't it?"

"I'm afraid it is, my dears. You have to find for yourselves what's right and wrong. And then make sure you do the right one."

"All the time?"

"All the time. Until you have no more need of time."

"It sounds impossible," said Rebecca.

"On your own I expect it is," smiled the lady. "But who knows what you cannot do, with a little help from your friends."

"Is that why we are here?"

"If you are willing to accept our help. By our rules we can never force you."

"So I can go back home whenever I want to, and be a little horror?" asked Rebecca.

"If that is what you choose."

"Oh I would never do that!" cried Rebecca. "I'm going to stay with you and all your friends and learn how best to be good."

"Very well, that gladdens my heart," said the lady. "But it may not be so easy. There might come a time when you prefer to go back and be a little horror."

"Never, never, never!" cried Rebecca.

"We shall see," said the lady.

"You said our friends would help us, if we let them," said Rebecca. "So I'm just going to leave it all to them."

"I fear it is not quite so simple," said the lady. "Certain steps you have to take on your own. You cannot drive to victory all the way on a four horse winged chariot. Otherwise you'd be no better than an angel, would you?"

"I suppose not," said Rebecca.

"What do we have to do now then?" asked Richard. "It sounds as if we have reached the end of our ride."

"You must present yourselves to the Emperor."

"Who is he?"

"He commands the armies that enforce the laws that rule the worlds of time."

"Is he very frightening?" asked Rebecca.

"Only if you fear the law," said the lady. "So that depends on you."

"What do we have to do when we see him?"

"You must ask if you may step outside his law, so that you can better help all those who are inside it, when you return."

"Do we have to return?"

"That is the law."

"Then I *hate* the law!" cried Rebecca.

"If you hate the law then I think you will hate the Emperor," said the lady. "And then he may well appear to you like the demon under the Fallen Tower."

"Is he really like that?" asked Rebecca.

"No, of course not," said the lady. "He would simply be reflecting you, being lawless, to teach you a lesson. The choice is yours."

"I never thought choices could be so easy and yet so hard," said Richard.

"That's why angels are content not to be humans," said the lady. "It is a life of difficult choices. Although if you make the right choices I am told that it gets much better, even than the perfect life of angels."

"Well I suppose we'd better go and meet him then," said Rebecca.

"That seems to me the right decision, if somewhat grudgingly made," said the lady.

"Where is he?" asked Richard. "Does he live in this big palace?"

"Oh no, he is much too grand for that," said the lady.

"He must be very grand indeed," said Rebecca.

"Turn round and you will see," said the lady. "He is standing right behind you."

Chapter 16: The Giant Emperor

THE children turned but could see nothing. Nobody was to be seen apart from the ranks of assembled angel soldiers.

"I don't see anyone," said Richard.

"Nor me," said Rebecca.

"Look further," said the lady, "toward the far mountains."

They did so. The palace was in a plain in a wide valley and when they approached it they had descended over a dark blue range of mountains that seemed studded with stars. They now looked to the far side of the valley and to the mountains that rose up there.

They were of a different colour, mostly reds, from scarlet to crimson, and studded with coloured points of light, like radiant gems rather than stars. And they rose to an enormous height, dominated by a huge promontory that was lighter coloured, like pink granite. From this there descended frozen streams, or glaciers, that merged on the lower reaches into stretches of snow. The summit of the promontory was also covered in snow and about it had been built what appeared to be a miraculously high wall of gold, regularly carved into turrets of fantastic shape, and with coloured inlays within them, like slabs of precious stone or rock.

"Is that golden wall round the top of the mountain his palace?" asked Rebecca.

"It looks like a kind of crown," said Richard.

"Look more closely," said the lady, "and you will see that it *is* a crown."

"Gosh!" cried the children together, as they suddenly realised the scale of the thing.

"It is a crown!" cried Rebecca. "And that huge mountain is like a head. What looks like pink granite cliffs is really a face. See, you can see the eyes and nose – and the ice and snow coming down from it is a beard, just as the snow on the top is like hair."

"It's a fantastic model," said Richard.

"Wait a minute, I think it's moving," said Rebecca. "There's a gap appearing above the line of the frozen rivers."

"There's going to be an avalanche by the look of it," said Richard.

"It's more what I would call a smile," said the lady.

Not a mountain range, but the head and shoulders
of an ancient King

And as they gazed the crevice at the top of the snow line broke wide open into a long dark gap within which they could see huge white regular slabs of sparkling stone.

"They're just like teeth!" cried Rebecca.

"They *are* teeth!" exclaimed Richard.

"Perhaps I should have told you," said the lady. "The Emperor is a giant."

"I've heard of giants but this is ridiculous," said Richard.

For they saw now that they were not gazing at a mountain range but at the head and shoulders of an old man, with long beard, red jewel studded robe, and a jewelled crown upon his snow-white head.

"We are at the gate of the world of giants," said the lady.

"It seems impossible," said Richard.

"You shouldn't judge everything by your own size," said the lady. "That's very short sighted."

"But we haven't anything like that at home," said Richard.

"Yes you have," said the lady. "It's just that you do not observe it. You yourselves are much bigger than that, in the eyes of an ant or a fly."

"But we are the biggest things in our world," said Rebecca, "except for a few animals like elephants and things."

"I wouldn't be too sure of that," answered the lady. "You live on what you call a planet and that is very big compared to you."

"But it isn't alive," said Richard.

"Is it not?" said the lady. "Again I would not be too sure. That seems rather a flea type opinion."

"A flea type opinion?"

"Yes, a flea would probably think the dog he lives on is a dead world too."

"Fleas can't think," said Richard.

"What a lot of things you take for granted," said the lady.

"It's scientific observation," said Richard.

"Have you ever spoken to a flea?" asked the lady.

"Of course not," said Richard.

"You might be considerably enlightened if you did," said the lady.

"But fleas can't talk," said Richard.

"How do you know?" asked the lady.

"It stands to reason," said Richard.

"I don't think it does," said the lady. "And it seems to me that if that is what you call scientific observation you are living in a world of blind and superstitious ignorance."

"Let them come to me," cried a huge voice. It was deep and awesome as thunder, and rolled echoing all round the valley.

"Was that the mountain talking?" asked Richard. "Mountains can't talk can they?"

"You will have to believe your ears," rumbled the voice of thunder, and broke out into a chuckle that was like an erupting volcano.

"And believe your eyes," it continued after a while. "Fear not, my little ones, you are coming for a ride."

And to their sudden alarm they saw travelling with tremendous speed through the sky, a cluster of great pink objects that looked like elongated air balloons.

"Flying boats! Or air ships!" cried Richard.

"No! Fingers!" cried Rebecca.

And before they knew what was happening, a gigantic finger and thumb had plucked them all three, two children and the dog, into the air, rushing at tremendous speed toward the mountain side.

"He's not going to eat us, is he?" cried Rebecca.

"We'd not make much of a mouthful," said Canis.

"I'll never squash an insect again," said Richard, "now I know what it feels like to be one."

But they were dropped lightly and gently onto the crimson coloured soft surface of the giant emperor's robe. There they gazed in wonder at the panoramic view that they could see from his shoulder.

Below them, like a tiny model, was the four square palace with the troops drawn up on four sides of the rainbow circle. There stood the lady with her triumphal car, like a tiny dot before them. And across the valley was the far mountain range, dark blue with glittering specks like stars. And they saw that they were indeed stars in the mountains, and that what they looked at was in fact the whole of starry space set out before them, like a range of hills.

"Is that where we've come from?" said Richard.

"There stands the universe," came the great voice from above them, and it rumbled right through them, for they stood on the very shoulder of the body from which the great voice came. But great as it was it seemed perfectly aware of their spoken thoughts and able to converse with them just as if they stood face to face with an ordinary man.

"Is that everything there is?" asked Richard. "I mean it's very big. And it seems enormous when you are inside of it. But it does not seem to be all that very much from here."

"It is enough," said the great voice. "One little thing at a time."

"Is it the only one?" asked Richard. "Are there more and more and more, ranging far beyond those starry hills?"

"There is only one," said the voice. "That is what *universe* means. *Uni* means one. What need is there for others? All the worlds can be contained in that one."

"Is it yours?" asked Rebecca.

There came a deep rumbling like a gentle earthquake, and the children realised that the mountain was laughing.

"I look after it," he said in the end. "But I would not say I *owned* it. It just is. Just as I am I. If it belongs to anyone it belongs to those who are within it. That is who it was made for."

"Did you make it for them?" asked Rebecca.

"What big questions you ask," chuckled the giant, tumbling them over in the soft furry crimson grass of his cloak with the vibration. "They are far too big for me!"

"Won't you tell us? Or don't you know?" asked Richard.

"I can answer little questions like how large is the universe. How many grains of sand comprise the sand in all its beaches. How many seas and rivers are in all the planets of creation. How many shining suns. How much they weigh compared with one another. How bright they are. What they are made of. How many and which of the whirling orbs sustain organic life. But the answers to the big who and why questions you will have to discover for yourselves. That is what you only discover by going into the Gardens of the Blessed and eating the fruit of the Tree of Wisdom."

"Will we learn our True Names there too?" asked Rebecca. "And find our True Goodnesses?"

"If you can find your way there and still want to," said the giant. And they felt him rumbling away quietly with mirth.

"Don't you think we can?" asked Rebecca. "Is that why you are laughing?"

"I believe you are capable of anything," said the giant, "if you set your mind to it. In that sense you are bigger than me. But please excuse me. I do not mean to laugh at you. It just seems to me so funny that questions so great should come from things that are so small."

"What do you mean?" asked Rebecca.

"That a little child can come to the fount of the universe and ask the mighty questions. When those who think themselves great in power or learning or wisdom within that range of whirling stars do not know how to begin."

"It seems simple enough to us," said Rebecca. "We just did what we were asked to do. And because we liked the Fool – and his dog." She ruffled Canis' ear.

"Yes, it is very simple," said the great mountain. "Too terribly simple for some. Love and trust has brought you so far. Keep to that and you should find your way safely the rest of the way."

"You mean we have yet further to go?" asked Richard. "It will take us aeons in a place as large as this, with us so small."

"Time and space mean little here," said the giant. "That is an illusion held by those deep in the depths of the starry mountains. When you strike the surface and come out into real light and air, in the world above the firmament of stars, time and space are no longer limitations."

"Why are you so much bigger than us, then?" asked Richard.

"Because I know more," said the giant. "I know all the laws of the universe and how to keep them going, and every hair or scale or feather on every animal, fish or fowl that walks or swims or flies or crawls throughout all of what you call time and space. That is why I seem bigger than you. But when you find what you have come to see, you may find yourselves as big as me."

"That's very grand," said Rebecca, "but I don't think I want to turn into a mountain."

"You only think I'm a mountain because you see only a part of me," said the giant. And he stood up.

To the children this was like suddenly going up in a fast elevator. As if the ground beneath them shot upward into the sky. Except that there did not seem to be any sky. Just a great light blue turquoise light all round them as far as the eye could see.

And far far below them, if they strained over a fold in the crimson cloak, that seemed to them like a giant earthwork, they could see far below, as if laid out on a table, the little mound of twinkling indigo blue that was the entire universe.

"Where are we going? I can't see anything. There's nothing upon nothing for miles," said Richard.

"That is only because your eyes are limited in their range," said the giant. "The light is so clear that it dazzles you. You will soon get used to it and be able to see as far as me. And after all I have not gone very far. I am still standing before my little table. I have to attend to this little experiment before me for a little while longer but my companions will look after you and take you into the garden to meet the others. See, here they come."

"I can't see anything, can you?" said Rebecca.

"I suppose it will be another huge face like a mountain," said Richard, "bearing down upon us."

"Wait a moment. What is that?" cried Rebecca, pointing high upwards into the air.

"It looks like a star," said Richard, "and I'm sure it wasn't there a moment ago."

"Yes, and I think it's getting bigger," said Rebecca.

Chapter 17: At the Shepherd's Lodge

A ND as they watched they saw the star, at first a tiny point of diamond light, grow brighter and larger, and it was plainly descending.

As it did so it gradually began to take on shape and they saw that it was not in fact a star but what seemed to be a great building descending through the sky, and the starlight was shining from what might have been the place of a weather vane on its summit. It had a threefold structure. In the centre was a dome, from the top of which the star light came, and on either side of the foursquare building there was a tall tower rising, pointing upward with a spire to the sky. The whole building, its central hall and side towers, was of stone of brilliant white.

Finally it ceased its descent and remained in the air before them, as if it were about a quarter of a mile away in terms of earthly distance. Faintly they could hear music coming from within it, and a spicy pinewood smell seemed to drift across to them.

Then the doors of its central tower were flung wide open, and the sound of music rolled out towards them and the scent of all kinds of woods and flowers and hedgerows.

"It's beautiful," said Rebecca.

"It's not going to be like that horrible tower once we get inside, is it?" murmured Richard.

"No, you can feel it's different," said Rebecca.

And as they watched, it seemed that a radiance and a vapour (it was like a cross between the two) surrounded the building out as far as they themselves were, so that it was as if it stood in a vibrant lake of silvery purple mists. And a figure came to the open doors, they could see his outline dark against the light that blazed from within. And he slowly walked towards them, across the lake of light, as if along the bright path of reflected light that shone from the radiant doorway.

As he approached they saw he wore robes of white, and that he had a tall staff, curved at the top like a shepherd's crook. And Canis leaped forward to meet him, running round and round him joyously like a shepherd's dog.

"Canis knows him," said Rebecca.

It was not in fact a star, but a great building descending through the sky

The young man stopped before them and smiled.

"Welcome to my house," he cried.

"Oh, is it yours?" said Richard. "We were rather expecting to meet a giant."

"I can be a giant if I want," said the young man. "Watch!" And he disappeared in a flash from before their eyes.

"Oh now you've done it," said Rebecca.

"I didn't mean to offend him," said Richard.

"Now I suppose he'll come back as something big and horrible," said Rebecca.

"How is this?" came a reverberating voice from before and below them.

They peered nervously ahead. There was something huge and blurred beneath the building that hovered before them.

"How do you like my hat?"

And then they saw. They realised that the young man was now of giant size before them, and wearing the building like a hat. It looked something like a bishop's mitre, and the shepherd's crook that he carried reared up like a vast golden serpent into the sky beside it.

"I think we'd rather have you the same size as before," quavered Rebecca.

"Very well," said the young man, immediately appearing before them again. "As you wish. But I hope that when I appear large," he said to Rebecca, "you don't think that I'm automatically horrible."

"Oh no, I suppose not," said Rebecca, "although it is difficult to like something that is so much bigger than you."

"Perhaps not when you get to know it," laughed the young man. "But all strange things are a bit frightening. And especially when they are big, I admit. I suppose it is not good manners to appear to other people much bigger than they are. I didn't mean to show off, and I'm sorry if I startled you, but you did ask me. And when people ask me things I like to do as they wish, although sometimes it turns out that they wish that I had not!"

"We'll be very careful what we ask for then," said Richard.

"That's very wise," agreed the young man. "But don't be afraid to ask, I like doing favours for people."

"We have come seeking," said Rebecca, "for our True Names and our Goodnesses."

"That is a very sensible thing to look for," said the young man. "I wish that more people asked for things as wisely as you."

"Oh we're only doing what the Fool told us," said Rebecca.

"There is wisdom in knowing whom to take notice of," said the young man. "There is no lack of people willing to tell you what to do. And very often the more insistent they are, the less they should be taken notice of. You did well. And you have come to the right place."

"That's because we have been helped and guided by Canis," said Richard, pointing to the dog.

The young man bent and patted Canis' head. "That is another sign of wisdom," he said. "To be able to learn from creatures who seem less gifted than yourselves."

"Oh but he can talk," said Rebecca.

"So can they all," said the young man, "but very few humans can understand them. So usually they have to teach by example. Many dogs, for instance, are part of a dedicated cosmic society, formed to teach certain human beings the qualities of love and devotion and faith to a master."

"Some dogs are nasty though, aren't they?" said Richard. "Guard dogs for instance."

"Even guard dogs show devotion to the duty to which they have been called," said the young man. "But it is true, some dogs, horses, and even cats, fall away from the ideals of their mission. It is not only human beings who are fallible. And very often it is humans who, because of their higher intelligence, which can be a great burden, set a bad example which is followed by the animals. Or treat the animals so badly that they become as bad as their human masters."

"Anyone would think you didn't like humans very much," said Rebecca.

"They cause a lot of trouble," said the young man, "but I love them as much as any other creatures. Their trouble is that they have such large brains that they get themselves into trouble. For instance, if you only had the brains of a jellyfish you wouldn't cause much trouble, would you?"

"I'm still a bit frightened of jellyfish," said Rebecca. "I always think they might land on me in the water."

"Oh don't be frightened of them," said the young man. "There is more harm caused by fear than anything else. Do you ever stamp on spiders just because you are frightened of them?"

"No, I ask Richard to catch them and put them out of the window," said Rebecca.

"Well I'm glad you are not frightened of me," said the young man, "and that I am not frightened of you. Although when I took on my giant size, you looked just like creepy crawly little spiders to me."

"Oh but spiders have eight legs, not four. I mean two arms and two legs," said Rebecca.

"I know," replied the young man. "Although there is more reason to be frightened of humans than of spiders. But come, let me show you the wonders of my house."

And he turned, and smiling, beckoned them to join him on the silvery walkway of light that stretched across the shimmering lake. He put his arms about their shoulders as they hesitated, and they walked together, Canis bounding in circles all round them, towards the doorway of light.

"Is this building really your house?" asked Rebecca as they approached it.

"In a way I suppose it is," said the young man. "But as you saw, I can also wear it."

"It's really too grand to be a hat," said Rebecca. "Rather more like a crown."

"Yes I suppose so," said the young man. "Either way, it is very heavy. Therefore I prefer to take on a smaller size so I can go inside it. And it has other uses then."

"What kind of uses?" asked Richard.

"I will show you," said the young man, "but it is not really a house, in the proper sense of the word. It was not meant to be lived in. It is more in the nature of a gatekeeper's lodge. A place for passing through."

And so saying, they reached the double doors. The singing of mighty choirs and the scent of incense swamped them as they entered the blaze of light.

"It's like a brilliantly lit church, or a cathedral," murmured Richard.

"At Christmas time," whispered Rebecca. "You can feel all lovely Christmassy kind of things in the air."

"Yes, I sometimes call this my Christmas house," said the young man. "It has that feel about it."

And as they passed in through the door they passed also through the brilliant light, that hung like a curtain before it, radiating its illuminating power to the world outside. Before them they saw, towering to great height, a mighty pillar that extended outwards like a bowl at the top.

"Whatever is that?" asked Richard.

"Have you not seen one before?" asked the young man.

"It looks a bit like a huge font, where they christen babies," said Richard.

"It would have to be a big baby, it's so tall," said Rebecca. "It's more like a water tower."

"And so it is," said the young man. "It is really a magic fountain."

"It doesn't *look* like a fountain," said Rebecca. "A fountain should have water jets squirting high into the air and making spray and rainbows."

"That's quite true," said the young man, "but this magic fountain is blocked."

"Who blocked it?" asked Richard.

"Go close to it and you will see," said the young man.

"It gives me the shivers a bit," said Rebecca. "It reminds me of something. Something nasty. I know – it's a bit like that tower, where that horrid couple tried to trap us."

"It's made up of lots and lots of grey bricks, or stones like bricks," said Richard. "And look – each one has a name on it."

"Let me see," cried Rebecca.

They bent closely and examined the stones and sure enough each one had a name on it.

"Are they memorial tablets like grave stones, saying when people were born and died?" asked Rebecca.

"No," said Richard. "They've got no dates on them."

"It shows the names of all the living," said the young man.

"What, all of them?" said Richard.

The young man nodded.

"Including us?"

"See if you can find your own stones," said the young man.

No sooner had he mentioned the possibility than Richard and Rebecca came upon two stones, set side by side each other, and on one was deeply inscribed Richard Duncan Knight and on the other Rebecca Julia Knight.

"Look, and there's the names of all our friends," said Richard.

"And of mum and dad, and granny," cried Rebecca.

"Fancy finding our own names in all the hundreds and thousands," said Richard. "What an amazing chance."

"There is no such thing as chance," said the young man. "You find what you look for."

"What are those stones? And why are our names on them?" asked Richard.

"They are a record of all who are blocking the flow of the magic fountain," said the young man.

"Do you mean that we, our stones, are stopping it from flowing?" cried Rebecca. "How horrible! Can't we take them away?"

And she started to scrabble against the stone that bore her name. But it was dark and as hard as granite and wedged in tight.

"You can remove them if you will," said the young man, "but not before you can replace them with something better."

"What with?" asked Rebecca.

"With a stone of gold and crystal that bears your true name."

"What will happen then?" asked Richard.

"This model of a dark tower will become a shining bright tower, and a model of the true goodnesses of all whose names are appearing in it."

"Won't the new bricks block the fountain the same as the dark bricks in there now?" asked Richard.

"No, because it is a fountain of light. Light spurts from the source of all being, and jetting high into the air becomes clear crystal water that dissolves all evil it touches. It transforms all that is sick or ailing or neglected into beauty and health. And that will form into a lake in a beautiful garden surrounding it. And from the garden four great rivers will flow into your dark world, and into the other dark worlds in the Mountains of the Stars, to transform them into as wonderful a place as this. And, as I said, we stand here only at the gates of wonder."

"What do we have to do to get our stones with our true names on?" asked Rebecca.

"Will you entrust your wand and your jewel to me?" asked the young man.

The two children looked at each other doubtfully.

"They were given to us when we started our journey," said Richard.

"And I don't know whether it is right to give them up," said Rebecca.

"That must be something for you to decide," said the young man, "on the grounds of whether you feel you can trust me."

"How can we tell what is best to do?" asked Richard to Canis.

"You must feel with your own heart," said the dog. "Does it warm within you when you think of giving him your treasures?"

"It feels a bit heavy when I think of giving them up," said Rebecca. "But the feel of this place, and the feel of the shepherd man or porter at the gate or whatever he is, seems to make my heart go a bit quivery."

"Me too," said Richard.

"Then I think you have your answer," said Canis.

"Please sir," said Rebecca, "if you say you want them we will give you our wand and our jewel."

"We feel that probably they were given to us so that we could give them up at the right place and time," said Richard. "Nothing lasts for ever does it?"

"Only here," smiled the young man, taking the sparkling wand and the round jewel from Richard and Rebecca. "And another rule of this place is that whenever you give something up you receive something better in its place. Here, take these, they are the keys to all you truly need and desire."

And he placed into each of their hands a little key. One of gold for Richard and one of silver for Rebecca.

"Find the lock that will take those keys," he said, "and your mission will be almost complete."

Chapter 18: The Whirling Maze

"WHICH way do we go?" asked Richard.

The young man smiled down at Canis, who barked and wagged his tail.

"Your faithful dog will show you the way."

"Come on," said Canis, "we are nearly there!" And he scampered, with his nose down, round the tall dark font.

"Look," said Rebecca, pointing at it as they went past. "Our bricks. They are beginning to glow."

And sure enough, although it was not *very* noticeable, the two dark stones that bore their names had begun to grow a little lighter in colour, a little more translucent, and even to glow dimly a little bit, at least compared to those around them.

"Are there any others as bright as ours?" said Rebecca. "I wonder if ours are the brightest. What does mum and dad's look like?"

Then she gave a startled cry for Canis had turned and snapped at her, even showing his teeth.

"Never ask questions like that," he growled. "That is the kind of thing they ask down in the dark tower. If you talk like that your silver key will turn to lead in your hand, too soft to turn any lock."

Rebecca looked nervously at the key in her hand, and wondered whether it shone a little less brightly. Richard looked furtively at his also, for he had had similar thoughts to Rebecca. But the keys seemed well enough.

"I'm sorry Canis," said Rebecca.

"Never mind," said Canis. "You can't help being human I suppose. But thinking you are better than anybody else is the quickest way to become far worse."

"Even up here?" said Richard.

"Especially up here," replied Canis. "Nothing that is mean or spiteful or deceitful can last up here very long."

"We can't help being what we are," said Rebecca.

"I know that well enough," said Canis. "But breathe in the air of this place. Listen to the music that sings through it. Is it not like the spirit of Christmas, when everyone feels full of joy towards everybody else? Breathe in the atmosphere and it will lift you up beyond all mean and petty thoughts."

And so they did. They found they were going through a great hall, that would have been like a church, except that it was festooned with coloured lights, and balloons, and all manner of decorations. And such decorations! They shone and glistened in all the colours of the rainbow and many more colours besides. Colours such that you could hardly imagine. And all around the sides of the hall it seemed that merry parties were going on, full of chatter and laughter. And high above them light streamed in onto the scene below, through windows of many coloured glass that all showed scenes from the Christmas story. Of a star guiding three wise men. Of shepherds in the fields at night being greeted by an angel. Of a baby in a manger, surrounded by an ox and an ass and other lowly animals. And also other Christmas scenes – a tall broad Christmas tree laden with presents with a fairy on the top. A jolly red cloaked Santa Claus laden with gifts from the North Pole, reindeer pulling his sleigh. The same merry figure walking the snowy roof tops and nimbly descending the chimneys through glowing hearth fires to leave his gifts at the bedside of sleeping children.

"Come, this is the way," said Canis. "Follow my nose." And he put his nose down to the ground, the way that dogs do, and trotted off into what they saw was a wide circular maze, outlined on the floor with patterned tiles. Its extent was equal to that of the dome that was high above their heads.

"We have to tread the maze, to find the true way to the centre," said the dog.

And so they did. It was not a puzzle maze. There was only one path for them to follow. But it went round and round, and back and forth, until every patch of ground within the circle had been covered. And at last, after a short final straight bit, they found themselves in the middle.

"They do say," said Canis, "that the distance we have travelled, walking through the maze, is the same as the height from its centre here to the high point in the roof." And they looked up and marvelled at the height of the pitch of the dome above them. And they admired the bright and beautiful pictures painted on the inside of the dome. It was all the starry sky, with angels pushing the stars around as if the stars were angels' lamps. And they also saw mighty constellations depicted there, those that surround the northern pole – the Great Bear, the Swan, the Throne of Cepheus the king, the curling, coiling

Angels pushing the stars around as if they were their lamps

Dragon. And they realised that the point of the dome was the North Pole of the heavens, about which all the stars turn throughout the night, all the way down to the zodiacal creatures at its rim.

"What do we do now?" whispered Rebecca. For it was very awesome and still, standing here in the very centre of the maze.

"What do you see before you?" said Canis. "At your feet, hidden in the floor."

And looking down they saw a little picture in shining mosaic within the tiny central circle of the maze. It was of a naked dancing figure, surrounded by a wreath of holly and mistletoe, dancing in a night sky, holding in each hand a little spiral of gold and another of silver. It was difficult to see if the figure was male or female, but around the wreath were emblems of a lion, an eagle, a bull and an angel.

"That looks somehow familiar," said Richard.

"Aren't they the emblems the Fool put round the attic door?" said Rebecca.

"Look a little closer," said Canis.

"Those spirals the figure is holding," said Rebecca, "they each have a little hole in."

"So?" said Canis.

"Are they key holes? Do you think our keys fit?" she cried.

"I never heard of a key hole in the floor before," said Richard.

Excitedly, they put their keys into the picture, Richard's gold key with the golden spiral key hole, Rebecca's silver key into the silver spiral key hole. And together they turned, for they quickly discovered that neither would work unless they were turned together.

And as they turned them a most strange thing began to happen. The whole floor of the maze started to turn, not round and round, but over onto its back so that they found themselves upside down, under the floor. Only they soon forget that they were upside down because above their heads was another great dome, exactly the same in shape and size as the one before, but with different pictures painted on it.

At least the ones around the rim, of the Zodiac, were the same, except that, because the children were upside down from the way they had been before, the signs now seemed to go round the other way.

And the paintings on the outside of the dome, although they were of stars, were not the familiar ones of the upper dome. Richard knew enough from reading books however, to realise that they were stars of the earthly southern hemisphere. They were mostly sea pictures. Of Argo the great ship that bore the heroes in search of the Golden Fleece, of Cetus the great whale, and other sea monsters, and high above at the summit of the dome shone the Southern Cross.

"Come on," said Canis. "Never mind staring and star gazing. We have to tread our way out of the maze again now. Don't forget your keys."

And putting his nose to the ground he led the children the circuitous way back out of the maze.

The children took their keys from the lock and hurried after him, backwards and forwards, round and back through the circular maze. But now they found, perhaps because they had turned topsy turvy, that the exit to it was at the far side from the way they had come in, even though it was in the same part of the pattern on the floor. In other words, if it had been the westernmost point of the circle they had entered, they now left it at the eastern side.

Now they found they were passing through another part of the building. It would have corresponded to the choir had they been in a church. There were high seats towering on either side of them, except you could hardly call them seats. They were more like niches in the walls, something like what are called misericords in abbey churches. Little ledges for the monks to rest upon to save them from standing for long hours. But each niche was occupied by a model of an angelic figure, every one with a musical instrument of some kind, and they played slow and stately solemn music in contrast to the merry noise of the upper side of the building whence they had entered. It was like a great mechanical organ, with figures, played by some unknown mighty hands.

And at the end of a dark blue strip of carpet they came to long low steps leading upward to a throne. And they were well aware of a powerful presence seated upon that throne, for they felt the power of her eyes upon them as they approached in awe, treading silently, unconsciously in time with the stately music of the model angels on either side of them.

Behind the throne was a rich curtain tapestry that showed all the fruits of the earth. And this theme was continued upwards by the

soaring pillars of stained glass windows that also showed, glowing in the coloured glass, pictures of every bird and beast that you could think of, or even imagine. For there were birds and beasts represented there that were never seen on earth, and some that one hears about only in legend, such as centaurs, unicorns, amphisbaenas (which are two-headed creatures), phoenixes, basilisks, winged serpents and many more besides, too wondrous to mention.

The children stopped at the foot of the steps before the throne, not daring to proceed any further. They looked up at the tall beautiful woman who gazed down at them with eyes that seemed to see through to the very core of their being. It was the kind of look from which no secrets are hid. She saw all that they were and had ever been. All the good things, all the bad things. The mean things they had done and were ashamed of, and the good things also, and even better things which they could do if they really did their best.

The lady was fair of skin, with great violet eyes, and she wore a glittering silver crown upon her head, and a long cloak of blue and silver which tumbled about her feet. Behind her head and shoulders, as part of her throne, there was carved a great golden sunburst, an image of the rays of the sun, that shone with a deep golden light. And at her feet, partly concealed by the folds of her robe, that billowed like waves of the sea about it, a large silver crescent moon, that shone also with its own deep silver light. And one of her silver shoes was resting upon it.

Her eyes were the more powerful because she wore a veil that hid the lower part of her face, although it was made of such diaphanous silk that they could see that beneath it she was smiling. Upon her lap she held a large book, with thick black covers, and with one hand she held a marker between the pages.

"Richard Duncan and Rebecca Julia is it not?" she said, in a deep low voice.

"Yes Miss," answered Rebecca, feeling it incumbent upon her to curtsey. And Richard nodded and gave a little bow. Somehow there seemed a need to be serious and formal.

"Your names are in my book," she replied. She opened it slowly and gazed long upon the pages that she had marked. "I see that you are rather special."

"Are we?" gulped Rebecca.

"In what way please, ma'am?" asked Richard.

"You have the power to pass the secret gates."

"Is that – good?" asked Richard.

"It is very good," said the lady. "But …" she paused, "it brings a high responsibility – and not a little danger."

"What kind of danger?" asked Rebecca.

"The danger that comes to all who fly too high," said the lady. "For the higher you find you can fly, the farther it is to fall."

"What have we done to be able to fly so high, like you say?" asked Richard, beginning to feel a little bit proud of himself, until Canis gave him a very low warning growl.

"It is not what you have done, but what you have been given," said the lady. "But … " and again she paused, "to those who are given much, much is expected in return."

"I suppose that's only fair," said Richard.

"What do we have to do?" asked Rebecca.

"To complete the quest that you have started on," said the lady. "But now comes the greatest test."

"Oh I don't like tests," said Rebecca.

"You have done well enough so far," said the lady, "so be of good heart. And you show goodly humility. For those who do not fear the task are those most likely to fail."

"What do we have to do?" asked Richard.

"Pass beyond my veil," said the lady, and she indicated the tapestry of living things behind her. She rose to her feet and stood to one side of it.

"I should warn you that it takes your deepest dedication. Are you willing that in order to do the greatest good, you may find that you yourselves may even cease to be? For it is said that no one who has passed my veil has ever returned to tell the tale of that which may be found there."

"No-one?" gulped Richard.

"So it is said and written."

"And is it true?" quavered Rebecca.

"Only you yourselves can see," replied the lady.

"What shall we do?" said Rebecca to Richard.

"I don't know," said Richard, "I suppose we could run for it."

"You may refuse, with honour, if you choose," said the lady, as if she were reading his thoughts. "You will find yourselves back as you were before you started on this quest, with all memory of it gone."

"I suppose that means we might well have been here before," said Richard, "and failed the test and forgotten all about it."

"That doesn't help to decide what it is best to do now though, does it," said Rebecca. "Oh what shall we do? How can we decide the best way?"

"What did I tell you before?" came a low doggy growl from beside them.

"Oh yes," said Rebecca. "The answer is in our hearts."

"Let's ask them then," said Richard.

And the two children stood for a full minute, trying to feel how their hearts felt.

Then as with one voice they said, "we want to go through."

"Very well, the way is before you," said the lady, and with a regal gesture that seemed so gentle as to have no force in it, she pulled the throne aside. Behind it lay revealed a narrow slit within the curtain, through which she motioned they should pass.

And as they started to mount the steps the angelic trumpeters above and behind them blew forth a mighty fanfare that stirred the blood and gave them courage to try their best and meet whatever was to be found beyond the veil.

Chapter 19: Beyond the Veil

THERE was utter silence as they came through the other side of the curtain. And they found themselves in a world that was devoid of sight or sound. Nothing was to be seen before them but a shining silver mist. It was like being in the middle of a vast grey-silver ball, except that the inside of the ball seemed to be an infinite distance away. They were, it seemed, in the middle of nothing. They turned to look behind them, and discovered that the curtain through which they had come was curtain no more, but black hard shiny solid rock. In fact they stood on a perilously narrow niche, on a blank rock face, with nothing extending before them but the empty air.

"Now we've done it," said Richard. "It looks as if we've been tricked and trapped."

"Oh what are we going to do?" cried Rebecca.

"I don't know," said Richard miserably. "What do you think Canis?"

The dog shook his head doubtfully, and although he tried to put a brave face on things, his tail sank a little between his legs. "I've never been as far as this before," he said, with flattened ears.

"Where do you think we are?" asked Rebecca.

"Well logically I suppose we have come out of the other side of the great building that was the young man's hat when he felt like being a giant. Except we could be upside down now because we turned topsy turvey under the dome. But I don't think that logic or common sense work here very well."

"I suppose we can't be far from the young man though," said Rebecca. "Whether he is big or small or right way up or upside down. And he did say he liked helping people."

"But how are we going to get to him now?" asked Richard.

"We'll just have to do the best we can," said Rebecca, "and anything is better than nothing. I suppose we could shut our eyes and think of him as vividly as we can, and shout 'Help!'"

"Sounds a bit silly to me," said Richard.

"Silly or not," said Rebecca, "who is there to see us? And anyway we couldn't be much more silly to begin with than to be halfway up a cliff on a ledge, with nowhere to go."

"All right then," said Richard. "Here goes. Can you remember what he looked like? Should we imagine him like a giant wearing the cathedral place like a hat?"

"No, let's think of him as our size," said Rebecca. "I am sure he could grow as big as he wants to help us. But when he talked to us he was just like you and me."

"All right," said Richard. "Start imagining him then. First his smile, and then his face. And his white robe, and his shepherd's crook. Ready? Now call him."

"Help!" they shouted together. "Help! H...e...l...p!"

A stern woman's voice that echoed like a giant's, made them jump and open their eyes.

"Whose puny voices disturb the silence?"

They saw the voice came from a figure that was not a giantess, but who certainly was much bigger than them. She appeared to be floating in the air, far out from the rock face, above the abyss.

She was similar in some ways to the lady through whose veil they had but recently stepped. She sat on a throne at the top of shallow steps, but her robes were a dull silvery grey, shot with dark crimson and scarlet. An iron helmet was upon her head, and in one hand she held a set of golden scales that swung gently up and down, first one side and then the other, on their narrow balance beam. In the other hand she held aloft, point upward, a naked sword, that was so sharp that it made you feel the pain of cuts even to look at it.

"Please, we didn't mean any harm," said Rebecca.

"We seem to have lost our way," said Richard.

The stern woman laughed. A laugh of scorn that echoed round the silence.

"You meant no harm? You lost your way? Do you think good intentions excuse you to wander where you have no right?"

Rebecca gulped. "Good intentions are better than none, I should think," she called.

"I see," replied the woman scornfully. "The little one has learned a little wisdom."

"What about you?" she thundered, gazing at Richard. "Has the cat caught your tongue? And don't tell me your little sister led you astray."

"No, we came together," said Richard stoutly. "And we have come to seek our Real Names and our Goodnesses."

"Whose puny voices disturb the silence?"

"He! he! he! he! he!" The woman burst into peals of derisive laughter that made the children's spirits sink. "He! he! he! he! he! And what do you think you will find out here? Do you know where you are?"

"No," the children quavered. "Perhaps you will tell us."

"In the place where you will find nothing."

"Nothing?"

"Nothing. You are on the outside of all things."

"I don't understand," said Richard.

"Of course you don't!" called the woman, with a steely laugh. "There is nothing to understand."

"Well I don't believe it," shouted Rebecca in a sudden temper. "There *must* be something!"

"So there is. But you have left it," said the woman haughtily.

"Do you mean that all there is, is behind us?" called Richard.

"Behind you? You fool!" cried the woman. "All that is behind you is illusion. Behind that dark rock face it is a world of dreams. Worse than nothing exists beyond there, where you think you have come from."

"That's where you are wrong!" shouted Rebecca. "There are lots of things in there. Lovely things!"

"Nothing that is real," replied the woman. "And that is just as well. It is a place of selfish dreams and nightmares."

"No it isn't!" cried Rebecca. "Well, some things in it are pretty nasty. But my mum and dad, and our granny, they aren't bad dreams. Nor is my hamster or my rabbit or our cat. We all love each other and that isn't just horrible old dreaming like you say. And there's lots of wonderful things in there."

"Yes," said Richard, taking up the theme. "Trees, and woods and streams and meadows. And the sea and the sky. And lots and lots of interesting things. Books and mechanical things, and toys and games. And good people."

"Why did you leave it if it is so wonderful?" asked the stern woman.

"We told you. We have come seeking our Names and our Goodnesses." Rebecca cried.

"How do you know that is not a fool's errand?" asked the woman.

"Because we trust those who asked us to come," said Rebecca.

"And who asked you first?" she demanded.

"A fool," faltered Richard.

"There you are. By your own admission." Said the woman. "Only a fool or a joker would send you seeking where nothing can be found."

"He wasn't that kind of fool," said Richard.

"And we've met others on the way, just like him, who have told us to go on, and helped us and guided us," said Rebecca. "There was that nice shepherd we met outside the great gate."

"Oh, you've met him, have you?" said the woman.

"You know him do you?" shouted Richard. "Then how is it all dreams in there if you know him too? Is he one of our delusions?"

"No, you speak with some wisdom. There are real things within that cruel rock."

"Then why did you say there was not?"

"If you knew what truly greater things there are," said the woman, "you would think of all within that rock to be as nothing."

"Have you ever been there?" shouted Rebecca.

"It is not my place," said the woman. "My place is to stand guard outside it with my whirling sword." And she swung her sword round and round in an arc of fire. Sparks and flames leaped from it and sizzled off in all directions. "And to turn back all presumptuous wanderers."

"But the young man and the throned lady said it was a gate," said Rebecca. "What kind of gate is it if it leads to nothing or to nowhere?"

"I did not say it led to nowhere," said the woman. "I said that nothing here exists. It is a gulf of emptiness between what is real and what is not. I know you *think* that the world you come from is real enough," she continued, before they could protest. "So does a picture show look real as long as it is lasting. And then the lights go up and all is over, and you return to the real light of day. Let us say there are different levels of being real. And when you have been used to one, then others seem to be more shadowy."

"And there is more than one place, then?" asked Richard.

"Behind me, and beyond me," said the woman. "On the far outside of nothingness."

"I don't understand all this," said Richard. "Are you saying that we have been living in a dream that is inside nothing, and that nothing has something real on the other side of it?"

The woman nodded. " Very well described," she said.

"Sounds most peculiar," said Richard.

"Sounds like an egg," said Rebecca.

"What?" said Richard.

"We've just come out of the yoke," said Rebecca. "We are into the white, and what we can see all round us is the inside of the shell."

"That also is true," said the woman.

"Well how do we break out?" said Richard.

"When the chick is ready to hatch," said the woman, "and that will not be for aeons yet. That is to say, if the egg does not become addled and have to be destroyed."

"What is an aeon?" asked Rebecca.

"Millions and millions and millions of years," said the woman.

"Well that doesn't count because we've already been told that we are outside of time," retorted Rebecca. "So we can go outside whenever we want to."

"Not quite," said the woman. "Whenever you are *ready* to."

"Well we are."

"You may not be the best judge of that," replied the woman. "First you have to satisfy *me*. For I may not suffer anything evil or unworthy to go beyond this place."

"Who said we are evil?" said Richard.

"You would not be in there if you were all good," said the woman. "But if you are so vainglorious as to try it, there is an infallible test."

"What is that?" said Richard.

"You have to tread the narrow edge of the blade of my sword." She held it out straight before her, its point directly towards them.

"If you are not straight enough in your intentions and desires you will fall from the perilous sword bridge and be lost, floating for ever in nothingness through all eternity, for that is the penalty of overweening pride – utter permanent aloneness."

And as she spoke, the sword, in a marvellous manner, extended itself and grew so that its point reached the edge of the ledge where the children stood.

Chapter 20: The Test of the Balance

"IT'S terribly narrow," said Rebecca.

"I know," said Richard. "But I don't see how we have any choice but to try it. Who's going to go first?"

"And know also," continued the woman, staring fiercely at them along her sword arm, "that even should you reach the cross hilt of my sword, you will then be weighed within my scales to see if you are worthy."

"I think she is just trying to frighten us," said Richard.

"And she is succeeding," said Rebecca.

"We mustn't be frightened," said Richard. "We must concentrate on living up to the faith of those who sent us here. They would not have done that if they did not think we could succeed. They have believed in us. Now we must believe in them. So if we keep thinking of that, and of them, maybe that will keep us upright and straight along the narrow way."

"Yes, it was pride she spoke of as the great danger," said Rebecca. "And that means thinking of ourselves. But how can you stop thinking of yourself when you are in great danger?"

"You think of someone else, and follow their example," said Canis.

"How do you mean?" asked Rebecca.

"Follow me. And keep your eyes on me. And worry about me rather than yourself," said the dog. "Come on. Before you have time to have any doubts about it."

And so saying, he trotted onto the perilous sword bridge, as narrow as a ribbon.

"Come back! No stop!" cried Rebecca. But Canis kept on going. Before she had time to think again she followed him on. And Richard behind her. And before they had time to think about their own safety, so concerned were they with the safety of the one in front that they found themselves at the comparative safety of the sword's golden hilt, like a crossroads, in the centre of which they stood. The seated woman now towered above them.

"You may still have the chance to return, if you dare," she cried. And her voice was even louder and sterner. "Otherwise you must be weighed within my scales."

"What are we weighed against?" asked Richard, more or less to himself, as the swinging balances were brought close to them. They were now huge, compared to themselves, each pan being like a round cauldron of shining brass.

"You are weighed against a feather," came the great voice. And a white fluffy feather came floating down from on high and settled gently into one of the pans. It hardly deflected it downwards, so light was it.

"That is a feather from the Dove of Peace that laid the egg," she said. "It carries no weight of evil within it. If any of you weigh more than that, then your side of the balance will go crashing down and you will be spilled into the emptiness of the everlasting nothingness."

"That's impossible!" cried Rebecca.

"You were proud enough to try to pass the test," came the woman's stern voice. "Throw yourselves in shame into the void if now you realise the stupidity of your presumption."

"I'm not giving up without a try," said Rebecca, "even if it is impossible."

"Nor me," said Richard. "We can't just give up now. Who's going first?"

"No one. Let's go together."

"But we'll weigh even more together, won't we?" said Richard.

"What does it matter?" said Rebecca. "Each of us is bound to weigh too much on our own. So we might as well all get spilled out together."

"You're right!" said Richard. "Come on, Canis."

And all three leaped into the near side pan of the balance.

There was a sickening swinging for a few moments, and then slowly but surely they started to dip. Down and down they went, as they far outweighed the beautiful feather in the opposite pan.

"Oh we are going to be tipped out!" cried Rebecca, as the pan began to tilt to a steep angle as it neared the bottom of its traverse.

"Can't we doing anything?" shouted Richard. "At least let's all hold hands." So the two children held hands, and with the other hand one of the paws of Canis the dog. "At least we'll all be lost together," he cried, "and won't be for ever alone."

"Won't be alone?" cried Rebecca. "Remember the young shepherd. He said he liked to help people. Let's call on him for help. Like we did before."

And they shut their eyes tight and thought of him. Only to their minds this time he did not appear like a young man, but as a boy, golden haired and smiling, little older than themselves, and with his shepherd's crook green and bursting forth with spring shoots and flowers. And they began to feel the pan stop in its slow descent, and then start to go up again.

Hardly daring, they gradually opened their eyes. And to their great surprise and delight, they saw that as well as the feather in the opposite pan of the scales, there was the young shepherd, weighing down the other side to make a perfect balance. He was smiling and waving and shouting great joy and encouragement to them.

And the pans of the balance softly settled, gently swaying level, and they cheered with joy and relief.

And as the scales settled to rest in perfect balance so did they become transformed. The pans flattened out into platforms, upon one of which they stood, and the chains upon which the pans had swung became solid, and coiled golden sprigs out of themselves, like frost forming on a window.

The crossbeam became fixed and solid, and they saw it to be a golden lintel across two golden gates of finely traced scrollwork.

And the great stern figure of she who had held the scales and sword slowly disappeared. It was as if she evaporated like morning mist. And there they stood outside the golden gates, the boy and girl and the dog, and on the other side the young shepherd boy holding his flowering crook, covered in little white flowers, whilst sitting upon his shoulder was a pure white beautiful dove.

"How do we get through there?" said Richard, for the gates seemed firmly locked. And there was nothing above, below, or behind, or even beyond them to be seen. It was as if they floated in space.

The young shepherd boy smiled, and taking the gently cooing dove, he cast it into the air. It made several long swoops around them, and they saw that it held in its beak a tiny branch of wood, with grey-green leaves and fruit upon it.

"An olive branch," said Canis.

As it swooped around them the dove appeared to be growing in size. The second time round it seemed as if it had grown from its normal size to the size and bulk of a peacock, although still in the form of a dove. And after the third or fourth gyration it was more

His shepherd's crook was green and bursting forth with
Spring shoots and flowers

the size of a large hawk or an eagle. But still it wheeled and gyrated about them, round and round, and above and below, and then it was difficult to tell how big it was, for as it grew, so its circles of flight grew greater so that it was farther away.

Finally, as it reached the confines of the sphere in which they were confined it must have become of enormous size, but still it wheeled and then, as it reached the edge of the sky a tremendous thunderous cracking began.

The children gazed up and around them with fear as the silver sky became clear and glass-like no more, but jagged cracks spread rapidly across it, black against the silver. And with a loud rumbling crackling cracking noise as it did so, like ice flows breaking up, or the start of an avalanche, or a derelict bridge or building starting to fall.

And then light began to shine through some of the cracks. Light so bright that it seemed like lightning. Particularly when a forked crack grew larger and wider and a forked jagged stream of light burst through.

And all in all it seemed to the children as if the sky were falling in all round them, with the thunder and lightning of the most tremendous storm.

Chapter 21: Through the Golden Gates

B UT as they looked across to the shepherd boy, who stood outside
of the gates at the foot of the other pillar, they saw that he was
not only smiling, but capering with joy, his staff held high in the air,
and he looked across to them and cried "we are nearly home!"

And at that cry the gates before them swung open. With a last
roar the sky disintegrated and fell away, and a pure golden light like
that of the rising sun at dawn shone through the open gates towards
them, causing their faces to shine like gold as they looked upon it.

And on the other side of the gates at their feet, they saw a
golden yellow path, with gleaming bricks in it, and on either side
of the path, as far as the eye could see, the most beautiful and
perfect gardens. They were formal and in intricate laid out patterns
near the path but becoming rolling parkland beyond. And in the
parkland and among the trees animals roamed. Deer, bears, dogs,
sheep, creatures they had never seen before, even dinosaurs, that
they had seen only in books of prehistoric life. And none of them
interfered with or chased the others, even those they supposed
would be enemies.

As they walked forward in wonder through the gates the
shepherd boy knelt on the path before them and prised up two of
the stones. Smiling, he pressed one into each of the children's hands.

They stood in amazement holding their stones, for each one
seemed to glow with a light of its own that came from deep within
it. And on each of the stones was their name, their present name,
deeply carved. But as they looked at the name so other names
appeared below it, and so on deep into the centre of the stone until,
far into the heart of the stone, in strange characters they could not
in their ordinary minds have deciphered, was a final name that,
when they looked upon it, caused their hearts to burn within them,
as though they had at last met someone, or received a letter from
someone they realised loved them and knew them far better and
more deeply than anyone else had known them, even their friends
or their mother or father, indeed better than they had ever known
themselves. It was like finding a long lost loved possession, that
had been lost so long ago that it had been almost forgotten about,
and the re-finding of which brought back memories of great joy of

wonderful times past, and at the same time the realisation, now that one had found it, of wonderful times to come.

"What are they?" asked the children breathlessly.

"Paving stones on the way to the one true centre," said the young shepherd, smiling broadly. "And the record of your own True Names. You will see that you have many, for many are the ways that you might be named in different times and climes, but in the centre of all is your One True Name, of which all the others are outward forms."

"Can we keep them?" asked Rebecca.

"They belong to no-one else," smiled the young shepherd, "unless we include the Great Magician who made them, for he owns all in the end."

"Will he mind?" asked Rebecca.

"Oh I think not," smiled the shepherd boy. "Otherwise he would not have let you find them."

"It was you who found them really," said Richard.

"And all those who helped us to get here," said Rebecca, fondling Canis' ear.

"We were only doing what the Great Magician wanted," said the boy.

"How do you know what he wants?" asked Rebecca.

"We ask him of course," said the boy.

"How do we do that?" asked Richard.

"The same way you asked for help from me," said the shepherd boy. "You think of him with love, and wish."

"But what does he look like?" asked Rebecca.

"If you really want to know you will see," said the boy.

"Is it really safe to?" asked Rebecca. "He sounds very powerful. And did you say he was a magician? He won't change us into something awful and nasty?"

"If he should change you I think it would be for the better," laughed the boy, "compared to which your present state would seem like an ugly monster. But I fancy he will like you just as you are."

"First however," continued the boy, "we must meet the Lady of the Garden, who rules over all the flowers and plants, and birds and beasts within this place, and over the fishes in the lakes and pools."

"Is it a big garden?" asked Rebecca. "It looks more like a park to me."

"It goes on for ever," said the boy. "No-one I know has ever come to the end of it yet."

"Are there others living here then?" asked Richard.

"A few," said the boy. "But one day it will be open to all."

"I'm not sure that will be a good thing," said Richard. "However nice it is at the present, when crowds and crowds of people come, there will be lots of noise and rubbish, and stupid people pulling up the trees and frightening the animals. Can you imagine this full up with motor cars and deck chairs, and ice cream vans and hot dog stands?"

"When I say the place is open to all," said the boy, "I do not mean they are forced to come here. It may be they prefer the kind of place you describe, in which case they might not wish to be here, which will be to their eternal and infinite loss. And the entrance, as you have discovered, is not so easily achieved. But do not worry about overcrowding. Were the whole world to enter in those gates the garden would be large enough for all of them. There are no limits to the space that is needed here. Each one can be alone in the midst of their own horizon if they wish to be, because this is the Garden of the Heart's Desire. Anything that you wish for is yours."

"Is that really so?" cried Rebecca.

"Try it," smiled the boy.

"I'd like – a great big scrumptious ice cream," said Rebecca. "Like the one granny bought me on my birthday at that special café we went to. It was all different colours and flavours."

"How about one like this?" said the boy, and he stooped by a flower bed, and picked a number of flowers, which all bent their heads towards him as he did so, as if they wanted to be plucked. And he arranged them into a little bouquet and handed them to Rebecca.

To her amazement she found that they were not flowers as she had thought, although they were in the perfect shape of flowers. Upon a soft plate of green that were the leaves, each blossom was a perfect model flower in different coloured ice cream.

"Oh!" she said, "It seems a shame to eat it, it's so beautiful."

"Are *all* the flowers in the garden made of ice cream?" asked Richard, amazed.

"Only if you want them to be," said the shepherd boy.

"How strange, living in a garden of ice cream," declared Richard.

The animals gathered about them

"I did say, only if you wanted," said the boy. "It would become very boring after a time. It's nice to have a treat or two like that at first, but soon you find there are greater, more satisfying pleasures."

"I can't think of any," said Rebecca, her mouth full of a dahlia that tasted of the most exquisite strawberry ice cream she had ever had.

"You are just greedy," said Richard. "You'll end up like those greedy pigs in the Dark Tower we came through if you are not careful."

"I won't, will I?" cried Rebecca, somewhat in alarm.

"If ice cream for ever was all you wanted," said the boy, "and you did not care who suffered so long as you got it, then neither she, nor you, would ever have escaped from that place. But the fact is that you are both capable of better things than that."

"Finish your ice cream and enjoy it," he said to Rebecca. "It is a free gift given in love. There is nothing wrong with accepting gifts in joy. In fact that is what all things in this garden are for. Come on," he said to Richard, "I think you had better have a treat as well."

"I prefer chocolate," said Richard.

"That is easily found," said the boy. And breaking a large flake of bark from a neighbouring tree he gave it to Richard, who found that it was a slab of most delightful chocolate, milky in some parts, plain in others, in fact of whatever flavour he chose to fancy, and some new flavours he never knew existed, but which the chocolate seemed to think he might enjoy.

"Come along then," said the boy. "You can eat as we go."

And they walked on slowly through the park along the golden path. And the children were glad and amused to see that Canis held proudly within his jaws a bone that the shepherd boy had picked for him from a toadstool in the grass.

And as they walked so they gradually gathered a crowd about them, of animals that had been wandering and grazing in the park.

There was a great stag with huge spreading antlers. And sheep and goats. And little squirrels, and rabbits and hares and mice. And a grand tawny lion with shaggy mane. A slinky beautiful leopard or cheetah. A lynx like a great cat with sticking out furry ears. And on the animals' backs there rode birds. Lots of little sparrows and coloured finches, some of them perched on the branching antlers of the stag. And on the lion's back there was a sleepy looking barn owl, blinking wisely. And flocks of bluebirds and swallows whirled about their heads.

Soon the path led by a lake, and as they walked so they saw that fish were swimming alongside them, of all shapes and sizes, some putting their heads out of the water, and smiling in fishy ways. One or two bigger ones even waving their fins. And one or two leaping right out of the water, their scales shining rainbow colours in the air.

And presently they came round a curve in the lake, to a rustic bridge that led toward an island. And the boy led them over, the children and Canis behind him, and all the animals following.

Chapter 22: On the Wondrous Island

THE island itself was a riot of flowers and growing things. It was almost like climbing into a flower basket. But little paths led through the clumps of blossoms so that none of the animals or the children need tread on them, and the flowers were swaying gently to and fro in unison and singing, and each of the blossoms was a little face. And with their singing they gave off a beautiful scent that varied with the notes of the tune they sang so that it was a melody of perfume as well as of sound, coming from the glorious variegated colours of the blossoms from which the singing came.

And then the children noticed a deeper strain to the song as if others were joining in, and they realised that the animals about them were singing too. The stag and the lion and the other big creatures in deep bass voices. And the birds were singing their hearts out as well, although much higher up the scale. And they all ranged round a little mound of rocks, that were piled up in the centre of the island.

The rocks themselves that comprised the little hill were clumps of crystal that glowed and changed their colour and brightness in unison with the song. And the smaller creatures, the rabbits, the stoats, the weasels, the squirrels, the mice, even butterflies and humming birds, and multicoloured insects, sat between the stones of the hillock looking up towards its top where, upon a throne of pure white marble, a most beautiful young woman sat. Her hair was yellow and her skin was fair and she wore a circlet of multicoloured flowers as a crown, each of which had its own little face and joined in the song. And her dress, which flowed down to her bare feet, was of green and decorated with patterns of leaves and plants and flowers, and she held a golden sceptre in one hand and in the other a heart shaped mirror that flashed with a dazzling light whenever it caught the sun.

She smiled upon all the company and slowly raised her golden sceptre. The song of the flowers and the animals and birds came to a natural close and they stood facing her in a pure and golden silence.

"I see we have three visitors," she said, with a sweet and welcoming smile.

All the animal eyes turned upon Richard, Rebecca and Canis.

"Come and sit by me," she said.

"Did you bring your little gold and silver key?"

And the two children and Canis shyly stepped forward through the animals and carefully up the little hill of rocks, where they found that there were little coloured flagstones for their feet.

They climbed to the feet of the young lady with the flowery dress. She motioned them to sit on two little pedestals at the foot of the marble throne, half facing her and half facing the animals below, whilst Canis sat like a good dog at her feet, and even gave them a respectful and affectionate lick.

"Ah my good brave dog," she said. "Ever faithful and true. You have led the children home."

"Did you say home, please Miss?" asked Rebecca, hesitantly.

"This is where you belong," said the maiden. "Don't you like it?"

"Oh its lovely," said Rebecca, "and I've never felt any more at home anywhere, but – we do have another home. From here it seems long ago and far away, but that's where we are from and where we live with our father and mother and our gran – as well as our rabbits and hamsters – and I am sure they are all going to miss us."

"That is your home too," said the maiden, laughing. "Home is where the heart is. And one day you may find that there and here have become the same place."

"I don't understand," said Richard.

"Never mind. You don't really need to," smiled the maiden. "It will all happen naturally, just like growing up. Or as birds learn to fly or fish how to swim, and that was not learned out of books was it?"

And all the birds and animals, and even the fish that had gathered around the shores of the island, their shiny faces poking up through the little billows, laughed merrily at the thought.

"But I see from what you carry in your hands, you have learned already most of what you need to know. Gaze into those golden crystal blocks and you will learn all there is to know of your true selves because in them is written your true names."

"We know," said Rebecca, "and we are grateful for these treasures to the shepherd boy who…"

And she looked around but found to her dismay that the shepherd boy had gone.

"Oh where is he? Our friend?" she cried. "Without him we would never have reached here, and we never properly thanked him."

"Never fear," laughed the maiden. "You will see him again before you go, and you can thank him properly then."

"Are we going from here then?" asked Richard. "Somehow there does not seem anywhere else to go."

"That is because we are so near to the centre of all things," said the maiden. "Although it is a centre so great that it encompasses everything. A part of you will stay here, now that you know of us, but you still have much to do at your other home. Lives to live, and loves to love. Then one day, and it will be the last long day, you may return here for ever."

"I'd love that," said Rebecca.

"And there is plenty to explore," said the lady. "And even a great library," she said to Richard, "with the story of everything that ever happened anywhere, and how everything that was ever invented worked, and how all that ever lived grew, so if you have a liking for reading you will find yourself much occupied."

"It all seems like one wonderful holiday," said Richard.

"It is. And what is there wrong with that?" said the lady. "But now you have come for something else have you not?"

"I'm not sure what they are," said Rebecca, "but we were told of our True Goodnesses."

"Did you bring your little gold and silver key?" asked the lady.

"Yes," said the children, holding them towards her.

"You gave your wand and your jewel for them to enter into the outer gates, did you not?"

They nodded.

"Now is the time and here is the place to exchange them for my sceptre and my jewelled mirror. But when we exchange them it will also mean goodbye."

"Goodbye?" faltered Rebecca, gazing round at all the dear creatures.

"For a time and a space, yes," said the lady. "But we will all meet here again. Have no fear of that. For all that you think of as your life is a great spiral, like a whirlpool, and all must sooner or later come to the centre, and that is where you will find me, and all the other dear creatures here."

"And Canis? What about him?" asked Rebecca, doubtfully.

"He has his way to go, the same as you. His tasks to do. But you will see him again, in doorways here, in gateways there, at

unexpected times and places, ready to guard and to guide. And now that you have been here, that will be something of your own duty to all your friends and relations, and even those who are not your friends, when you get back home on Earth."

"Oh dear," said Rebecca. "It sounds so right. It is all so joyful and yet it is also sad. Why do we all have to part from each other?"

"All parting is only a seeming so," smiled the maiden. "You will see me, if you develop the eyes to see, in all the flowers and growing things of nature. In all the fish, the animals and birds. For I am the queen and empress of all living things. And all the others you have met upon your way here, they also are to be found, each in their way, wherever you go, because they help to make the world."

"But where does the world, or the worlds, come from, and everything that is?" asked Richard. "And what is it for? And what purpose does it serve?"

"Questions, questions!" smiled the maiden. "And wise you are to ask them. But the answers are too big to be given in words. You have to see and feel and *be* them."

She smiled gently upon them.

"But if you really want to know," she said, "you have the keys in your hand. Give them to me for the magic sceptre and jewelled mirror of your own True Goodnesses and then much will be revealed to you."

The children slowly advanced their keys, and put out a hand to pat Canis' head, who rubbed his back against their legs.

The lady took the keys and placed in their hands her sceptre and the bright jewelled mirror.

As soon as she did so a deep rumbling came from the rocks below them. It rapidly grew louder and louder, and then with a great whoosh a huge fountain jetted up from behind the throne and shot high into the air, and far above their heads, and the spray began to fall like gentle rain.

And as they looked up they saw that the softly falling spray was as a veil before the diamond bright sun that hung high in the sky above them, and that a most glorious rainbow was forming about it. In fact it was a full rainbow. A full circular rainbow, and a triple one as well. Three full circular rainbows in the spray of the fountain.

And then the rainbow itself began to take on form and they saw the figure of the shepherd boy, who was capering and dancing and waving to them.

"Come up into the heart of the rainbow!" he cried.

Chapter 23: To the Heart of the Rainbow

AND Canis, with a bark of joy, leaped into the air and ran straight up towards him as if he had invisible wings. And Richard and Rebecca too, before they had time to doubt their ability to do so, did the same, and ran to join the shepherd boy. It was like running through a tunnel, or a funnel, of rainbow coloured light, and the falling waters of the fountain were like mist upon their faces, tingling and refreshing, and they ran so easily that they might have been running downhill instead of steeply up.

The boy was silhouetted against the diamond white disk of the sun.

"Catch!" the boy cried, as they came to where he played. And he threw to Richard and Rebecca each a brightly coloured ball, and then another and another and another. And they had no trouble in catching them because they were like coloured balloons that floated in the air and they needed but a touch to send them bouncing up into the air or back and forward to each other, and Canis too leaped into the air from all fours and hit them with his nose, and even balanced one on the end of it as he capered on his hind legs for a time.

"Come along!" cried the boy. "Up toward the sun!"

And he led them in a merry dance on upward toward the diamond disk behind him.

"Is it really the sun?" asked Richard.

"Of course it is!" cried the boy. "But not your sun. This is the sun behind all suns!"

"We seem to be going faster and faster," gasped Rebecca.

"It's the attraction of the central sun," cried the boy. "It pulls all things towards it. And the nearer you are, the stronger the pull."

"Is it like a black hole in space?" asked Richard.

"It isn't very black is it?" laughed the boy. "I suppose you could call it a white hole in created things."

"What is through it?" cried Rebecca.

"We will soon see, won't we," laughed the boy, as they sped even faster towards it. "It's big enough to hold everything."

And as they approached it faster and faster, so indeed it got larger and larger, and brighter and brighter, until they struck what must have been its surface.

He merrily juggled a whole oval of coloured
spheres in the air

And as they did so it was to the peal of a great cry of laughter from the boy, that echoed like joyous thunder all about them, and he suddenly appeared like a giant before them.

"You've turned into the giant shepherd again," said Rebecca, "that we met outside the gate."

"Had you forgotten you were in the land of giants?" cried the young man, laughing. And he merrily juggled a whole oval of coloured spheres in the air, that had now grown up to his size.

"What are they?" gasped Richard.

"Worlds. Ideas for worlds. Each one more beautiful than the last!" he cried. "If you were standing inside one I expect you would call it a universe."

And he snapped his fingers in the air and they streamed off and up and into the air, glinting in the light like a stream of soap bubbles.

"How did you do that?" cried Rebecca.

"Ah! I'm a magician you see, as well as a clever juggler," he cried. "Come and see my table."

He pointed a finger at them and beckoned, and they found themselves wafted into the air before him to look down on the surface of a square table below.

"We must see about getting you home," he said. "Look down at the top of the table."

Chapter 24: The Way Home

AND as they did so it lit up, almost like a television screen. But brighter and clearer, more in fact like a window. But a window in space. Because there below them they could see Myrtle Cottage in its little garden. And as they watched they found they could zoom in and see inside the windows and even through the roof and walls, for there was granny sleeping in her afternoon nap. And there were their own bedrooms, with their toys over the floor.

"It's time for you to go back there, with the things you have won," said the young man.

"Oh I do want to go home, but we shall miss you, and all the lovely things up here," said Rebecca.

"But we are never very far away," said the young man. "You see how easily I can see you when I want to. And you can see me too. And all the things up here, by building pictures in your mind."

"Isn't that just imagination?" said Richard.

"*Just* imagination?" said the young man, in pretended horror. "*Just* imagination? That's the way you see things that are truly real. But of course you have to practice. And you have to keep the windows of your imagination clean. Otherwise they get so dirtied up you can see nothing through them."

"What will keep them clean?" asked Rebecca.

"The things you have been given on your journey here," said the young man. "Your Own True Names and your Own True Goodnesses. Keep hold of them in your mind's eye and you will never be lost and never be alone, no matter what trials and tribulations may seem to come upon you when you are in the dark worlds where people are still learning to see."

"We will be able to see better than them, then," said Richard.

"Yes, we'll be able to tell them all about it, and lead them to doing the right things and getting their own true names and goodnesses," said Rebecca.

"It is true you must try to help those who have not been so lucky to see what you have seen," said the young man, slightly sadly. "But it may not be so easy as you think. Many there are who will not believe you. And many who will laugh at you, or even hate you for what you try to say."

"Oh that's awful," said Rebecca.

"Each one has the right to find their own way," said the young man. "That is one of the laws I have made."

"*You* have made?" cried the children.

"Yes. I made it all," said the young man.

"Who are you then?" said Richard.

"It is for *you* to give *me* a name," said the young man, "by what you see of me."

And before their eyes he turned into the emperor they had seen before the Hill of the Stars, and into the bearded old man they had seen as the priest of the stones, and the man with his head hanging down into the abyss, and then into the Fool they had first met.

And beside him there appeared the young woman from the island below, with her flowered dress, and they put their arms in love round one another, and they looked down at the children. And she took on all the different forms, of the veiled lady on the throne, the stern lady with the scales and the sword, the maiden on the victory chariot, the young girl with the lion.

And Canis appeared beneath their feet, and he had grown to giant size, even greater than a lion.

"Farewell!" the three of them cried.

And Richard and Rebecca found themselves sinking downwards into the table. And as they looked back they saw the young man and the young woman with their dog, and behind them a great white tower building, and although it was in shape like the horrid tower they had seen on their journey upwards, this was the beautiful and clean original, whilst the dark tower had been but its shabby and deceptive imitation.

The children turned their eyes down to the table again and saw Myrtle Cottage coming up, as it seemed, towards them. And they saw through the slates of the roof, into the attic, with their own forms sitting on either side before the little door. And as they did so, so they found themselves back, with a bump, inside those bodies, safely within their own heads. And even the imagination bodies they had made were gone.

"My goodness, I feel stiff," said Richard, stretching himself.

"Me too," said Rebecca. "And I feel as if I've just come back from such a long long way."

"So do I," said Richard.

"Do you think we've been asleep?" said Rebecca.

"I've had very vivid dreams if we have," said Richard.

"Me too," said Rebecca. "Did you…?"

And they compared notes about what they had seen and where they had been, and they found it was all exactly the same.

"If it was dreams, then we've dreamed it together," said Richard. "So it must be true. How else do you tell that anything is true but by seeing things together?"

"Come on, let's tell granny," said Rebecca.

And they rushed pell mell downstairs and tapped on granny's door.

"Goodness me," she said, "is it nearly time for tea? I must have just dozed off for a few minutes. I'm glad you came and called me."

"You will never guess where we have been and what we've seen," said Rebecca. And they started to tell her all about it.

"Well, well, well," she cried, "what amazing adventures! And all from a pack of cards. Are you sure you have not been peeking at my secret pack?"

"Your *secret* pack?" asked Rebecca. "I didn't know you had a secret one."

"That's why it's called secret," said Granny. "Well, if you haven't, you must have seen those things some other way. I only use them on very special occasions."

And she went to her cupboard and took out a little box which she unlocked with a little key from about her neck. Inside it was a bundle of black silk. Unwrapping the silk very carefully she showed them a very strange looking pack of cards.

"These are very old," she said. "An old gypsy gave them to me when I was very young, and they were very old and well used then. No one but me should touch them because they are very close to me, like old friends. But from what you tell me that you have seen, I think it must be all right for you to do so. Because I think they must be your friends too."

And she gently handed the cards to Richard and Rebecca. They carefully laid them out on the table. And to their surprise they saw that the suits were not the same as ordinary packs of cards. They were like the images they had been told about by the Fool – some were swords, some were wands, some were cups, and others were round jewels or coins or what might be backs of mirrors even.

And more to their wonder still, there was not just a single Joker, but lots of picture cards.

"Look," cried Rebecca, "there's the Fool, with Canis the dog. There is the great Emperor. There is the Hanging Man…"

And excitedly they found pictures of every one of the characters that they had met.

"What do you make of this?" asked Richard.

Granny smiled. "Ah, there's more than meets the eye," she smiled, "in granny's pack of cards."

LaVergne, TN USA
08 October 2010
200139LV00001B/41/P

"Badness is only spoiled goodness."
—C.S. Lewis

Comb City

I am not…

A) Black.

B) Good at Donkey Kong.

C) Living at the Argyle Hotel any longer.

D) A stick like my sixteen year old brother, Timmy.

E) Jewish.

F) Afraid of Gargamel.

G) Sure if I'll find any cool friends around here.

I'm Philip Winston. I'm almost eight. I have blonde hair, I have two birthmarks on my arm, I have a loose tooth I can twist around all the way. Since the start of summer, we've been living in Massachusetts (which is hard to spell because of the double S's and twin T's). Our new house is in a town called Leominster (sounds like Lemon-stir). Just so you know…it's not that great. It's not that rad to me. But my father needed to leave California.

Today is Saturday and I'm watching TV, chugging on Tang. The Smurfs is almost over. It's the one where evil Gargamel creates Smurfette. He brews a potion of crocodile tears and bird brains. His cat, Azreal, helps too. They send Smurfette to the village, hoping she'll destroy everything. But Papa Smurf discovers Gargamel's plan. He saves her with 'plastic smurfery' and, in the end, they all start to sing their La La song.

A thousand Chinese names cover the fingerprinted screen.

After a Fruit Roll-Up, maybe I'll try to find those Smurfs.

=o=

I like…

A) Those boxes of french fries you can heat up in the microwave.

B) Playing house with Jenn Carr in the hotel lounge.

C) Summer vacation.

D) Being the monkey in the middle.

E) Making scary faces at the people who take my dad's picture.

F) Snap Pops.

G) Hugging my Hefty Smurf figures.

Now I'm bored, though. There's nothing left to do here. My brother's at the mall and I can't find any cartoons on cable. It's hot, but we don't have a pool (like a real one, not those dumb baby kinds).

I decide to go looking for their village. I sneak through the backyard, jumping over booby traps and trip wires.

Bet you didn't know… but I'm an expert on the Smurfs. Once, my father called a man named Big Wig and he sent every episode to our suite. So I know almost all of them are blue. I know they live in a big secret mushroom patch. I know Azreal is always lurking, I know Brainy is a jerk, I know Papa is 543 years old.

As I search bushes and weeds, I hear Jokey Smurf laughing.

"Afternoon, Phil."

It's my dad. He stands on the banking. He wears a plastic jumpsuit, sunglasses, and his favorite hat from Burberry. Dad carries a large green can while he sprays each apple tree. I can still see the new stitches on his neck. My father looks like an alien, I think (close to the one from that space movie he did).

"How's you cuts, dad?"

He shrugs. "Fantastic, Phil. I told you before. Just a few incisions here and there. Ten years gone."

"Okay then."

"In a few weeks, you'll see. Sure, I look like somewhat of a ghoul now, but at least no one from the studios can see my recovery."

"Well, *I* can see you."

My dad looks like he's frowning on the inside. "What are *you* doing anyway?" he asks.

"I'm not doing *any*thing," I tell him.

"Looks like you're up to *some*thing. Did you get your beauty rest last night?"

"Not so much. I unpacked my room, though."

"If you don't sleep you'll go bonkers, pal. Why can't you get any Z's?"

I give him a nasty face. "Aint my fault."

"And did you do your jumping jacks today?"

"Yes." I'm white-lying.

"Good. It'd be nice if you lost some of that gut."

I can see that metal discs are tied to the tree branches. They're swinging, shining and hurting my eyes. So I blink a lot. "What are those thingys?" I ask and point.

"They're pie pans. They keep those damn birds away. I guess the light scares them. Mr. Tremaine from across the way told me about it. Thought I'd give them a try." He sprays more.

In my head, I think, "That looks silly." But I just tell my dad, "Oh."

He says, "We'll have the best trees in town."

"Why you wetting 'em?"

"This stuff… it's poison. Gets rid of the bugs that munch on apples."

"But we don't have any apples."

"Not yet. But soon. Bugs will eat the leaves too."

"Well, kill 'em all," I say, "Because I hate bugs."

He squirts a few leaves with white liquid. Dad says, "That kid Lee came over. But I told him to come back later. I know you'll have a tantrum if anyone comes between you and your toons. Why don't you go find him, pal? Lee wants to be your friend."

Just so you know… Timmy says that Lee's mother must be an alcoholic.

I tell my dad, "Lee's always spying on me. I don't *want* to play with him."

My dad sprays more. "Then what's your plan, Phil?" He sounds like he could be a little mad.

"I'm looking for mushrooms."

"They're not the kind from restaurants. They're not the kind from the Ivy. If you eat them, you'll have to go to the hospital and get your stomach pumped. It'll hurt probably and the photogs will be there," he says, all snappy.

15

I Kung Fu kick the brownish lawn. "I'm not going to *eat* them. I'm trying to find the Smurfs."

"They're not *real*, Phil. We already talked about this, maybe a million times, back in California."

"Like *you* know."

"Don't get smart."

Climbing the hill, I dodge deep quicksand. "Dad?"

"Don't come too close."

My father drops the can. He shakes off his gloves and slow-pokes over to me. "Go find something to do, Phil."

I give him a meaner look.

"What's up your crack? None of those faces."

In my brain, I say, "I miss Jenn Carr." In my mind, I say, "I miss Mr. Shaw and his multiple choice pop quizzes." In my head, I yell, "I'd go to sleep if I could ride in mommy's limo at night like I always did!" In real life, I just sort of tell my dad, "I hate it here."

"Hate is a pretty strong word. Maybe say, 'I don't like it.'"

"*I don't like it.*"

"Why?" he asks.

"Well… 'cause it's stupid. It's boring." I can smell the Erickson's BBQ'ing next door. Just so you know… they're getting divorced.

My dad crouches down and his suit squeaks a little. "It's not so bad," he says. "It's great here. And, for now, no more movies. No more meetings. No more of mom's old stuff lying around. This place is… fabulous. Everything's just new."

"Everything's wacko."

"*I* don't think so," he tells me.

"Everything's weird."

"*I* don't think so."

"Everything's nutty," I say. "Completely nutty."

"*I* don't think so."

I let out a long, half-whistling breath.

My dad picks up a glass filled with cubes and brown liquid. He dunks his middle finger in, stirring it. After, he takes a long sip. Dad bends down near me and his suit screeches more. "You'll love it here, Phil. I promise. It'll be everything you've ever wanted." He pinches at my round belly.

"What's so *great* about Leominster, anyway?" I ask. "I bet you didn't know... but Timmy calls it *Lame*-inster."

He tells me, "Timmy's always being a wise ass. He's a punk."

"No, he's not!"

"Don't listen to him. There are lots of wonderful things about this place."

Dad says that Leominster, Massachusetts is...

A) "Pant loads of fun."

B) "A blast."

C) "The town where Johnny Appleseed was born. He went around planting apple trees and maybe he planted the ones in *our* yard."

D) "A nice place to take a breather."

E) "Called 'Comb City' because of all the plastic factories that make combs and pens."

F) "Not full of demons like Los Angeles."

G) "100% just fine for us."

I watch another boy from down the street. His name is Levi and he's hopping around.

Dad says, "So, Phil, Leominster's really *the* place to be." He squeezes my shoulder. "Hey... you have an eyelash hanging. Close it up."

I shut my eyes. Dad then blows. It's hot. His breath smells like sweet Crown Royal and a sneaked cigarette.

He says, "Okay. Unlock 'em."

I open my eyes.

"No surgery needed," he says.

"Thanks."

"So... you feel better?"

"No."

"You will."

"Maybe you didn't hear... but Timmy says that Leominster's full of retards 'cause of all the smoky air from the factories. Timmy says they're killing everyone. And soon, we'll probably be dead too."

"Timmy's a dipshit, Phil!"

I give him a nastier face than before, just like Grumpy Smurf.

"Sorry. *Sorry*," he says. "If you stop acting this way, I'll get you a Happy Meal later."

In my skull, I tell him, "I really really miss mom." In my noggin, I say, "I'd blow up our new house if I could." In my head, I cry, "This is a nightmare." But when I start to speak, I tell him, "*Fine*. But I want a cheeseburger Happy Meal. And make sure they put the toy in the box. Sometimes they forget and that makes me steamed. I don't like to get *steamed*, dad. And anyways, you'll just have to go back."

"Okay, Phil. Now scram."

"Dad?"

"What?"

"Don't feel bad about loosing all your jobs. I bet you'd still be a great movie star."

He sprays more poison and I think his face might look a little sad. "Alright," he says. "Thanks, pal."

=ₒ=

I'm in the backyard. I watch for enemies. I search for the giant named Bigmouth, hunting for Hogatha, the evil witch. There's danger everywhere.

"Smurfy," I whisper.

Skipping over trap doors, I see one. It's a small, brown, spotted mushroom.

I call out, "Papa Smurf? Vanity? Clumsy Smurf? Lazy? Hefty? Can you hear me? Can you see me? I'm a good guy, guys. I'm here to help."

An orangy cat zings by. Flashing his teeth, he hisses.

I gasp. It must be Azreal. "*You*. I *know* what you're up to."

I hear Gargamel shouting in the forest. I think he's coming closer.

"I'll stop you both. You won't find the Smurfs and you won't hurt them." I pick up dad's canister and begin to spray Azreal. I wet his eyes, but he quickly jumps away. Chasing the cat, I soak his mouth, his ears and his dirty paws.

18

Dirty One

He tries to crawl away.

"Beware! Beware! I'll save you all."

$=_0=$

My father has stuck Band-Aids on his stitches. Our neighbor, Ms. Minx, is standing on the front lawn with her son, Jeffy. Jeffy boo-hoos and points at me so I give him silly faces.

Ms. Minx screams, "Our cat collapsed in the driveway! He crawled up two streets and puked blood in the fucking driveway. Pepper's dead!"

My father claps his big hands once. "How do you know my son did anything?"

The lady says, "Lee from Stearns Avenue came and told us. He told us that your boy killed Pepper!"

Dad looks at me. "What did you do, Phil?"

I tell them that…

A) "I didn't kill Pepper."

B) "I killed another cat."

C) "His name is Azreal and he's evil."

D) "I'm a good guy, not a bad guy."

E) "If you cry too much, you'll throw up.

F) "Maybe *your* cat will show up soon."

G) "But Gargamel might get him."

My father yells, "Get in the house, Phil! Now!"

$=_0=$

I sit on my new mattress and I've stopped crying.

The door opens half way and then, all the way. It's Timmy. His mohawk points at the cobwebs that hang from the yellowy ceiling. Bet you didn't know… but Timmy has secret tattoos.

He asks, "So, you killed someone's cat?"

"*No.* I guess, but…"

"I always knew you hated pussy," he says and laughs.

19

"It's not funny. *Not* funny. He was evil. Don't you believe me?"

"I don't know. You're always making stuff up. But don't have a shit fit, Phil. Who cares? You'll get away with it. People forget about stuff. They'll forgive you 'cause you're a kid. So... raise hell while you can."

My brother gets blurry because of my tears. "I feel... not good," I say, sort of quiet.

"I feel not good too."

"I want to go back home."

He smiles. "Yeah. But this dump is where we live now. Hey... I think it's sucky just as much as you. Dad wants to disappear so he can make a dumb fucking comeback someday. Loser. He's washed up."

"What are we gonna do, Timmy?"

"I guess it doesn't matter. The fumes from the factories will make us stupid soon anyhow."

I can hear the neighbor's sprinkler go click, click, click.

Timmy shakes his head like he's saying 'no' and he tells me, "Some old lady asked for my autograph today. Must have seen our picture in a magazine or something. She said she thought mom was the most beautiful woman she had ever seen on TV."

"What did you do?"

"I told her mom was gone. Then I signed her arm."

"That's nice."

"I wrote 'suck balls.'"

=₀=

It's after six and the sky looks like strawberry frozen yogurt.

My dad comes in. I know he's still mad. I know he might spank me. I know he apologized to Ms. Minx, I know he took pictures with her, I know he wrote a check. Dad's tossing an apple from hand to hand. On his neck, a row of wet brown stitches ooze blood and dad's skin is shiny, puffy and pink. He looks like a zombie to me (close to the ones from his first monster movie). I feel scared. In my head, I shout, "Go away!" In my thoughts, I tell him, "Everyone hates me now." In my brain, I yell, "I'm trapped in heck!"

20

"No Happy Meal, Phil. I brought you a snack, though," he says, holding out the fruit.

I hug my Hefty Smurf figures. "I don't want it."

"Alright."

"Leave me alone."

"Fine, Phil."

"Mom would never have brought us to a place like this! Never!"

He quietly says, "Well, she's the one who overdosed."

"Stop talking please!"

"She did this to me too. It's not just you. I should still have a wife. And a People's Choice Award too."

My dad slams the door.

But I crawl inside a big moving box with Hefty Smurf. I touch his round bicep and his hat. I begin kissing his nose and his heart tattoo, over and over. I rub my finger between his legs. I lick Hefty.

From Kissing

Marry Me

That afternoon premiered like some show.
I played a broken boy who was lonely and bored and blonde.
After twelve seasons, each day felt like another
repeat. All my scenes were the same.
But, once again, cameras began churning.
4...3...2...
ACTION!

Footballers crashed, pantry to porch. Launching blows, they tackled and broke through the windowpane. A spritz of crystal crumbs gouged their faces.

And we began scoffing.

"Steroids are wicked gross," I said. "*Nasty!*"

Bundles of thread were safety-pinned to my cut-offs. I was twisting, tying, braiding, binding.

"Fuckin' A!" Sherrie grumbled. She thrust her two middle fingers at the School Break Special. "All these shows are fake. They aint real, Butch. They aint like us."

Sherrie was my second cousin and most days, we'd watch Sally Jessie or Jem or Dance Party U.S.A.

"TV's *so* queer," she said.

Knotting the last rung of color, I smiled at perfect black and blue zigzags. "This bracelet's done," I told her.

"Who ya gonna give it to?"

"You."

"Where am *I* gonna put it? Already got thirteen," she said. "Just keep it."

"Can't give *myself* a friendship bracelet. That's *retarded*."

Sherrie poked at her new spiral permanent. Bunching the kinks, she locked them with an orange banana-clip. "I gotta get home."

"*Kids Incorporated*'s on in ten minutes. Don'tcha wanna stay and watch?"

"Can't. Homework. Fuckin' fractions."

"Eighth grade's hard, huh?"

"It rots. Two more years and then you'll see."

I snatched a dusty white Sweetheart from the candy dish. It read, "Marry Me." Slipping the Necco in, I nursed noisily.

"Alright," Sherrie said, "Have fun with What's-His-Face tonight."

Soon, the lights paled to death.

There was only darkness.

Chomping on my chalky heart, I waited for the next scene.

Monsters

Monsters were growling, grinning, snarling, spinning.

Predator ripped through black slush and mire. Bawling, the beast rumbled, rocketing near. As he shot toward heaven, fat dollops of sludge drizzled down over us.

And the crowd jolted.

Foxboro Stadium was thumping like an earthquake. (The booms, the T-shirts, the kids. The swearing and hooting. The gasoline, the pretzels. And high-fives. The clapping, the howling. The mad dads too.)

But I watched Milo Morgan. I stared at the heart-shaped, violet bruise that shone on his bicep. The boy drooped, hunched. He was sucking up another Slush Puppie.

"Cool… huh?" Milo said, catching my gaze.

"Yeah!"

"Black Jack's the best! That one *rules!*"

Since summer, Milo had lived two floors above me and we'd sometimes watch *Alf* or *Batman* or *Dukes of Hazard*.

"I think *The Crusher's* comin' up!" he told me.

Suddenly, one truck cart wheeled, toppling twice and, soon, sparks burst from beneath his jutting fangs.

And the flocks froze.

"Holy shit!" Milo cackled.

In an instant, plumes arose. Black swirls soared, choking the stars, crowding the crescent moon.

"HEY!" he yelped. "Let's go take a piss!"

"Um... I don't gotta go right now."

"*I* do! Don't be *gay*. Just come on!"

A Friendship Band

"That guy's fuckin' dead!" Milo whooped. "Wipe outs are the best!"

Wrenching down my Jockeys, I began to pee and a dim, murky drivel seeped over the seat.

"This is my third truck show, ya know," he called out.

"Awesome."

"Yeah. Just *wait* till the finale."

I could hear his voice swell, bouncing between cinder block slabs.

"Hey... Butch?"

"Yeah?"

The cuss-covered door squeaked behind me. Instantly, I spun round, squirting my stonewashed leg.

And I saw him.

Milo was smirking at me.

For six long seconds, I couldn't budge. My eyes were locked on the curves of his smug smile.

"What are you doin'?" I finally asked.

"Nothin' Just messin' around."

"Well... *get out.*"

"No," he sneered. "I aint movin'."

Gushing with grins, Milo bent over and flicked my dark magenta head. It hurt.

"Yours is way fatter than mine," he told me.

I quickly tucked myself away then kicked the silver knob. Toilet froth blasted as butts and cups bobbled about.

"We should get back," I said.

"Yeah. In a sec."

"We're missin' the show."

He scuffed closer. He pinched my best bracelet. "So... uh... what's *this* thing anyway?"

"A friendship band."

"Oh, yeah?"

"I make 'em all the time."

Slowly, Milo slid his pointer between my wrist and the purple strap. "Looks kinda... *girly*."

"*No sir*. It's cool. It's the oldest one I got. The thickest too."

But the bathroom door whooshed open. Cackling crowds of men charged through.

"I'll go out first," Milo said. "Meet me by the Pepsi machine."

Nosebleeds

It was dark.

Milo hauled me beneath the booming bleachers. Hand in hand, we tripped through shadows and neon ribbons of light.

"These are the shitty nosebleeds," he told me.

"Where are we *going*?" I griped.

"This way."

Above us, work boots were beating, bumping, pounding, pumping.

"Look," he grinned. "I wanna show you somethin'."

With a crooked smirk, Milo reached down and shed the beat T. Every lump of his muscle bulged through caramel skin.

"Why... why'd ya do that for?" I asked.

Dirty One

He stroked the butterscotch bumps. "See. These new muscles started comin' out. It's cause of all my sit-ups. Aint they cool?"

Inside me, jitters twitched, snapping like pistons.

"If ya want... ya can feel 'em," he smiled.

"Uh..."

"Go ahead. I don't care."

I was colored in crimson. Fighting fidgets, I began to paw Milo's nubs. My shaky palms steered breast to bellybutton.

"Aint I *hard*?"

"Yeah."

"Neat... huh?

"Wicked cool."

"Hey," he snickered, "got a triple dare for ya. Will ya do it?"

"We're gonna get in trouble."

"Don't be a *gaylord*."

I glanced away. I thought of Dallas. I thought about Falcon Crest.

Milo said, "*I* triple dare *you*... to French me."

"But..."

And he began kissing.

Milo pecked and puckered and bit. With long laps, he licked my pimpled chin and two goopy streams of dribble stretched between us.

"Don't I feel good, Butch?"

"Yeah."

My penis grew. It curved against my thigh, swelling solid.

"Kissing's cool," he told me.

> Our scene faded and I felt numb, washed in electric waves of thrill.
> I could see new scripts. (The gazes, the rubs, the smiles.
> The laughing and hand-holding. The sleepovers, the walks. And
> twilight. The giggling and making out. The close-ups too.)

Pretty

Scooping through my chest, I dug out soldiers and Snorks and Smurfs. At the bottom, a heap of flyers lay, pig-piled.

27

I had only saved my favorites. (The Jockeys, the French cuts, the red bikinis. The Caldor guys, the K-Mart guys, The Lechmere guys. And bumpy muscles. The thongs and the Hanes. Polka-dotted silk ones too.)

Thumbing to each dog-eared page, I fanned them across my bed so I could see all the pretty men. They smiled. They gawked at me.

And I spat a bubbly brown phlegm gob in my hand.

I began pulling, gasping, tweaking, rasping.

"Milo..."

After twelve quick strokes, it began to leak over my leg.

"Put it iiiiin."

Faggots

Once Ma mixed her second Bay Breeze, I edged down the hall. In silence, I hid and watched.

Faggots began flashing on our fingerprinted screen. It was a news show called, *AIDS In The U.S.A.*

I could see everything. (The vials, the doctors, the swim trunks. The towels and dancing. The hand-flicking and the sneezing. The mothers and bodies. The shorts, the lights, the powder.)

One fruit cried, "Thought I had the flu... but it never went away. This is *terrible*. This is *awful*."

Red-faced, I sunk backwards.

"Serves ya right," Ma snapped. "Fuckin' fudge packers."

Play

That next morning began like an episode.
But, I just couldn't act as my character. I couldn't lie or pretend or fake-laugh.
Still, we plodded through another scene.

Star beams bounced off his links. Hurdling, B.A. cut through Malibu's sparkling midnight surf. As machine guns sputtered, he dove behind a range of rock.

And I began hacking.

Bed-headed, I watched an old A-Team.

I could feel the scorching fevers that flared beneath my skin. Flames burned and blazed (like bonfires, like hot pins.)

"Poor little guy," Ma said. "Ya look like death. Better rest and take it easy."

"Ya think... maybe... I could getta Happy Meal for lunch?"

"Butch... *no*," she hissed. "Have some crackers or bologna or something."

"Okay."

She placed three grape Chewables by the set. "Take these. And drink some Coke too. Least ya had a good time at the truck show last night. I told ya it would be fun. See... ya need to be friends with boys too. Boys gotta play with boys. So... call that nice kid from upstairs. Tell him 'thank you.'"

My face sloped into a jumbo smile.

Dick Disease

"You twerp! Got a couple days off! Lucky duck!"

Sherrie sat, legs like a pretzel. She had just begun making another band. Her ponytails of pink and orange thread were taped to the TV tray.

"I'm sick," I whined. "For real!"

Her eyeballs plunked back. "Yah, right. *Faker!*"

I tiptoed over to the medicine drawer. It was packed with bottles and Band-Aids and Kotex. Sifting, I snatched out a fistful of Cherry Ludens.

"Hey... ya wanna snack?" I called out. "We got Fruit Roll-Ups."

"Can't! Remember? My diet?" Sherrie poked a pouch of blubber hanging from her hip. "Mom wants me to loose ten more pounds. If I don't, she said she'd put me on those Deal-A-Meal cards."

I fake-frowned, stripped a drop and tossed it in. Quickly, the candied sweetness bled over my tongue.

Sherrie asked, "So... did ya have fun with What's-His-Name?"

Since that special Sunday, I'd wanted to talk about Milo. I had wanted to tell her everything.

"Know what?" I said. "Somethin' happened."

"Like what?"

"Um… I had my first kiss."

"Thought you already did! What about Shannon B.?"

"Don't count."

"Well… then… who?"

And I began to wish and wish.

"Okay… see… a couple nights ago… at the Monster Truck Show…"

"Yeah?"

"Well… like… *Milo kissed me.*"

Sherrie squinted. Blink less, her lips curled. "You kissed *a boy?*"

"Well… *he* kissed me. It was a dare."

"That's nasty Butch! GROSS!"

"But…"

Sherrie kicked on her crimson Reeboks. "That's why you're so sick."

"Whattaya mean?"

"You kissed him and now… *you* got the dick disease. *You* got AIDS."

"No sir!"

"That's what happens to boys that mess with other boys. They end up being big fairies and fudge packers. And they all die."

Right then, I thought I might burst (like a bomb, like a firecracker.)

"THAT AINT TRUE!"

By Heart

I had memorized every single word.
Patting cowlicks, I reached for one last pocket of air.
Cameras rushed in.
4…3…2…
ACTION!

I knew his number by heart.

Curling up like a capital G, I sucked back the goo. It filled my throat and packed my mouth. With a gulp, sweet snot slowly crept down.

And his line ticked.

"*Whose this?*" Milo huffed.

"It's Butch. From downstairs?"

"Oh. Hey. What's up?"

"Nothin'. Whatcha doin'?"

"Dumbbells. Push ups. I'm just workin' out," he groaned.

I swabbed my drippy nose with an electric blanket. I told him, "Stayed home from school today. I'm *wicked* sick."

"That sucks ass."

"Yeah. Just got into a fight with my dumb cousin too."

"Girls blow," he said.

Twice, I glanced at *Facts Of Life* giggling on mute.

"Hey... um... Butch?"

"Yeah?"

"Can I ask ya somethin'?"

"Yeah."

"And promise ya won't laugh?"

"I swear."

"Well... ya think... ya think *I* could be famous? Someday? Like Ricky Schroeder, maybe?"

"Sure. You could be a star too."

"Cause... ya know... life seems kinda like some sort of TV show anyway. Feels like I'm actin' all the time. Does that sound queer?"

Smoothing golden tufts of downy, I grinned. "Nope. That don't sound queer."

"Hey... um... Butch?"

"What?"

He began whispering, "Ya think I'm... good lookin'? Good lookin' enough to be on the tube?"

"Yeah. Yeah."

"Ya think... I'm... *sexy*?"

"Sure."

"Ya think I'm *hot*?" he asked.

Again, my penis began to bloat. It peeked out. It pushed through my front flap.

"Totally."

Michael Graves

No Gerbils

> *I was the only one being taped.*
> *Sherrie hadn't come to the set in four days. Like everyone*
> *else, she hated queers and faggots and gaylords.*
> *No one wanted to see a fairy on TV.*
> *But I felt different from all the others. (No dresses, no gerbils,*
> *no rainbows. And no glitter. No flags or chaps. No triangles. And*
> *no high heels. No make up. No confetti. And no moustache.)*
> *I knew I was a fag too.*
> *But I knew I was still me.*

One Day

I waited outside Honey Farms, cradling a new *Teen Machine* and I flipped past pinups and glossy centerfold pullouts. Each star was batting, beaming, laughing, leaning.

But then, I saw her.

Sherrie bopped toward me with long sassy strides. She clutched her Walkman. She grooved. She lip-synced.

"HEY! HEY!"

"Oh... *hi*," my cousin said. She panted and pried the phones from her head.

"Whatcha doin'?" I asked.

"Nothin'. Fuckin' exercisin'."

For thirty two seconds, we shifted around, blowing sighs.

I could only watch the bare traffic that crawled by us. I prayed and I prayed.

"So... um... ya think you're gonna come by soon?" I finally asked.

"Don't count on it."

"Sherrie... this aint no big deal. *I'm still me.*"

She tapped her speckled jelly shoes. "Butch... now..."

"Now, I'm a faggot. But *really*, I'm the same old me. And ya know what? Milo's *wicked* cool. He's awesome..."

32

"What? You think you're gonna marry him or something?"

Twirling my blonde ducktail, I smiled. "Maybe we *will* get married. One day."

"*You* can't! Gaylords *can't* get married. And gaylords *can't* have no kids."

"I can if I want!"

"Look," she said, snaking her hips, "We aint friends no more. 'Cause I don't wanna die. And you got it. You do, Butch. That's why you're still sick. *Duuuuuh*. If you don't believe me, ask your doctor."

But I did believe her.

Tiny puddles of pain flushed in my eyes. Right then, I hated Sherrie (more than Dad, more than the devil).

She shrugged. "I'm sorry."

"LOOK! JUST PLEASE DON'T TELL ANYONE I GOT IT!"

So Much More

Bulbs blared, cooking my skin.
And I was frightened of being cancelled.
I wanted other things. (The face, the clothes, the premieres.
New stories. The earrings and longer hair. The money, the
fans, the limo rides. The mansion. And parties too.)
I wanted so much more. (The Emmy, the cool friends. The interviews. The
diamond ring, the big wedding, and the husband. Puppies. The straight teeth
and baby boys. The dinners, the pictures. The valentines. And the Oscar too.)

A Little Bit Funny

With a wet face, she jerked up the dial and beats began surging from her peach plastic box. As DJ scissored, she thrust about.

And I bit down.

A raspberry Ring Pop was locked between my molars. Cracking its sugary diamond, I watched another Full House.

"BUTCH! BUTCH! Turn off the set!"

Ma boomed in, ruby with rage. Her arms gripped around a stack of my weekend flyers. "Why ya got all these Sunday ads for? Found 'em in your old toy box."

Quickly, I tried to think of good lies.

"It's just... junk," I told her.

"Ya must've saved 'em for *some* reason," she said.

"Um... no."

Ma shook her peppery bob. "Just *tell* me. Why ya got 'em'?"

"I... I dunno."

"Throw 'em away, Butch. *All* of 'em. Ya keep stuff like this... somebody'll think you're a little bit funny."

Fucking Bitch

> *Another scene was set to begin.*
> *But I hadn't rehearsed. I wasn't sure how to play.*
> *Quaking, I hid from the lens.*
> *4...3...2...*
> *ACTION!*

Milo's first friendship bracelet curled around my fourth finger (like an emerald band, like a diamond ring.) I tugged it tight, squeezing the skin scarlet.

Behind his door, *Max Hedroom* droned. The tube buzzed and beeped.

And I knocked hard.

"Milo?"

For sixteen seconds, I listened.

"Milo? *Milo?* I can hear ya. I know you're there. I need to talk to ya...about some stuff."

There was no answer.

I began to grow dizzy from my dick disease and I could feel it driving, sweeping through me.

"Ya don't have to come out if ya don't want to, but I gotta tell ya somethin'. I think... I *know* that we're sick. We're very sick. With AIDS. We... have it. But it's gonna to be okay. It *will*. 'Cause we can do it together. We can do it. I'll take care of you… you'll take care of me. Like… we don't have to be like everyone else. We can be… together. And maybe one day…"

But his door swung open.

Milo was sneering. He stood, bareback, in only briefs.

"Hi."

"I AINT SICK!" he shouted. "I AINT GOT *THAT!*"

"No. Ya do. And I do too. *We're fags.*"

"I ain't no queer!"

"Listen…" I said, holding out his bracelet. "I made this for you."

Milo pinched my left ear. He twisted twice. "SHUT UP!"

Sobbing, I caved to the damp hallway carpet.

"You're a FUCKING BITCH!" he screamed. "Be quiet. GO HOME!"

He slammed the door, cussed five times and, in seconds, his TV shot up all the way.

"Milo?"

I could feel my innards split. They began to bust (like a grenade, like an M-80).

"BUT I GOT IT FROM YOU!"

I Got the Cure

I knew that there would be a big finale. (No Christmas, no high school, no wardrobe. No vacations and no friends. No summer, no stories. No birthdays, no sundaes. And no Sherrie.)
I knew that soon, my life would be over. (No Ma, no laughter. No graduation, no semi-formals, no happiness, no yearbooks. And no pictures, no dreams. No debuts. No cliff-hangers. And no Milo.)
ACTION!

"Hello there, Butch," Dr. Magnum said with sideway smiles.

"Hi."

I sat in red Fruit Of The Looms. My legs were criss-crossed.

"Jeez. Can't believe how much you've grown. Looks like ya started to get some big boy muscles."

"I guess."

As always, crops of silver hair reached out from beneath his collar and cuffs.

"How's school?" he asked.

"Okay."

I didn't smile. I couldn't.

Dr. Magnum slid a drawer open. Scratching his buckled brow, he pulled out an instant Polaroid camera.

"Listen," I said. "I know what's wrong with me. And I have to tell ya."

"Well… go ahead."

"I'm sick… with the flu. But it aint *really* the flu."

He sat on the spinning, squealing chair.

"See… I kissed a boy… and now… I got AIDS. "

My doctor broke with a cackle and he clapped once.

"It's true. It's true!" I said.

"Well, I betcha didn't know… but *I'm* a lot like you." Dr. Magnum said. "See… *I've* kissed boys too. Lotsa boys. Really, all kinds of boys kiss boys. Nothin' to be ashamed of. Just gotta keep quiet about it."

As fat tears ballooned in my eyes, I pushed down the moaning. I tried to hold back.

"But… see… I just wanna be …all these things."

"Oh yeah?" he said, gliding closer.

"I don't *wanna* be like all those other faggots," I blubbered. "I wanna be more famous. And I wanna be rich. I wanna be cool. And I wanna be married. I wanna be skinny. I wanna baby too."

He cupped his smirking mouth. "Well… you have to be what you are. You can't change things."

My face gleamed with grief while whimpers began to squeak free. "PLUS, I'M DYING!"

"Look, Butchie, *I'm* your doctor and *I'm* gonna make sure you're okay."

"Really?"

"Really. *I* got the cure."

"And I'll live?"

"Yep. I promise. And we don't even have to tell your Mother about it." Dr. Magnum aimed his camera. "So… take off those shorts and let me have a good look."

Dum Dum

Everything was hushed.

I slid up my briefs and rubbed away leftover tears.

Still clad in latex mitts, Dr. Magnum tightened his holiday necktie. He said, "Don't forget to give the nurse a sample."

"What do you mean?" I whispered.

"A sample. Of your urine."

"Oh. My pee?"

"Yes, Butch."

My oily bottom still burned. It still ached.

Suddenly, Dr. Magnum began to grin. "Hey… you wanna Dum Dum?" he asked, pulling out one pink pop.

"No thanks."

"Aw… come on, Butchie."

"I don't want one."

"Just because you suck on it… doesn't mean you're *really* a Dum Dum."

CUT!

Bath Time

My Tunnel

I'm bent over and my head tingles.

"Let's have a look, now," Papi says.

I pull apart my rear. Wriggling, I see a private hair on the bathroom floor. I sigh. It floats away.

"Wider, Otis," he says.

I open more.

"Bigger."

Even more.

"How's my tunnel?" I ask. "Did I get it all? Is it okay?"

"You're filthy down there. Get in the tub."

Papi always says: "A boy's gotta be clean. He should be clean as a whistle."

To me, that's silly. Dumb. *Duh.* Because whistles are filled with spit.

Only Baths

I'm not allowed to take a shower.

Only baths.

Papi tells me: "Otis! You're too *young* for showers. You might slip and fall and break your head open. You could die!"

See… he *always* goes on.

But, someday, maybe I can turn that middle knob. Maybe I can wash standing up.

I Hate Baths!

I hate baths!

They're icky! They're yucky! THEY ARE!

First: I rub and scrub, scratching my curls clean. Globs of sudsy dribble ooze over me. But then, I dunk under. And one day's filth is set free. Sludge. Grime. Flakes. I can't see it since Prell makes the water white like half-n-half. Still... I *know* it's there. IT IS!

Next: I soap up my arms, my belly. The gunk skips away and floats by. *All* around me.

Then: I clean my privates. Dove can sneak inside, burning bad. But things get very very very slick.

After: I scour my bottom with a washcloth. It usually needs fifteen wipes to rub clean. All the tiny chunks worm loose and hide. Sometimes, if I wash *too* much, it might start to bleed.

In The End: I'm alone, sitting in a pool of sand, sweat, and shit.

If I could take a shower, it would all just suck down the drain. But, for now, it's filthy water.

And I'm *never* clean.

NEVER!

Arcade

If I really want something, I'll smile non-stop. I'll tug on his arm hair.

"Can I go to the arcade? *By myself*? It's just downtown. They got Pac-Man and Mrs. Pac-Man. Probably Asteroids, Spaced Invaders, Frogger too."

"You aint goin' alone, Otis. No way!" Papi says.

"Please? Pretty please? The Farley boys'll be there."

"You could get lost. You could get kidnapped. What if there's a knife fight? Somebody might do somethin'."

I tell him, "No fair! I'm not a baby anymore!"

"I don't wanna hear fresh talk!"

"Well... why don't *you* take me then?"

He pushes my hands away and he glares. "Stop it," Papi whispers. "Stop. In this house, you're my little boy. It's different out there. What do you think people would say, huh?"

It's Bath Time

After Lotto Live, Papi starts in on me. "Otis? You take that medicine drink?"

"Yeah," I say.

"Swear on Mama's grave?"

"Yes."

"Well... it's bath time. Come on now. Lemme get the water goin' for you. And don't start sassin'. If you do, no picture show."

Squirming in bikinis, I wait for the tub to fill up halfway.

Papi tells me, "Feel this."

I step on the bathmat and dip four toes.

"That too cold? Or just right?"

"It's good."

He cranks the silver X's, twisting them tight. "Get in. Quick before it cools. Remember to wash *real* good this time. No more skid marks, Otis. The brown ones or the red ones."

Cussing, he coughs and goes. Papi leaves the bathroom door open.

Like always.

He'll clomp in every now and then. He'll say things like: "Scrub good." Plus: "Use elbow grease."

Picture Shows

I *do* love picture shows!

They're my favorite! THEY ARE!

I like *Prison of Secrets*. I like *Seduced by Madness, The Carol Conners Story*. I like *Diamonds and Love*.

On the tube, *anything* can happen. Those people scream and kiss so hard. They slam phones, they get married, they cry out loud. And everyone looks gorgeous.

Mama once told me: "I betcha *you'll* be on TV one day."

See… when all the stars come on, I feel like I might disappear from this place.

Company

We don't get much company. Except for Junebug. And, of course, The Farley twins.

Papi will call their pop and say: "The grass out here needs a haircut."

They come after lunch. One is Ted. One is Tad. I don't know which is which. Papi pays them two dollars an hour. Each.

Ted or Tad gives the whole yard a buzz cut. Ted or Tad rakes up all the wet green clippings. They work and work and sweat and sweat. Partway through, the twins take off their white T-shirts.

Papi doesn't know, but I watch.

I stay real real quiet.

And I keep watching.

I do it to the pillows.

Medicine Drinks

I hate those pills!

They're scary. Because one might get stuck going down. I could choke! IT'S TRUE!

Instead, I *always* have my special drink.

First: He taps out the blue one and the tiny orange one.

Then: Papi uses a butter knife to press them. He mashes and grinds until it's only pretty powder.

Next: He stirs the dust with instant hot cocoa. Papi starts mixing, mixing, mixing, mixing, mixing, mixing.

Last: I drink it *all*. Every bit.

Papi says, "Better finish it, Otis. If you don't, you won't feel right. You won't feel good. You won't feel like yourself. Remember what Dr. Ferguson said? Gotta take 'em right. Gotta take 'em everyday."

Usually, I can't taste the pills much.

In the Tub Again

The yellow phone shrieks.

"Touch hole!" he shouts and then zips to the parlor, quick as he can.

See… Papi *always* goes on. Yakking. Joshing. Swearing. Especially when Junebug calls.

I squeeze the shampoo into my palm. There are three fat dots and one squiggly line. A smiley-faced man. But he begins to look sad. His eyes drip, sliding off my skin.

Papi shouts: "You scrubbin' nice?! You bein' good?"

He'll be back to check on me soon. He *always* does.

I'm ready to wash, but then, a big, extra large plan packs my whole head. It's something new. Something like the picture shows on five.

Maybe I *can* have a shower.

Under

All around me, creamy slime shines. And I pretend I'm floating in a milkshake. Not my own muck.

Soon, I'll have to come up. I'LL HAVE TO! But I hold my breath. I keep on.

Big bangs boom, thundering down the hall.

Closer.

And closer.

And closer.

And closer.

Soon.

Just about now.

"Otis? OTIS!!!!"

I shoot out, waves spilling over.

"PAPI!!"

"Otis!"

I'm hacking, I'm coughing, I'm grinding. Snot pours from my nose.

"Jesus, Mary and Joseph!" he screams.

"Sorry!"

Papi yanks me out, pounding my back a dozen times.

And I cry.

"God!"

But I'm not sad. I'm not even *that* scared. Just think I should.

He hollers, "You tryin' to go see Mama again!?"

"No! I promise. Tonight's drink just made me so tired."

"You can't sleep in the tub, Otis! Do that in our bed!"

Half to Death

"Otis Kipp! You could be dead right now! This is serious. Just wait till Junebug hears. You scared me half to death!"

Guess I *do* feel bad about lying and faking.

But, see... Papi doesn't know.

He'll *never* know.

NEVER!

Tomorrow? A Shower?

We get in.

After some sneezes and one 'fuck', he's ready.

First: I pull the bed sheets up to our chins. Tight.

After: Papi covers us with an old lacy blanket. Looking to each side, he makes it even and fair.

Last: I spread aphgans out. The rainbow one, the U.S.A. one too.

"Get ready for prayer," he says.

"Wait. Wait a sec. I'm really really sorry about almost dyin'."

He moves close. "Well... don't worry."

44

"So... what about tomorrow? A shower? 'Cause... see... I can't sleep standing up."

"I *guess* so. But I'll have to sit there and watch. I'll have to make sure you're alright."

"Okay," I say with a wiggle.

"You're gettin' older now. Time to try grown-up things."

"Yeah... see... I'll be twenty two in September."

Papi socks his pillow three times. "I told ya Otis, *don't* say that number. *I already know.* Now get goin'. I wanna' do it."

A secret smile breaks across my face. And I just keep on. "God bless Mama n' Junebug n' Dr. Ferguson n' the Farley twins."

Curls and Curls

I watched Leominster's traffic circle me. Curving close, Exit 19 snaked around our backyard. There were so many vehicles: Trans-Ams, convertibles, big rigs, vans, station wagons.

Sirens began to scream. Honks, screeches, and beeps wailed non-stop.

"Glitter, glitter, glitter, glitter," I said and spun fifteen revolutions. Magic was gushing from my body. It churned around the slide and seesaw. With that luster, I said, "Protect me... and Reba ...and Mom too. Don't let anyone crash into us!"

=□=

Later, in the bathroom, my sister, Reba, complained, "Leeee! Your hair!"

I was glaring at myself. Endless chocolate knots sprang into the atmosphere. Ringlets wrapped all around my head.

"Jesus Christ," Reba, snapped. "Wish mom would do this."

"I'm *sorry*. Not my fault she's working early and late all the time."

She orbited me, clutching a bouquet of brushes.

"Can't you hurry?" I asked.

"Shut up! Your hair sucks."

My chin fell to my doubled fists. Tubes and canisters crowded the vanity. There were tons: gel, mousse, hairspray, VO5, toner.

Reba grabbed a puff and stabbed the gnarly nest.

"Owww!!!"

"Quiet!"

She yanked, jerking hard. My head snapped back all the way.

"Come *on!*"

Tiny pops began to crackle. Finally, the brush tore through. Coils of ripped-up hair sailed to the floor.

"God! Don't you ever comb this bush?"

"I try, but it's too hard. Wish I had hair like yours."

She scowled at her own strawberry locks. Patting and wrenching, Reba sighed. "*My* hair don't do nothin'. *My* hair blows."

She snatched up a can of Aqua Net and doused her feathered head. A sweet mist showered down over us. The glue cooled my skin, fading to hard stickiness.

"Finished?" I asked.

"There's nothing I can do. It's impossible. Gotta call Jeff anyways."

=₀=

I dodged the pavement cracks all the way to Mrs. Tremaine's house.

Like always, Mrs. her poodle yipped. His name was Martin and he was seven inches tall. Martin had soft black fur.

"Hey there, Sugar Pop," she said, untying a basket of wet pillowcases.

"Mornin'."

"Lord. Got so much dang laundry to do." Her muu-muu fluttered and exposed thick brown thighs. With a smile, she slapped the dress down.

"Is it too early to come by?" I asked.

"Course not. I git up at five-thirty every single day. Just gotta keep it down. Mr. T's still in dreamland. Sleepin' late again."

I tiptoed closer. "I'll be extra extra quiet."

"Ya'll ready for school?" she asked.

"Guess so."

"How *is* grade five?"

"Always the same."

Martin waddled over. Shifting on three tiny limbs, he wobbled and crashed.

"Poor little man," Mrs. Tremaine said. "He's always fallin' down. Wish to Christ he never lost that leg."

She draped a bed sheet over the line, clipping it with giant wooden clothespins. The pink cloth sailed free. Countless clusters of black holes freckled one side.

"What happened to your sheets?"

"Ya know how Mr. T's always sleepwalkin'? Well, he just gits up in the middle of the night, lights a Lucky, and lays back down. He's famous for smokin' in his sleep."

"That could be dangerous," I said.

"Say... will ya help me git all my new returns together?"

= o =

Humming, Mrs. Tremaine dragged a stuffed garbage bag along. Rainbow flip-flops cracked and smacked the heels of her feet.

"Where did ya find all these ones?" I asked.

"Well, mostly from the plaza trash. Can't believe people just throw out their bottles and cans. Each one is worth five whole cents!"

She ripped open the shed door. I stepped in and stale fumes washed over me. One horsefly buzzed by.

"Dang!" I said, swatting.

A giant city of tin skyscrapers lined each wall, each shelf. There were hundreds: Coke, Coors, RC, Shasta, Slice.

"Now don't forget," she said. "Look for our state on top of each one. If ya don't see it, it *aint* no good."

Right away, I went to work, building new goo-covered towers. "So, when you goin' to turn 'em all in?"

"Dunno, Lee. Someday."

"Well... there must be a thousand bucks worth by now."

Mrs. Tremaine grinned, popping out a crushed-up Miller can. "Just look at ya hair today! It's so wild."

"I know! I hate it! Wish I had straight hair."

"Why don't ya just chop it off?"

"Then my big ears'll stick out. Kids'll call me names. And mom won't let me anyway. I can't do *nothin'*."

"Mmmm. See... *I* got real curly hair too. So, I go to my sister's salon. She puts in some straightened."

I fingered a kinked curl. "What's that?"

"It's some sort chemical. They pour it on your head and all those waves just disappear."

"Really?"

"Yep," she said. "All my girlfriends do it too."

"But *I'm* a boy."

"So."

"And I aint black like you."

"Sugar Pop... it don't matter. Ya can do anythin' ya want."

"Well... gotta try somethin'," I beamed. "Even Reba says my hair's impossible."

"Then, *go* to the salon."

She folded up the bag. Leftover tonic dripped to her toes. "All done for now. I'm gonna git more cans later."

We stepped out, shortcutting through the flower garden. Gingerly, Martin crouched down and peed on a marigold.

=ₒ=

"Lee!"

I spun, my Nikes shredding over the pavement.

It was a girl from my class. Her name was Joanne Murphy and she was the tallest girl I knew. Joanne had wispy blonde hair.

She galloped toward me, clutching a shoebox. Joanne was covered in florescent jewelry. It clinked with every stride. Pink kitty cats swung from her lobes while rainbow jelly bracelets crawled up her arms.

"Did you finish the social studies work sheet?" she asked.

I stamped my sneakers. "Nope. Forgot."

"You can copy mine if you want."

"Hey, what's in your box?"

With a smile, she lifted her lid. "Cookies. For class. Peanut butter ones."

"Yum."

"Have one."

"Really?"

"Of course."

I reached in and nabbed the largest.

"Your hair looks great today, Lee."

"This mess. Naw," I said, chomping fast. "*My* hair blows."

"*I* love it."

"Really?"

"Yep. Nice and curly." She shuffled ahead. "So... ya know... I hope John isn't mean today. I *hate* boys."

"But... what about me?"

"You're different. You're a sweetheart. And John isn't."

"He's just..."

"He's a asshole, Lee."

John was Joanne's brother. He had stayed back two years before and ended up in our grade. They both looked so much alike: same nose, same chin, same eyes, same ears, same face.

But John was evil... the evilest.

She twisted her neon rings. "Why don'tcha show me another one of your spells?"

= 0=

My teacher handed out more activity sheets. His name was Mr. Tambo and he always gave me C+'s. Mr. Tambo didn't have any hair left.

We had just begun learning state capitals. I knew I'd never remember them all. There were too many: Richmond Virginia, Topeka Kansas, Montgomery Alabama, Jackson Mississippi, Augusta Maine.

"Your quiz'll be next Thursday," Mr. Tambo droned.

But whispers began to sweep up from the back row. "Hey Curls..."

I quickly glanced back. John and Ricky Henderson clucked between muffled laughter. Their desks were crowded with Garbage Pail Kids and torn-up notices.

"Curls and curls and curls and curls," he chimed.

Joanne swerved around, scowling. Both her middle fingers popped up.

"Don't forget about St. Paul, Minnesota," Mr. Tambo said. "Everyone forgets about little Minnesota."

But then, shots blasted the back of my head. Three or four sopping bullets clung on. The balls stuck, embedded in my walnut locks.

"Gaylord," John snapped.

A huge swell of giggles arose.

I faded to pinkness.

"Curls and curls and curls and curls... just like a little girl."

= □ =

In the bathroom, more matted waves locked around me. The spirals bound, pulling tighter and tighter.

"Sparkle, sparkle, sparkle, sparkle."

Whirling, I squinted through blackness. Power pulsed inside of me. It was beaming beneath my skin. It was racing through my organs. And I envisioned new straight, spiked hair. "Go away. Vanish. Disappear. Now. Now."

Finally, I fumbled for the switch and white neon bulbs exploded.

I could see myself.

Still, curls curved all around my head.

I was ugly... the *ugliest*.

= □ =

Mrs. Tremaine said straightening my hair would cost thirty dollars. I went home and pried open my coffee can bank. But there wasn't much at all. I knew I'd have to find the rest myself. Barreling upstairs, I headed for Reba's room. I burst through, colliding with a tacked-up Kirk Cameron poster.

"Lee!" she screamed. "FUCK YOU!"

Dirty One

Reba was sprawled across the bed, denim shorts bunched at her knees. An issue of Sassy sat on the nightstand. It lay open to a shiny Chad Allen centerfold. Both Reba's hands fiddled between her legs.

"GET OUT!"

"Sorry!"

I slammed the door and rested my head on Kirk's lap. After almost two minutes she began to hack. "You can come in now," Reba finally called out.

Breezing through, I flopped on a thrashed, pink beanbag. The insides squished as I sunk in.

"Try knocking next time. Dink!"

"Sorry."

"Jesus. So... what do ya want anyways?" she asked.

"I'm broke. I need money."

"Why? You're only nine."

"I'm gettin' my hair straightened."

"You *are?*"

"Yep."

Reba sighed. "Well, maybe it'll help."

"But I don't have any cash. I gotta pay for it."

She snapped her retainer in and out of place. "Sell something. Kids sell stuff all the time. Like cups of fruit punch or some shit."

The telephone started whining. Reba instantly picked up the cream rotary resting beside her. "Hello... Jeff? I was just thinking about you."

I burrowed through the attic, squeezing by pink puffs of insulation. In back, Nana's old potholders were buried, boxed. There must have been a hundred: red ones, blue ones, yellow ones, gold ones, black ones.

I carefully dotted the table with each knit square. Using glitter and chunky bubble letters, I drew a sign. It read, "4-SALE!!!!!!"

As I waited, toots tinkled from Route Two. But only thoughts of my straight, handsome new mane drifted through me.

=o=

"Curls and curls and curls and curls. Whatcha' sellin' Curls?"

John and Ricky whizzed over on brand new Huffys. They braked, skidding before me.

"Tryin' to raise money for a new haircut?" John asked.

They both tittered, clucked.

"Why don'tcha be quiet," I said.

John swept blonde tresses off his forehead. "Know what you look like, Curls?"

"Huh?"

"A fuckin' nigger."

Ricky broke into a fit of chuckles. Scratching at his crew cut, he doubled over.

"You do! You look like an ugly nappy faggot nigger."

And then, a massive body blacked out the light.

"Hey!" Mrs. Tremaine shouted. "You two shits got somethin' to say?"

"No... no," John stuttered. "We gotta... um... get back home."

"Then why don't ya fuckin' get goin'. Now!"

Quickly, John and Ricky pedaled off, their gears clicking. Both boys glanced back twice.

With a sigh, Mrs. Tremaine kicked at the lined pavement.

"I hate them," I whispered.

"I see why. Ya outta pop 'em in the face."

"They're just... horrible. I wish they'd go far away. To, like, Jackson, Mississippi or some place."

"Well, don't worry, Lee. Maybe someday they *will* go away."

Martin limped over. He pranced in circles.

"Ya can come help me find more cans if ya want," she said, finally grinning. "But, first, how 'bout I git some of these beautiful potholders from ya."

＝ᴅ＝

I sat at my table with my head slung back. Peering through beams of sun, I watched heaven strut by. It was crowded with so many things: clouds, kites, jets, balloons, plastic baggies.

Dirty One

"Lee!"

I shot up.

Joanne smiled and skipped closer. A new pink heart pendant swung from her neck. It swooped side to side, ringing with the rest.

"A sale!" she shrieked. "Cool."

"It's stupid. It's dumb. Nobody's gonna buy 'em."

Joanne scanned the turf, fingering each square. At last, she snatched up two purple potholders. "These please. How much?"

"I *aint* gonna charge you. If you *really really* want 'em... they're free."

"Thanks Lee! You're the greatest! What are you gonna do with all the money you make?"

I froze. "Um... can't say. It's a big secret."

"*Oh*... okay. Well... I have something for you too," Joanne said.

"What?"

"It's a special present. A spell of my own."

"Really? What kind?"

She grabbed my hand and squeezed. "A *strong* one."

$$= _0 =$$

We sat Indian-style. Rotting crab apples spotted the lawn around us.

Gently, Joanne linked onto my pinkies. "Repeat after me, okay?" she said.

"Okay."

"1... 2... 3... 4... 5..."

I copied her.

Magic rushed, burning between us. It flickered, seared.

"...6 ...7... 8... 9. Please make John die."

The words just came.

I snatched back my hands and crashed to the side.

"Bet this one'll work," Joanne said.

$$= _0 =$$

Twice a year, the nurse checked our entire school for lice. Her name was Ms. Bloomfield and she wore sweaters in spring. Ms. Bloomfield had short, permed hair.

I was next in line. Mashing down the tangles, I shuffled on. Cases of awards and medals glowed beside me. There were so many: soccer trophies, football trophies, baseball trophies, track trophies, spelling bee trophies.

"Curls and curls and curls and curls."

I twitched.

"Bet *you* got lice," John said.

"No, I don't."

"There's probably a ton of bugs in there. They couldn't get out if they tried."

"Be quiet. Dink."

He grabbed my shoulder, digging in. "Know what?" John said. "I hate you. *I hate you.*"

Ms. Bloomfield busted out into the hall. Shuffling through stacks of paper, she coughed, again and again.

I knew I'd be able to escape him because now, it was my turn.

But the telephone rang. Ms. Bloomfield scrambled back to her desk and plucked up the line.

"You know, Curls, one of these days, I'm gonna mess you up."

Tears bulged in my eyes.

"I'll get you," he grunted. "I will. I'll show you what little faggots get."

"*GO AWAY!*"

I shot into Ms. Bloomfield's office.

"Curls and curls and curls and curls... just like a little girl."

= □ =

I cast another spell.

Beside me, traffic bolted on, grinding, revving.

"Shimmer, shimmer, shimmer, shimmer," I said, closing my eyes, reeling about. The magic sparked in my bones. It was pouring out. It was flooding the backyard. "Give me straight hair. Make me normal. Now. I command you."

=o=

I was sneering at my dim reflection. As always, the locks stood, tall and puffed. They were impossible.

"Leeeee!" I heard Reba scream.

Big bangs thundered from above.

"Leeeee!"

My sister raced down stairs, through the parlor and into the bathroom. Breathless, she panted in the doorway. Wet hair clung to her forehead and cheeks.

"LEEEEE!"

"*What?*" I snapped.

"Jeff just called."

"So..."

"He said some kid from grade school got in a massive crash on Route Two. Guess it was really really bad. Some kid named John something. Do ya know him?"

=o=

I sped. I stomped through muddy gutters.

And then, I found Joanne.

She sat by the corner, a tin box wedged under her arm. "Wanna a brownie?" she asked. "They're for class today and..."

"Joanne..."

"See... there's some with nuts and some without..."

"JOANNE! Is.... is John dead?"

My chest was sinking and swelling. I pulled at a knotted curl while puddles filled my eyes.

"Lee," she giggled. "*No.* He's alive."

"Well... is he okay?"

57

"I *guess*. He's got two broken legs. Some cuts too."

A tear slid down my face. "We did it to him, ya know! It's our fault! Because of our spell!"

"He was *supposed* to die."

"But..."

She grabbed my wrist and tugged me closer. "He deserves to be dead! John would do the same to me... and to you too. Maybe next time that spell *will* work. All the way."

I began to sob, rocking in place.

"It's okay, Lee. How about that brownie?"

= 0=

John was absent for a long time.

But one half-day, I saw him again.

Flopped in a wheelchair, he sat by the principal's office. Both his legs were sealed in white plaster casts. Each had already been decorated with so many names: 'Milo Morgan, Elmer Mott, Ben Erickson, Denise Rockefeller, Otis Kipp.

I poked at my burry crown of hair and inched over. "Hi John."

"What do you want?"

"Well... I just wanted to tell you that... I'm really really sorry about your legs and everything."

"Shut up," he hissed. "Just shut your ugly face."

"Soon, you'll be able to walk and run and ride your bike again. Soon, you'll feel twenty times better. This... this should have never happened."

"Get away from me."

With blazing cheeks, I scurried toward Ms. Bloomfield's. My sneakers squeaked across the lobby linoleum.

"Hey Curls," John called out. "Someday... someday, I'm gonna stick my dick right up your ass. And I'm gonna rip you open. I'm gonna slice you up."

"Huh?"

"You heard me," he said. "I'm gonna fuck you. Better watch out."

Dirty One

At that second, I could feel the power begin to zoom inside me. It charged through my brain. It raced through my heart. *It filled my body.*

I hop-scotched back. "Know what?" I said. "I hate you. More than anyone or anything."

He chuckled. "Curls... you're not even a boy. You're a little girl."

"Be quiet. Right now."

"Curls and curls and cu..."

I lunged ahead, whacking his cheek.

And I reached for John's golden hair.

"Fuck you! FUCK YOU!"

Two giant chunks tore free.

=₀=

Cackling, Mrs. Tremaine twirled around the breezeway. She gripped a fan of money between her two brown hands. "Sugar Pop! Look! I'm rich!"

"What's goin' on?" I asked.

"See, me and Mr. T. got my brother's truck and went down to that redemption center. Cashed in all the bottles and cans. *Finally.*"

A smile erupted on my face. "How much?"

"Oh, not sure. Looks like a billion bucks, though. Don't it?"

"Yeah."

With glee, Martin squawked at my feet. I picked him up and stroked his neck.

Beeps were bleating from Route Two.

"Got in a fight today," I said. "With that mean boy from the potholder sale."

"Did you win?"

"Um... yeah. I guess. But soon... he'll be back to get me."

Mrs. Tremaine smiled. "Then you'll stand up to him. Again."

"I dunno."

"Sugar Pop, a boy has to do what a boy has to do."

"Yeah."

"Ya did a *marvelous* job bein' so brave. So… what do ya say we go to the salon? Ya can get some of that straightener. *I* got the money. It'll be an early birthday present."

"Well…"

"Changed ya mind?"

"I dunno."

"Well… *I* like your hair the way it is anyways. It suits ya."

"Think so?"

Mrs. Tremaine pulled at my curls. "It's big and wild… and handsome.

Do It

Denise Rockefeller curled around a lacy sheet. Combed in thrill, she whispered, "I love you."

Doug Cleveland was bare and kneeling beside her Cabbage Patch Kid. "It'll work. It'll get bigger," he said, stroking.

"Almost ready?" Denise asked. She pinched at thick veins bulging in his thigh.

"Almost."

Each time their bodies met, prickles of static snapped her skin. Denise had never seen a nude boy until that day. She was awed by his outty, his wild underarms. Denise marveled at Doug's chest.

"It's close to four. My mom'll be home soon."

Doug was pumping faster and with both hands.

"Come on," she whispered.

"Almost there."

"Let's make love."

"Yep."

"I've waited for you for twelve and a half years. I'm ready," she said.

"Uh huh."

"Do it."

"Denise! I'm fucking trying!"

Eight minutes later, Doug was sprawled among teddy bears.

As Denise placed the goopy Trojan in the trash, she could hear scratching behind her bedroom door. "Wallace!" she yelped, "Shush!"

=□=

Denise Rockefeller stretched across the peach love seat.

It was ten past four on a Thursday.

Broken sun peeked through blinds, glazing the parlor with stripes. Rains of dust glimmered inside each beam.

She was picking at the silver braces that crowded her mouth. Opening wide, she scratched at hooks and brackets and wires. Denise had been waiting for Doug's call. While her brain began to fill up with jumbo question marks, she wondered where he might be. Lovingly, she imagined him dirt biking through the sand pits. She could see him buying her a stuffed kitty with fluff and fake diamonds for eyes. Doug might be at the arcade or Doug might be at the skate park. Her snapshots were also framed in doubt. Denise saw her boyfriend necking with other girls and she saw herself, lonesome.

"God," she said and sighed.

A bowl of onion rings steamed on a TV tray. Denise nabbed one. She tore open the hoop, yanking out its innards. As she snacked only on the golden shell, crumbs sprinkled onto her lap.

Wallace, the black bunny rabbit, scampered from his cage. Bounding closer, his lop ears flapped like lazy wings.

"You want some?"

Denise tossed an onion to the buckled rug. Wallace pounced. With a chomp, he nibbled and then, hopped away.

"Be a good boy."

Suddenly, five loud raps sounded from the front door. She struggled up.

It was Ricky Simmons, her new best friend. A massive bag filled with newspapers hung from his shoulder. As he slouched, an autumn gust exploded on the stoop.

"Hey," Ricky said and grinned.

"Hi."

"What's up, princess?"

"Nada."

"Your Mom home?"

"Nope." Denise waved him inside.

"Can't stay long. Gotta finish all my routes before supper," Ricky said.

"How many you got now?"

"Just four. Fruit Street. Second Street. Ninth Street and Horace Lane. You know… my Dad's got three weekend routes too."

"Geez."

"It's wicked cool, though. Got different routes and different papers. Means I get all the different crosswords."

"I like word searches better," Denise said.

"Nah. Too easy."

Ricky dropped his sack. Crouching down, he gave Wallace a few rubs. The rabbit wiggled as Ricky stroked his head and his back. Wallace bowed.

"Look." Denise began tugging at her raw, crusted earlobes. "Do these seem grody?" she asked.

"Not so much," Ricky said. "They're healing."

"Can't wait to get pierced again. I always get infected."

"I wanna get mine done, but my mom won't let me."

"Why not?"

"She says everyone'll call me a fag. I told her they already do."

Denise shook her head. "You're a not a fag, you're a homo. 'Fag' isn't a nice way to say it."

Ricky shook his head too. "Anyhow… so… whatcha' up to?"

"Doug's supposed to call."

"Are you two still in love, just like the movies?"

They both busted into a fit of giggles.

"Shush," Denise said.

Ricky snorted and smoothed out his shiny gelled bangs. "He's soooo cute!"

"I know. He's just… smart and cool and sweet," Denise said.

"Yeah."

"You know… I really really really… *love him*. I do."

"Denise…"

"I think about it. Alot. Because maybe we could be together... forever and ever."

"Don't be an airhead."

"I'm *not*. Sometimes... I can just feel it."

Ricky plucked a root beer sucker from the candy dish. Unspooling the wrapper, he slipped it onto his tongue. "But Denise... you're only, like, thirteen."

"So what," she said. "Listen... I gotta tell you somethin'."

"Yeah?"

"See... well... it's major."

"Just come on. You *have* to tell me. I'm your bestest friend now."

"Well, okay. Okay. Like... me and Doug... well..."

"You two did it!"

"No," she snapped. "No."

"Then... you didn't do it?"

"Like..."

"You *did* do it!"

"*We made love.*"

Ricky's eyes flung open. "Did he have a huge dick? Did it hurt?"

"*Stop.* Stop."

"Did you bleed? Did he shoot his load all over the place?"

Denise grabbed Ricky's shoulder and wrenched him back and forth. "Don't be such a perv, please."

Wallace began to thump his rear legs loudly. Wrestling about, he thrust himself into the love seat's cushion. He was pumping and slamming and biting.

"Wallace! Wallace!"

Ricky half-chuckled. "He can't help it."

"Little bunnies shouldn't do that. Wallace! Enough!"

The rabbit jolted up and shrank away.

She said, "Mom's getting him neutered next week. The vet thinks that'll help."

Ricky grimaced. "That's mean."

"Why?"

"Because they'll snip off his balls."

"Well... it's for the best."

"He just wants to fuck," Ricky said.

Clucking her tongue, Denise frowned. "Don't talk nasty. You know I don't like it."

"Here's your paper, princess. Your mom still owes me three bucks, you know."

=₀=

Denise Rockefeller sat up in the pastel recliner.

February vacation had passed, but she hadn't seen Doug. Her thoughts began to Tilt-A-Whirl. Doug might have been mad or Doug might have felt bored. Her non-stop chatter boxing probably scorched his ears and maybe, Denise spoke about highlights and vests and jelly bracelets too often. Maybe she could chat about metal music, darts.

"What's another word for inept?" Ricky asked. "What's inept mean, anyway?" He sat on the cream carpet as a *Telegram* lay in front of him. With a neon pen, he worked through another crossword puzzle.

"I dunno," Denise replied. "Look it up."

The Home Shopping Network blared on TV. A diamond bracelet was on sale for $99.99. The model waved her hand about, circling again and again.

Denise continued to suck on an extra large vanilla shake. Jerking her cup, she drew up the sweetness, swallowed and choked for air. She stared at the sparkling gems. "I like that one," she announced.

"Looks like something my grandma would wear.."

"*No.*"

"We goin' to the mall tomorrow?"

"Can't. Gotta see Dr. Walker. He'll probably tighten my braces again. He's soooo mean. It always kills."

"That's cruddy."

Denise chewed on the straw. "After, I'm meeting Doug."

"What are you guys gonna do?"

"Eat. Hang. And we should talk."

"About what?"

"Just… stuff. Like the spring dance."

Ricky sighed. "I gotta change this channel. It's for old bags." Snatching up the remote, he started cruising through cable stations. Ricky zipped by videos and cartoons talk shows. Red digits on the hot box sped forward. "There ain't dick on," he said.

"Never is," Denise added.

He stopped on forty-nine. A furry man was grinding himself into a girl. She shrieked, grunting loudly. "Fuck my cunt! Do it hard!"

Denise yelled, "Yuck! Change it!"

"Look at them. He's really doin' it fast… *and* hard."

Denise slurped. Loud gurgles bellowed from the bottom of her cup.

"Is *that* what it's like when you and Doug do it?" Ricky asked, jabbing his finger at the dusty screen.

"No," she said, "It's not like them. It's not like that."

"What's it like?"

"It's…"

"Is it good?"

"It's good. It's… like… well, we only did it once."

Ricky's eyes were fixed on the set. "If I had somebody who'd do it to me, I'd be doin' it all the time."

"We just haven't had the chance."

A veil of worry dropped over Denise. Maybe she was horrible at making love. Maybe Doug didn't like her groans and mews. He might have known she was acting.

"Come on!" the man yelled. He sputtered, whacking the girl's thigh. "Come on! Suck my fucking cock! Suck!"

Ricky hacked. "When are you two gonna do it again?"

"Soon. Maybe tomorrow."

"Oh."

Denise was crushing the paper cup. Its plastic top popped off and tumbled into her lap. "It's not like the TV, you know. We're in love… and I love him and he loves me."

"Did *he* make you suck *his* cock?"

66

She glowered. "No, Ricky. Turn that off! Gross!"

Ricky returned to channel fifty two and then clomped down to the basement for more Shasta. After ten minutes, Denise thought that he probably found her mother's magazines again.

= □ =

Denise Rockefeller breezed through McDonald's double doors.

It was almost five on a Tuesday.

Toddlers were shouting over their Happy Meals. One couple chewed on hamburgers and cheeseburgers and chicken nuggets.

As Denise weaved by customers, a cloud of fried fumes engulfed her. She peered around the dining room. Her eyes burned, but she found him.

Doug Cleveland sat by a portrait of Ronald McDonald. He was chomping, hunched over his Value Meal. The tray he had ordered for Denise sat across from him.

"Hi, baby," she said.

Like usual, strawberry cowlicks stood up around Doug's head. His jersey drooped low, revealing one gold chain and an old, faded hickey.

"Hey," he said.

She slowly bent down. Grabbing him, Denise cradled the back of his head. "I missed you."

They started to kiss. As she tongued her boyfriend, Denise could taste pickles.

Doug suddenly coughed. He yanked back, quickly returning to his meal.

"Geez," she muttered.

"How was the dentist?"

"Orthodontist." Denise tossed her purse onto the yellow booth seat and sat down. "It was wicked dumb. They tightened my braces."

"That blows."

"Yeah. My face is killing me."

Doug said, "I messed up my dirt bike... *bad*. Crashed into a rock bed and warped the friggin back wheel."

67

She was tearing open packets of ketchup. She squeezed the redness onto her coupon-covered placemat. "You have to be careful, Doug."

"Yeah."

"You could break your neck or something."

"Yeah."

She shrugged. "You know… I really really really missed you today. I did," Denise said.

Doug took a massive bite from his McChicken Sandwich. Globs of mayonnaise oozed out the side of his mouth. "Me too," he replied between chews.

"You swear?"

"Sure."

"Swear on you mother's grave?"

"My ma's not dead yet, Denise."

She glanced around. "Listen. I think that me and you should talk about stuff. I gotta say something."

"Alright."

"And I don't want you to get mad, okay?"

"I'll try… I guess."

Denise whispered. "Like… we made love three weeks ago. And we haven't done it since."

His eyes skipped away.

"When are we gonna do it again? *Can* we do it again?"

Sighing, Doug chugged on his Orange Crush. "That's kinda what I wanna talk about."

"Oh… ok."

"I've been thinkin' lately… and this ain't workin,' Denise."

She gulped.

"You're real nice. You are. But I don't think we should be boyfriend and girlfriend anymore."

Denise dropped her McFish sandwich. It landed in the puddle of ketchup.

Dirty One

Denise Rockefeller scuffed down Second Street.

The darkening sky rumbled above. Street lamps began to snap on, twitching with a bare glow. Each one hummed.

Slowly, Denise dragged a cube of wax across her upper braces. Mashing the square, she coated sharp bits and crooks. Her charm bracelet chimed with every twist.

Ricky Simmons was zigzagging from one house to the next. He tossed newspapers onto lawns and porches and doorsteps. With every sling, he'd recite the family's name and address. "The Parkers. Nine Fruit Street," he said.

Denise inched on, following her new best friend.

"The Collins. Eleven Fruit Street. Hey... I'm thinking about gettin' another route," Ricky said. "Maybe on Saturdays. There's this new contest. If you deliver the most papers, you get a free trip to New York City. *I* wanna' see that Statue of Liberty. I wanna see everything."

Sighing, Denise stroked the suede frill of her jacket. "Ricky... I can't believe this. I just..."

They both stopped beside a quivering lamp.

"I love him. And he's just gone. It hurts... like a stomach ache... or cramps... or a bad cavity."

"I bet."

"I miss him. I do," she shuddered. "I really thought we'd make it."

"Well... I guess not."

Tears sprung from her eyes, but quickly, Denise swiped them away. Her mascara began to smudge and smear. Since the breakup, she felt as though she were beneath a mound of electric blankets, huffing in hot, stale air. Her head was muddled. Nothing felt real anymore. She wondered if he swooned over someone else, someone with bigger breasts and black panties. Maybe he loved Jennifer Carr or Jennifer Maxfield or Jennifer White.

"I *have* to see him. I *have* to know why"

"You'll feel better soon," Ricky said, squeezing her shoulder. "Soon, you'll feel great."

"I don't think so!" she sobbed.

"You'll find a new boyfriend."

"I don't want a new one!"

Ricky zipped his button covered jean jacket. "You will."

=o=

Denise Rockerfeller slowly squatted down.

Wallace, just home from the animal hospital, was lying inside his cage. He didn't blink.

"How you doin'? Bein' good?"

Squares of dark fur had been shaved away and his bare skin was pale and stitched.

"It's okay."

Struggling up, Wallace whimpered.

Her hand coasted down the curve of the rabbit's back. "Now you'll be perfect. Now you won't be actin' up. You'll behave."

Suddenly, Wallace sprung, driving his two front teeth into Denise's flesh.

Moments after, she was bleeding in the sink.

=o=

Denise Rockefeller trudged up her ex-boyfriend's patchy carport.

It was six on a Sunday.

Thick winds gushed, blasting about. Flyers and magazines and bills clogged the front step.

Denise poked his doorbell. A loud, piercing buzz droned from the inside out. She forced a smile, teetering back and forth.

Mrs. Cleveland was suddenly squinting out the shade less window. A long cigarette dangled from her lips and, while she scowled, streamers of white smoke surrounded her. Puffing and yanking, she pulled open the door.

"Who are you?"

"I'm Denise Rockefeller."

"Never heard a ya," she said, scratching at her puffy painted sweatshirt.

"Doug home?"

"He's up in his room."

"Oh."

"Don't be too long. We gotta eat soon."

"Ok."

"Don't think we got enough meat loaf for three."

"Ok."

She shuffled upstairs, then down the hallway. A string of seashell nightlights lit her way. T-shirts and Def Leppard tapes were strewn all over. Padlocking her tears, Denise stopped at the postered door. Her worries continued to flip-flop, but she knew she'd win him back and she knew they'd be together again. Gingerly, Denise turned the golden knob.

Doug Cleveland was on his bed. He pumped a stuffed brown bear. Doug swerved and jammed and humped. His black briefs were knotted around his ankles. Moaning, he dragged himself over the animal's plush belly.

"Yeah," he muttered.

As Denise watched, disbelief shellacked her face.

"Fuck!"

With a groan, he turned.

"Denise! Jesus Christ!"

Doug jumped up. Covering himself with the bear, his cheeks bled to pink.

"*What are you doing?*" she sneered.

"What are *you* doing?"

"You can make love to a teddy bear... with yourself? But you can't do it to me?"

Doug was silent. His thick penis jabbed at the bear's button eye.

"Why? Why!?" Denise asked.

He didn't speak.

"Why?"

Yanking up his underwear, Doug dropped the animal. "'Cause it feels good. I like it."

"Then how come you did it with me in the first place?" she fumed.

"I dunno."

"How come, Doug?"

71

"Probably cause you made me."

Denise bolted down the hall, dodging the maze of mess.

"Don't tell anybody! Please!!" he called out.

=o=

Denise Rockerfeller coasted through the mall.

Crowds wandered end to end, chuckling, tittering. Their scuffs echoed everywhere.

Denise was chewing on Sour Patch Kids. She puckered and sucked. The red gooey clumps barely shifted, clinging to her top wires. "I gotta get home soon," she said, her words muffled.

Ricky Simmons was dragging beside her.

As they guzzled grape cola, the duo pushed by a cotton candy vendor. Syrupy clouds enveloped them.

"This place is sooooo beat," Ricky said.

"Yeah. Sorta."

"Anyways... that girl, Kelly C, she said she saw Doug at the Spring Dance."

Denise glanced away. "*So?*"

"Just sayin'."

Denise had only seen Doug exiting the lunch room or detention. Every surprise glance of him stung like her first ear piercing.

"He's a jerk off," she snickered, "I really really really hate him."

"I *know* you do."

"I'll find a better guy. Somebody more popular. More cuter. Somebody with a pool. Somebody who's... not a liar. Somebody who's... amazing."

A junior high couple barreled toward Denise. They were both blonde and they both gnawed on giant bowtie pretzels. Holding hands, they smiled.

She looked to the left, to the right. Still, Denise moved on, thrusting between them. Their link snapped and the teens broke apart.

"Look," Ricky said.

Whirling, she found him.

Dirty One

Doug Cleveland stood by a Toys R' Us display. Smiling part ways, he cradled a stuffed kitty cat. He pulled on its tail. He smoothed back its whiskers.

"Fuck," Denise whispered.

Dirty One

Introduction

I was unloading a paper sack. Jugs of bleach and Soft Scrub mounted at the foot of Mom's bed.

"I'll get it all clean by Tuesday. Tuesday," she told me.

I set out Brillo Pads. "Think I remembered everything."

"This is just right, Noah. So... you wanna have a waltz before I get going? You wanna have a dance?"

"Not today."

She smiled. "You never dance with me anymore."

"Mom?"

"What?"

"Everything's *already* clean so, you know, you don't have to clean."

She smiled again. "Everything's filthy."

"When will you go back to the factories?"

"This is my job, now."

All the grenades of pain and ache burst in my chest. I quickly shoved away that sadness because I knew he would never cry.

"I'll start downstairs," mom said, smiling.

"Okay."

Later, I hid inside my bedroom. Later, I peeled open a new paperback. Later, I thought of the boy who wallpapered my mind, the boy who I wanted to become. Later, I prayed in whispers, *"Make her... calm down. Make mom normal. Make her go back to work. Make her better because... I think she's sick. And please, please, please make the minutes go by fast. Make Monday come real soon,"* I pleaded.

Part One

The banana buses had gone. Even number seven. The walkers walked off and teachers ambled to their rusty cars. Leominster's grade school became deserted.

I was standing with thirteen year old, Ben Erickson. We stood by the chain of crosswalk lines that reached across Stearns Avenue. As he and I shifted in circles, yellow leaves crunched beneath our high tops.

Ben, like always, looked like a champion. He wore his sun-swept face and his golden, back-to-school crew cut.

Shana Krush was there too. She remained mute. She turned away, reading *Fangoria*.

We were the only ones around.

"God... please make Mrs. Erickson late. What about a flat tire? What about a pile up? What about a busted engine? I gotta have more time."

Ben began digging up rocks from bald patches in the crab grass. He launched them at traffic. A neighborhood pussycat darted across the pavement and sprung away from danger. Collapsing with laughter, Ben laughed and laughed.

Like always, I followed his lead. I laughed too.

"Thought I woulda hit her," he said.

I flicked him. *"Awesome. You almost did... right in the head."*

"Wish I woulda."

Ben's hands were soiled with black earth. He wiped them on his jean jacket, rubbing smears into the denim.

"Please make him just... touch me."

He flicked me back. "Shit," Ben said.

"Shit," I copied.

He cast a grin toward Shana.

Shana was propped against the giant maple, opening her math workbook. She wrenched her 'Reno' cap downward and Shana's head bobbed low.

"Hey!" Ben yanked down his sweat pants. He wagged his penis at her.

I pretended to not care, but I prayed, *"God! Please! I have to see it! Just one look! Please!"*

He then turned. My eyes pored over his thick peachy penis. It was bare, hairless and unlike mine. At once, glee machine-gunned, popping through my entire body.

"Gross!" Shana shouted. "You're a pig. You're a filthy pig!"

Ben tucked himself away. He rumbled over and tore the workbook from her grasp. As one page ripped free, it circled to the ground.

"Give it back," she snapped.

"No."

"Give it!"

Scrimmaging away, he scoured through her assignments. "Eight wrong! Eleven wrong! Nine wrong!"

"Be quiet."

"Ten wrong!"

"Be quiet! You're the one that stayed back."

"Six wrong!"

Shana clawed at his chest. "Give it to me you A-hole. Give it to me!"

I was giggling. I was also trying not to giggle.

"Help me, Noah," she said.

"Um..." I began.

Ben shot out his palms and pushed her. Shana rocked backwards, crashing to the sidewalk. She landed on a carpet of wet, yellow foliage. The hat tumbled off of her head and a dark curtain of hair escaped.

"Don't put your fucking hands on me," Ben said. "I'll punch your face again. Is that what you want?"

He tossed the workbook into the atmosphere. It landed beside her.

Shana moaned, "I dare you. I *dare* you."

Mrs. Erickson swerved down the street, tooting her little horn.

"Get up, Shana," I said. "Hurry. Here she comes."

Ben's mother parked beside the curb. "Let's go," she urged through the window.

Part Two

We buckled ourselves to the plastic-covered seats.

Mrs. Erickson was fishing through her leather purse, its contents tinkling. "*Sugar*. My matches are hiding again. I always lose 'em."

Tangy perming fumes wafted from her head. The highlighted curls looped around and reached outward. Her new coils were glossy.

"'Bout time," she said, locating the matches. Mrs. Erickson shoved a Basic One-Twenty in her mouth and lit up. Sucking hard, she coasted through a yellow light. "That means go faster," she said.

Ben was ogling his mother. He tugged on the shoulder strap and rolled his shimmering eyes. The window beside him began to slide down as a blast of wind swept inside.

"*Don't*," Mrs. Erickson said.

"Why not?"

"I'll get the chills, Ben."

"I can't breathe."

"*My* window's open. Roll *yours* up."

"It's *not* open," Ben replied.

"It *is*. It's cracked. A sliver," she said, her voice climbing.

"Mom..."

"Now!" she commanded and whapped his ear.

Ben did as he was told. Smoke began to engulf the van. White rings and corkscrews swayed in the October light.

"I like the new van," I announced.

"Not sure if I'll keep this one. I'm testing it out."

"It's nice," I said.

Mrs. Erickson glanced to the back. "So, Shana... heard you're going to Can-Cun next week. Another trip."

"Yeah."

"That should be fun."

"Not really," Ben sneered. "*She* aint going. Just her Mom and Dad. Shana gets left behind."

"Cut it!" his mother barked.

Shana's face ignited with shame. She clutched a violet bruise that spread across her neck.

Turning onto my street, Mrs. Erickson turned left.

I was always the first to be dropped off.

"Here you go, Noah."

She came to a halt beside my driveway. Sighing, Mrs. Erickson peered into the side mirror. She poked her tresses, patted her curls.

"Thanks a lot," I said.

I slid open the sliding door and jumped down to the concrete. Smoke crawled out, vanishing in the autumn orbit.

"Tell your mom I say 'hi.'"

"'kay."

"When's she gonna leave that beautiful house of hers? You think she'll start driving again?"

I stepped back. "She says it makes her nervous."

"Oh. Well... that's okay," Mrs. Erickson said. "Maybe I'll see her at church sometime soon."

"See ya tomorrow, Solider," Ben yelled across the seat.

"Bye bye," Shana said.

The Erickson's van vroomed away.

I was standing by the tip of my yard, watching Ben's shadow wave. He was waving to me out the rear. He waved, waved until the mini-van turned and vanished from sight. I found myself waving too. It felt like I was being tickled beneath my skin.

Everyday had become a day I gushed and lingered at his side. By four o'clock, I always missed Ben Erickson.

Part Three

I scuffed in. Draping my jacket over the spangled banister, I glanced from our parlor to our hall. Mom had done it again.

79

I carefully stepped across fresh Dirt Devil tracks lining the rug. Asterisks of sunlight gleamed on the polished end tables. Each family photo stood in its spot, sparkling, white-bright.

"Noah? Noah? You here?" Mom shouted.

"Yes."

"Did you wipe your feet?"

"Yeah." I stepped to the kitchen.

Mom was squatting over the floor. A large bucket of water steamed between her legs. Vigorously, she scrubbed the tile with a brush. As she scrubbed and scrubbed, white foam bubbled.

"What should we get for dinner?" she asked.

"I don't care."

"I could call out for some popcorn shrimp and cheesy fries. What do you think?"

"Fine."

"Did you get that Social Studies test back?" she asked.

"Yeah."

"What's the verdict?"

"Eighty-two."

"That's better than an eighty-one," she said and scrubbed.

I peeked inside the lazy susan, praying for Potato Sticks. There were none.

Mom rose from the floor and sighed loudly. She pushed up her cuffed sleeves. "Why don't you have a Fruit Roll-Up? Fruit's good for you."

I grimaced, rolling my eyes like Ben would. "Fruit's gross."

Mom stumbled over to the sink. She twisted the screeching faucets. Steam climbed upwards as she held her hands under the flow. Soaping up, she scrubbed between each finger, around each nail.

"I have to do the bathrooms," she said.

"You already did 'em. A few days ago."

"They need another cleanin'."

"Again?"

"They're dirty. And watch it when you go piddle, Noah. There's always pee on the seat. Yellow spots."

"Sorry."

Mom shook her hands off in the basin and grabbed a dishtowel. "When you have to go, just sit. Like me. It won't be so messy."

"I don't wanna sit down."

"It's easier, though. Right?"

"I wanna stand up."

Fresh blood was seeping from the cracks in her pink, chapped hands.

Part Four

I stretched across my bedspread, folding the Hardy Boys shut.

"God? Thank God you made me this way. Because girls are sort of... gross. I know they're nice, but... to me, they're nasty. That's why I like Ben. I'd rather play with him than some girl. And I want us to be best friends. Best buds. Twins. The same. Make me just like Ben. Please. Please. Please. Guess I gotta go. Oh...and forgive us for not going to church. We would, but mom's too nervous."

I eased up and, quietly, I dragged my bookcase across the scratched floorboards. It was packed with encyclopedias and Judy Blume novels. As the books trembled, I secured my shelves in front of the door. *Are You There God, It's Me*, Margaret toppled from its place.

No one could get in now.

I peeled away my brown slacks. Tugging at the thick waistband of my underwear, I dropped them. Faint curly-q's circled my penis. They shot up and darkened my vanilla skin.

Like Ben, I wanted to be smooth and soft. No hair. Then, beneath our Hanes, we'd be closer, closer to being the same.

The same.

The same.

Pressing mom's pink blade down, I pulled. First, to one side, then to the other. Strands of hair sprinkled the floor.

I continued shaving, shaving through the dry, dry pain. I shaved until they were gone. I shaved until nothing was left, but my new, magenta skin.

The same.

Part Five

I only played Mercy and Truth or Dare at recess. That Wednesday, I sat on the metallic bleachers. Lukewarm shafts of light fell down, bouncing off the silver slabs.

I was lighting a lighter over and over again. I watched the flame. I also watched the fifth and sixth graders that clogged the pavement in front of me. The girls were talking, trying to hide their gum-chewing. The boys were zipping through a game of basketball.

Ms. Mott, an outside aide, roamed about and eyed us all. Her vest flapped in the wind.

I saw Ben. He was speeding around, dribbling away from the others. Sweat gleamed on his forehead. No one could catch him.

I also saw Shana. She was waiting in line for hopscotch, gazing up at the crisscrossing airplane trails. Two girls cut in front of her.

Suddenly, Ben sped away from the pack. He flew up behind Shana, a massive smile dressing his face. He latched onto the sleeve of her 'Bermuda' sweatshirt. "Come on. I know you want some," he said.

"No! No!"

He began to spin her in circles. Cackling above the recess roar, Ben pulled Shana to the ground. He crashed down on top of her, pressing her face into the asphalt.

"Stop!" she cried.

Ms. Mott's whistle squealed and all the pupils gathered. "Move!" she yelled. Ms. Mott yanked Ben up by his shirt collar, stretching the white fabric. "Hey! Enough! Enough! *Enough*! Go! Take a seat on the bleachers. You can come with me after recess."

Shana hobbled to her feet, blood oozing from her sliced eyebrow. She smeared the redness.

"Someone bring her to the nurse," Ms. Mott said.

I prayed, "Make him come to me. Make him sit beside me."

With a snicker, Ben strode across the field. "See that?" he asked.

"Yeah," I said flicking the lighter until its flame scalded my fingers.

Ben rolled his eyes and sat down beside me. "Shana's a bitch. She should just kill herself."

"Forget Shana."

"She can't get enough." He whisked a hand over his head.

"You love getting in trouble, don't you?"

He smiled. "I'm just having fun."

Ben reached over and tugged on my jacket's zipper. Pulling at the golden tongue, a few metal teeth unhinged. He caressed the letters on the tab. "Y.K.K." he said.

"Huh?" I asked, lighting the lighter again.

"Y.K.K." he repeated.

I glanced down at the zipper's tiny letters. "Oh yeah," I said.

"You Killed Kennedy."

"Yeah."

I stared at Ben who stared and stared back at me. I then swatted his shoulder. I kneed his back. Slyly, Ben swatted me too.

He said, "You and me, we're like our own rebel army. I'm like, the General."

"What am I supposed to be?"

"A little soldier," he said and laughed.

I laughed too. "I'm not little."

"We should take the whole school hostage and demand a plane and a million dollars. Then we could fly to Costa Rica."

"How would we do that?"

"Like... I don't know."

"You're a punk," I told him.

Ben asked. "Ever been down to the old Foster Grant factories?"

"By Shana's?"

"Yeah, well, we gotta go. This week. After school. We'll plan our ambush."

I flicked the lighter.

"You should torch something," Ben told me.

Later, Ms. Mott was kicking out a fire in the field.

Part Six

I could hear Mom's favorite cassette playing. As I stomped up the golden stairs, I skipped every other step.

She was revolving through the hallway, spinning in a puffy, puffy violet dress. She ballooned with laughter. When mom caught sight of me, she broke from her dance, shameful.

"Thought you'd be home later," she said.

"Mrs. Erickson was on time today."

Quickly, I stepped toward my room, praying to get by.

"I was just practicing my twirls. Then I tried this thing on. Do I look dumb?"

"Yeah. Sort of."

"*Be nice.*" She rested her chapped hands on her hips.

"Sorry. I have homework, Mom."

I pushed through my door and shut it quickly.

The next afternoon, Ben and I would be together. The General. The little soldier. I knew that, by his side, anything could happen. Maybe we'd rob a bank or board that plane headed for Costa Rica. I didn't care because I knew that, somehow, Ben could camouflage all my hurt.

"*God? I love him. I love him because he makes me feel like…like…like every day is awesome.*"

Ben.

Ben.

Ben.

Ben.

Ben.

Part Seven

Mrs. Erickson veered through a busy intersection. Gouging out her cigarette, she scowled at the local drivers. A chorus of horns faded behind us.

"Mom?" Ben asked.

"What, Hon?"

"You can just drop us all at Shana's."

"What?" Mrs. Erickson said.

Shana jolted with a miniature grin.

Turning, Ben winked at her. His cashew-colored lashes twinkled up and down.

"Yeah... please?" Shana said.

"We're all going to go and do some school stuff. Homework." Ben said.

"Is your mom going to be there, Shana?"

"Please make her say yes."

"Yeah." Ben said.

Shana smiled. "Well... my aunt will be home."

"Oh. *Oh.* Okay. I have to go see the lawyers about your father anyway."

Mrs. Erickson beached the van in front of Shana's house. We all leapt down to the sidewalk. Bright chalk scribbles colored the pavement.

"Bye," Ben said.

"Call me if you need a ride."

Mrs. Erickson revved down the road and out of sight.

We stood there among the drawings. There were rainbows, diamonds, and orange stick boys.

We were the only ones around.

"Aren't we going to watch Godzilla?" Shana asked.

Ben stamped on a pink heart and smirked. "Noah and me are going down to the old factories."

"Am I going?"

Ben kicked at the pink heart. "No. *Hell* no."

"Why not?"

Ben molded his hand into the shape of a pistol. He shot Shana.

"Dickholes!" she shouted.

He grabbed my arm and led me away.

Part Eight

He and I were close. Thick prickers crowded around us. As we stumbled down a crooked trail, twigs cracked beneath our sneakers.

Ben shoved his pointer ahead. "It's this way."

A massive clearing stretched before us. In the middle, stood an old factory. It towered above the bluish pines. Wild ivy crawled over stacks of crumbling brick.

Ben basted his lips, peering up.

"Looks like a bomb went off," I said.

"Let's go in, Soldier."

I followed him in.

All the windows were smashed, jagged. Flocks of birds fluttered from beam to beam. They glided among the rafters, screaming at us.

"Didn't they used to make pens here?" I asked.

"Think so. My dad said all the smoke got into the air... it made people retarded and dumb so they closed it down."

"Maybe that's what happened to my mom," I said.

"She's messed up, huh?"

"Yeah," I said, quietly.

"That's what people say."

"Be quiet," I snapped. "Well... why does your mom have a lawyer?"

He jacked his shoulders up and down. "She's a psycho. She sues everybody. My dad. The neighbors. My other dad."

"Oh."

Ben scratched at his tummy. "Both our mom's are frigged."

"Yeah."

"You know, Noah, I hate our school. Shana. Everybody."

"Me too."

"Bunch of assholes."

"No shit."

"I like you, though.

I suddenly felt my own blood pattering. With blazed cheeks, I looked away to the block of ruins that surrounded us.

"Don't wanna go to seventh grade," Ben said. "Everyone says that's the best year... but you won't be around."

"I wonder if we'll still see each other," I said.

Inching closer, Ben dropped his book bag. "I hope so, Noah."

We stood face to face. Peanut butter skipped from his mouth.

"*I'm ready, God. I am. Please… make him kiss me.*"

Then, his lips met mine. Ben pushed his tongue inside. He licked my molars and pushed, pushed against the inside of my cheek. He pulled me to down to the dusty floor.

"*Make him kiss me and hold me till supper time.*"

"Don't worry," Ben said. "This'll be fun."

He unhooked my corduroys and then stripped me, bottomless. With a smile, Ben pet my smooth skin. "Neat. No hair. Just like me, huh?" he said.

"Yeah."

Ben quickly removed his sweatpants and mounted me.

I was pinned. "Wait," I said. "Wait."

"Don't worry, Noah."

Ben ground himself into my stiff penis. Hammering, he wailed faster and faster. His hands clutched my neck. Ben squeezed.

"No. No. Uh…uh," I gasped.

He squeezed and then squeezed harder.

I was breathless and I began to pray. "*God? I don't wanna do this. Make him stop. I don't wanna die. Make him stop.*"

Ben released his grip. He arched up and grunted. A stream of white juice spurted out of his penis, onto my stomach. Even onto my school jacket. The juice felt warm. I had never seen it before.

He moaned, rolled over and began yanking himself.

I felt like I had just stepped on a landmine. Fright dripped over me.

"*Why? Why? Why?*"

"I have to go," I coughed.

"Why?"

"I gotta go."

Struggling up, I pulled on my clothes.

"Noah? Get back here." Ben rose from the ground. His penis was standing up against his belly button. "Why you so scared? Soldiers *never* get scared."

Part Nine

I ran back the way we came.

"Did you have fun?"

I skidded to a stop.

It was Shana. She sat on a rock, gazing over at me. A tiny bouquet of expired dandelions flopped in her hand. She blew on their heads and white fluff scattered.

"What?" I asked.

"Did you have a good time, Noah?"

"We didn't do anything."

"He *wanted* me to see you two. He *wanted* me to watch."

Shana wiped her nose with the sleeve of her 'Tampa' sweatshirt.

"Shut up," I said.

"It's not *that* bad."

"What?"

"At least he didn't put it on your face. And he didn't punch you. He didn't pinch you. And he didn't call you names. He didn't call you a whore. That's how Ben does it to me."

"Shut up."

"But you're a whore too, Noah!"

Part Ten

I whooshed into the house, skating across the slick floor.

"Noah?" Mom rushed out of the parlor.

"What?" I said. I hurled for the stairs.

"Where you been?"

"With Ben."

"I've been waiting. You should've told me"

"Sorry," I said, climbing a few steps.

She squinted. "What's that?"

"What's what?"

Mom barreled towards me. Snatching onto my jacket, she examined the white stain left from Ben. "This. This... stain." Her rough fingers squealed across the nylon collar. She rubbed, trying to scratch away his mess. "What is that?"

I was grappling for excuses.

"What is that?" she repeated, louder.

"*God... what do I say? It's paint? It's Ben's juice. It's marshmallow fluff?*"

"Noah?"

"Maybe it's milkshake. We had some. I had one."

"Noah! God!" Mom yelled.

"I'm sorry."

"I can't believe you. I washed it yesterday. Why are you so messy? Why are you so dirty?"

"I'm sorry."

Later, I cried. Later, I paged through the dictionary, found the word 'whore' and felt as though it described me. Later, my mother and I danced for the first time that year.

A Snow Day

For Buki... the mega-watt star... the one who was saved... thankfully.

Sunday Morning

Cassidy was strewn across the floor. Lustered. Razzling. Her crimps fanned out like a silky pinwheel. Head-bopping, lip-syncing, she lay, awash in glitz.

Casey Kasem's Weekly Top Forty countdown buzzed through her headphones. The Walkman thumped on ten and a pop smash boomed across radio waves. She savored the bright, candied song while her dog, Chuckles, began prancing about.

Amid beats, Cassidy stared up at the parlor's overhead lamp. Two bulbs were burnt out. Lifeless. A graveyard of dead mayflies and Junebugs had been collected.

The DJ: "Tiffany soars up three spots on our countdown to number four. This youngster is hot, hot, hot! She's right on the heels of Sheena Easton."

Cassidy peeped at her parents through the open kitchen door. They were stiff, unsmiling and rock-faced too. Because they always looked as such.

Her father whipped his Folgers, adding more drops of cream. He huffed and dipped his bald head. Her mother tore through outlet flyers from the *Leominster Sentinel*. She was wearing a pants suit even though it was Sunday.

Casey again: "A former number one hit falls down the countdown. Who knocked this young super-group out of the top spot? Find out next!"

A commercial: "Fresher breath… Dentyne."

Cassidy slid the knob down to three, a light whirr. And her foamy, bubbled daydreams grew limp.

"Jews!" her mother exclaimed, opening the J.C. Penney advertisement. "Forty-five dollars for a blouse! That's *ridiculous*."

Her father shrunk, stirred.

"When will you talk to Cassidy?" she asked.

"*I can't. I won't. She's only eleven.*"

"You *have* to"

"Margo… *come on*," he said, pulling a mango cardigan tightly around his body.

Cassidy crawled behind the sofa. She was certain of their grumblings. Her parents had discovered the stolen rouge from Brooks Pharmacy. Or Ms. Diaz had phoned about that D+. As her doom neared, she cradled Chuckles.

"Ted Johnson!" Her mother's dusky, marmalade bob was now trembling. "Be an adult for Christ's sake. Be a man."

"I'm a man. I'm… ya know I am."

"Please!"

"Sssssshhhhhh," he hissed.

"She can't hear us. She's listening to the headphones." Her heels ticked feverishly. "Have you seen the paper lately? Have you? Everyone is talking. *Everyone*."

Her father inched close, swilling a deep breath. "Ya know… who cares what people say. *We* know the truth."

"Suck my cunt, Ted!"

"Don't use that word! Filthy!"

Cassidy feared punishment. She knew she'd be sentenced to her bedroom. Or her tapes and cassingles would be locked in the hallway closet again. Still, gulping down dread, she pulled herself from the floor and entered their hush.

"Hey, Sweets." Her father grinned. "Whatcha' doin'?"

"Nothing."

Her mother closed the clumpy sugar bowl. "Hon... you're father has to talk to you."

"I didn't do anything!" Cassidy shrieked.

"We *know*," her father said. "Ya didn't do *anything*."

"Oh. *Oh*. What then?"

"Cass, I have something to tell ya," he said, squatting down. "I don't work at the mall anymore. That's over."

Cassidy watched him quiver. His mouth moved slow and lame as if he were swallowing a banana split spoonful. He confessed that Bradlees had asked him to leave. Because a teenage boy from Electronics had begun talking.

"That little fink told everyone I did things I didn't do. But... Sweetie, I would *never* do something like that."

Her mother said, "I'm still working hard at the insurance company and, soon, your dad will get back on his feet. So everything is going to be fine."

"Oh," Cassidy replied.

"Yep," her father said. "Everything'll be okay. I swear."

Cassidy delivered a billion dollar smile. "I believe you, dad."

"Ya do?"

"Yes."

Her father reached out and grazed her hand. "And don't listen to what anyone says about me."

Cassidy's confusion see-sawed. She wondered if her father would find a new job. If they would move back in with Grammy. She wondered if he would vacation at Burbank Hospital again. Baffled, Cassidy began to sift through the newspaper.

"What'cha doin'?" he asked, jolting.

And she puckered. "Just wanted to look at the funnies."

Her father shot over to the massive heap. He rummaged through headlines and photos and offered her the comics. "Here ya go," he said.

Chuckles cantered in. He gagged while she searched for Blondie.

He Has AIDS

Sherbet-colored piles dotted the driveway.

"What's wrong with him?" Cassidy asked, tossing back ribbons of hair. "He just keeps puking."

Her father shuffled around and dodged the mess. "He's old, Cass. That's what happens."

"Maybe we could get him some medicine. Like... I don't know. Tylenol, but Tylenol for puppies. It's probably just the flu. Or a cold. It's not like he has AIDS."

Because

Ms. Diaz sat, quietly slicing a pen across extra credit comprehension questions. She had told the class to skim chapter fifteen in their social studies textbooks.

The girl behind Cassidy snapped, "*My* mom says *your* dad's a faggot."

"Shut up," she said.

"Aint it true?"

"Quiet!" Ms. Diaz blasted.

Decked in shame, Cassidy's cheeks smoldered, but still, she posed like a celebrity would.

The room slid back into silence. Children continued to trade notes and blocks of chewing gum.

Cassidy topped her mouth with Bonnie Bell. Her lips were glitterized. She dabbed at orange eye lids and then, spritzed on more Charlie.

Cassidy twirled her pen, pretending to finish the assignment, but really, she doodled. Her stage name. No more Cassidy Johnson. She needed something with glamour, style and flair. Gripping a dull number two, she wrote 'Cassidy Valentine.' And 'Wilson.' And 'Collins.' And then, 'Lee.'

CASSIDY LEE.

She smiled as though someone was taking her photo.

"It's time," Ms Diaz said. She arose, her face gleaming. "Your first essay will be due in two weeks, boys and girls. This is very, very important. There are so many rules you cannot forget. You *must* remember all your periods. You *must* remember all your capital letters. Spell out those numbers! This isn't math. And please, do *not* use the word 'and' too many times and never begin a sentence with 'because,' because it just sounds bad."

She's a Teen Superstar

Cassidy lounged on the couch. A Debbie Gibson hit thumped into her eardrums while Chuckles dozed silently beside her. She *did* have homework. Her essay was due in one week. The topic: the future. The length: One-hundred fifty words. Some classmates would write about becoming teachers or presidents and some would write about becoming lawyers or nurses.

Cassidy would be a teen superstar.

She planned to cut her debut record. Solo, she'd be known as a musician, songstress and dancer too. She'd sing so many songs. Dancy ones. Sugared ballads. They would all be runaway number one hits! Her music would blare from kitchen radios. And car stereos and headphones. And boom boxes. Cassidy's records would turn double platinum.

Of course, she would *have* to make music videos. In rouge and polka-dotted tops, she'd lip-sync her music, packing TV screens.

CASSIDY LEE!

"Everyone will love me, Chuckles."

The beagle released a groan.

Cassidy retrieved her tangerine Trapper Keeper and began writing the essay for Ms. Diaz.

The title: Teen Superstar.

Everything

Cassidy returned home by three. At the door, Chuckles retched and she pet his head. "You're my number one fan, aren't ya?" she whispered.

Her headphones played an old song by Sweet Sensation. Awhirl, Cassidy bumped with each electronic boom, dancing to the kitchen for a glass of Minute Maid.

She stopped, though. Because her parents were in the midst of another squabble.

Cassidy crouched down and spun the volume to two.

"Margo, don't treat me this way. Ya gotta believe me. I'm sick. But I can make it stop," her father said as his falsetto voice droned.

"Well… you must get better, Ted. Money's tight. There just isn't any. I need your rent and we can't even pay the vet bill. Go down to the factories. Apply."

"Margo, don't be so mean."

Hugging the doorframe, Cassidy's spirits fizzled. Their bickering always burned her ears like static. A Poison song. Some noise she couldn't turn off.

Her mother said, "I'm being *flexible*. I'm being *fair*. You're here for only one reason. Because if I had to, I could do it all on my own. It'd be good to get you out of my life. Out of my way. And you'd *never* see her again!"

He became crazed, wild-eyed. "If you hate me so much… I could stop it all. Just… everything!"

Cassidy stepped into the kitchen.

Her father's face slung into a smile. "Hey, Sweets."

"Hi dad."

Her mother clacked about. She grabbed her briefcase. "Have to get back to the office. See you at dinner, Cass. I'll bring home some Pop Rocks, okay? And don't forget to pick up the dog doo out front. Looks like a bunch of Tootsie Rolls."

As her mother disappeared, Cassidy's eyes shone with puddles.

"Remember the rule now." her father said. "Hey… let's spend some time together. Okay?"

The Promise

Her father drove to Barrett Park. She wouldn't say 'no,' but really, Cassidy thought the place was lame. With its jammed garbage barrels and crumbling monuments, this place had become a home only to squirrels and midnight punks.

"We got the place to ourselves, Cass."

They both sat on a wooden bench. Two planks of lumber were missing so their bottoms sagged through.

"Isn't this fun?" he asked.

She eyed acres of tall, grayed grass. A path that swerved through the park was overgrown. Bare. Fading.

"So, how's Ms. Diaz?"

"Fine."

"Ya got homework lately?" her father asked.

"Yep. I have an essay due," she replied.

"Really?" Her father brightened. "On what?"

"The future. Stuff like… my dreams. What I want to be when I'm bigger."

He buffed his bald patch. "When I was your age, I wanted to be a firefighter."

Cassidy tried to listen to the essay that he would write. Because he always yammered on and on. But she slowly turned the volume up to three as a frantic Martika song pulsed.

Since November, Cassidy felt as if they were all nearing combustion. While her father watched *Saved by the Bell*, her mother worked O.T. Cassidy's home rang with sad songs and gloom po-goed inside her more and more. She knew that life would soon flip to side B, a side she hadn't heard before.

If her parents split, Cassidy planned to become an orphan like the preteens on Jem and the Holigrams. Or *she* would divorce *them*. Tiffany did that.

Still, Cassidy longed for sundae nights and New Kids concerts, just as it once was.

Her father shook her. "Are you listening?" he asked.

"Yes. I'm listening."

"I'll fix things for us. I've fixed lots of things, lots of people. It'll all be better."

"Promise?"

"I promise."

97

In Another Place

"Sooner or later... *later*... *later on*... we'll have to put him down." her mother said.

"In the basement?"

She squeezed Cassidy's shoulder. "No, Hon. We'll have to send him to heaven."

"I don't want to," she squeaked.

"Me either," her mother said.

Hiking up his trousers, her father knelt down. "Cass... the dog isn't happy. He's sad and *very sick*. He'd be better in another place."

"No." She moaned.

"Cassidy," her mother began, "remember the rule? There's no crying in this house. Put those tears in your pocket or forget about watching the Mickey Mouse Club. Anyways, you're just going to get worked up and carried away like always. And what good will that do?"

Popped

The dog was snoozing atop the cream hassock. It's almost one in the morning.

"Chuckles... soon I'm going to be famous and then, I'll buy you a doctor and some pills and you'll be better than ever. I'll buy a mansion. And a limo too."

As *Friday Night Videos* cased the room in flickers, she wrote the last of her essay. It had swelled to more than three hundred words.

Cassidy squiggled about her future as a singing sensation. She wrote about sold out tours, howling fans and giant crowds too. Souvenir T-shirts, buttons, posters, hats, key chains, calendars, lip gloss, coffee mugs.

Cassidy would grace the covers of *Teen Star*. And *Seventeen*. And *Dynamite*. And *Bop* and *Big Bopper*. There would be cool pics plus awesome interviews. There would be two jumbo centerfold cutouts of the young and talented Cassidy Lee!

"Cass?" her mother suddenly said, easing through the front door. "Why are you still up? It's very late."

Nibbling on the tip of a glitter pen, Cassidy popped her head around. "Oh."

Her mother whispered. "Come on... turn off that nigger music and get to sleep."

"I'm doing my homework."

"*Tomorrow.*"

"But I have to finish."

Her mother gripped her half-hidden underwear in her left hand.

"Where you been, mom?"

"Working late."

Slater

Cassidy bashed herself into the wall and slinked down, slow and sexy. Sparklized. Agleam. She was crooning her way through the latest top five hit from Taylor Dayne. Cassidy flounced down the hallway and swung open the bathroom door.

"Dad!"

Inside, her father's hands were gobbed in Vaseline. He was tugging himself again.

"Shut the door!" he yelped.

She could see her magazines splayed across the vanity. Mario Lopez. Cassidy buckled over, shielding her eyes.

"Dad! Stop taking my *Tiger Beats!*"

Meat Loaf

A gaggle of girls spent the period milling over plastic trays, whispering about her. Plump and sour, they never stopped. Because they reveled in gossip. Fibs.

Those seventh graders: "He's a faggot. He takes it up the butt."

Cassidy ducked out of the cafeteria, her hunger dwindling. Wednesday's menu: Meatloaf with beans or a chicken pattie plus corn. She had committed to a new diet anyhow. All famous people were beautifully thin and she knew that pop stars didn't feast on meat loaf. Obviously.

Silence

Cassidy gazed beyond the frilly bathroom curtains. Outside, her father stroked Chuckle's ears and scratched his rump.

Suddenly ascending, he fetched a BB gun that lay hidden in the grass.

"Dad?"

And he shook. Fired.

"No!"

Chuckles began to leap, writhe and howl too.

"No!"

Her father shot thirteen, fourteen times, yet her beagle refused silence.

"STOP!"

Heaven

Cassidy plunged her face into the New Kids pillow.

"Do ya hate me right now?" he asked

"Yes!"

"I had to, Sweets. *I had to.* Ya gotta trust me. And Chuckles is better off. He's happier and he doesn't have to worry and he doesn't feel awful. Chuckles is up in heaven."

"You know... in that song?" she whispered. "Heaven's supposed to be a place on earth, dad."

He sighed. "I guess it's not, Cass. But I love you and... I love you so much. Please don't hate me for too long."

"Okay." She trembled.

Number One

Her sadness bubbled over as warm currents trickled from her violet eyes. Cassidy was crying in the hallway closet.

Because he was gone. Forever.

Bawling, she vowed to dedicate her debut album to Chuckles, her number one fan.

Dumb Fuck

Cassidy heard them through the wall.

Her mother shouted, "A BB gun? Jesus, Ted!"

"I tried my best," he said.

"Why didn't you gas him or something?"

"I don't know."

"Dumb fuck!"

Cupping her ears, Cassidy began to sing out loud.

Mega-Star

She skipped, her jelly shoes screeching over worn, grey tiles. From side to side, she ran her hands along the bulletin boards. Cassidy whizzed by colored turkeys from third graders and sloppy leaf collages from first graders. She trotted past Johnny Appleseed pictures and a hand-printed mural. Accidentally, she dislodged a few squares of art. They spun to the floor, stabbed with silver staples.

Awhirl, Cassidy stopped to look at her own class's board. A picture she had painted was hung at the top. Gorgeous orange and blue stars. Sequined fireworks. Cassidy proudly thought it was the best.

"Cassidy?" Ms. Diaz thrust her head out into the hallway.

"Hola," she replied.

"I'd like to have a talk with you. About your essay," her teacher said.

"Did you like it? Did I get an A+?" Or an A?"

She adjusted her dress coat. "Well, I'd like you to give it another try. I don't think you really *understood* the assignment."

"Yes I did."

"*No*. I didn't assign a *creative* essay. I'd like to know what you're going to do with your life, Cassidy. I want you to take this seriously. Look... I know things are tough at home right now..."

"Well, that's what I want to be," she snapped.

"Come on, dear. I want you to be realistic. A teen idol? You have to follow the rules just like everyone else."

"I can be that."

"I'd like the new essay by Friday. Okay?"

"CUNT!"

Ms. Diaz was paved in shock. "Why would you call me that?"

Cassidy flung her hips, sassily. "I'm going to be huge. I'm going to be big. I'm going to be a mega-star."

A Snow Day

Pulling back dust-covered blinds, she squinted out at the world and a vibrant light stung her eyes. Platinum snow had frosted everything. It trimmed her swing set, the lawn chairs and Chuckles' doghouse too.

She could also see her old, wooden playhouse. It had been marked in red. All over.

The words: FAGGOT. PERVERT. KID FUCKER.

Words

Cassidy sprang into the kitchen, only to find her father hunched over. She could hear him sighing hard, breathing fast as a motor. His shoulder blades puffed up and down. He was sobbing.

"Dad?"

He became still. "No school today, Cass. Not too much snow... just a few inches, but I guess the roads are nothin' but ice," he said and sniveled.

"Everything okay?"

"Sure. Sure. How about something to eat?" He began hunting through the oak cabinets.

Cassidy climbed onto a stool and dug her elbows into the countertop. She shoved aside some bills. "You broke the rule. Why are you crying?" she asked.

Cassidy's father dumped an avalanche of Corn Pops into a bowl and drowned them with two percent milk. "I just miss Chuckles, I think."

"Me too."

"Yeah."

"Mom at work?" she asked.

"Yep. She's *always* working."

"Even in the snow?" Cassidy asked, spearing her cereal with a spoon.

"Yep."

"Dad?"

"What?"

"You know… like… everybody's something. A nigger or a Jew or a fag."

"Cass! Don't cuss!"

"Everybody's the same, dad. It's just… words."

"I'm not gonna be no curse! I'm not gonna be no dirty word!" He began to weep fiercely, blotting tears with the sleeve of his cardigan.

Cassidy wanted to cry too. Because she felt stranded, numb. Yet instead, she performed as only she knew how. Cassidy smiled like a trillion dollar icon.

She said, "It'll be okay. Like you said, you can fix everything, dad. We can make our dreams come true."

He laughed a little. He ducked his head. "You're right, Cass. I know. Everything's going to be great. Don't tell your mom about this okay? Hey… let's spend some time together. I need your help with something."

Not Long

The car sputtered and chugged as Cassidy saw white vapor jimmy off her father's tongue.

"Where are we going?" she asked.

"Nowhere."

"Then why are we in the car? *In the garage?*"

He shut his eyes, scratching his bare crown. "We've got to check it. We've got to let it run for a while... to make sure it won't stall or break."

"How long will this take?" Cassidy wanted to sing songs and try some new dance steps. It was *her* snow day.

"Not long. I'm sorry, Sweets." He stared at her blankly for a beat. "Just don't wanna leave ya all alone, in the house," he said with a smile. "Your birthday's coming in a month. What'cha want?"

"A manager."

"Oh."

"Are we done?"

"Not just yet. Come *on*, Cass. Lay down if you want. Take a rest. I'll wake you when we're done."

Cassidy attached the headphones to her ears.

A commercial: "For first class healthcare..."

She could see him grip the steering wheel. Laying down, thinking about the day when one of her songs would be played, she smelled tart fumes. A quick band of static scorched her ears.

The DJ: "Here's the hot new track from Cassidy Lee!!!!!"

This Whole Galaxy

For Mommy... I love you.
For Tina... the Ancient Queen.

June 4, 1986

Comets blush in live rosy color. The neon ceiling smolders.

"WELCOME TO ROLLER PLANET!" I boom through the microphone. "LEOMINSTER'S NUMBER ONE PLACE FOR FUN!"

Like a nucleus, I'm perched at my booth while the rink spins around me... teens circle, skate over skate, weaving at top speed... a pageant... with naked knees... with concert T's. I snort one line and pinch out a Van Halen record.

"Sonny... hey!"

I bow my head.

Tom, topped in glow, grins like always. "How's it goin'?"

He still stands supreme. When he was only one room away, I had longed for Tom. I'd miss his peach-fuzzed chin, his winks, his lip-synced 'I-love-you's,' but today, I practice erasing him.

"Ready for graduation?" he asks.

"Aint goin'." I plunge the needle on the next track and a gloomy, glum beat swamps the rink.

"Does it still hurt?" he asks.

My eyes dash for his. "Does *what* still hurt?" I ignore the rattle from within, saying, "I don't feel anything anymore."

"Ya takin' the prescription?"

"Yeah."

He swivels in two circles. "It should kill the clap. Worked for me before. If ya need more, I'll talk to my dad. I'll make up something."

Pinning down the ache, I finger a new seven inch record.

"Ya got any of *your* pills? Any Ritalin?" Tom asks.

"*No.*"

"What?" he says and chuckles. "Ya gonna biff me in the face again?"

I think about his promises. About Malibu. About Sundays in the sand. About dozing, day after day. All our fizz-filled dreams scuttle back and my fury detonates. I yell, "You said we'd get away. You said you'd fix everything! And we've been lyin' to my mother for months and months and she almost found out! You know I'm too scared to do this alone!"

The brigade of beams fade and Tom disappears. As I turn away from that boy, he does not see my eyes overflow. He'll never know.

= □ =

Back then, I had told mom, "Have to work the Friday Night Date Skate." I'd coached my brother, saying, "We'll need a head start. Because she'll chase us if she can…"

After buying a beach bag and dubbing two mix tapes for the long ride westward, I was hungry for our new life.

Yes… now nothing at all. Yes… no escape.

Mom still lingers above us like the moon. Full. Half. New. Maybe we'll never steal away.

= □ =

Satellites of pain orbit inside my brain. Stretched before Solid Gold, I blink away tears.

"It's okay, Sonny," my eight-year-old brother says. "It's okay to cry. Okay?"

"I'm not going to cry, Levi".

He pets my newly-cut buzz, scratches my fuzz and shushes my hurt every minute or so.

I whisper, "It's just... Tom had a plan. He was supposed to save us."

"Ssshh."

"I feel like a pussy... but... *this hurts so bad*. I miss him... *and I hate him*. I hate his face. I hate his dumb hair. I hate his bones. I hate his guts!"

"Sonny..."

"It feels like I'm dying," I gargle.

"Ssshh. Ya aint gonna die."

"Feels that way. Like I'm all beat up on the inside."

"Pretty soon... those boo boos... they'll turn into scabs... and they'll get smaller and smaller... then one day you'll look and they'll be gone."

I thrust out a meager smile.

Levi asks, "Will ya read to me? Sleeping Beauty first?"

"Aren't you sick of this yet? We read these stories all the time."

With a blank look, Levi hands me the storybook. "Start at the start," he says. "But tell it your way. No princess."

I pry it open and begin. "Once upon a time there was a prince. A beautiful, handsome prince. After his first birthday, a witch flew to the kingdom. She was ugly, fugly. She was a bitchy witch. From hell. And she cast a spell. She said that, one day, the prince would be pricked by a prick and he'd fall asleep forever..."

June 5, 1986

"Stop goin' through my room!" I scream.

I've seen my mother fussing on the floor since the start of *News at Four*.

She claws her crater-covered face and yanks on her Bud Light T-shirt. "Ya can't go! Ya can't!"

"I didn't send away for the catalogue," I tell her. "Was probably my dick lick guidance counselor."

Mom screeches. "I can't take your brother. He don't take his pills... *my baby's sick*."

"He's not sick. He's... just... hyper."

"And ya don't *need* school, Sonny. You're *already* smart. And now Tom's gone so you can stay here with us. We can have daiquiris. We can watch scary movies. We can be perfect. We can be happy. Ya gotta stay," she cries.

I am crushing the college booklet. "You're paranoid… crazy. I told you, I'm not goin' anywhere." Suddenly, I can see Levi pee on the carport outside.

She threatens to pour Ajax in his Apple Jax or bind his feet with Britannicas and toss him into the neighbor's pool.

"Don't be a psycho," I say.

"I'll do it," my mother squawks.

"No you won't!"

"*I will!*"

June 11, 1986

Among the kitchen chaos, two bottles sit, brimming with tabs.

I buck from joy, swipe Levi's pills and dash off to swap them with Midol.

June 12, 1986

They're playing "We Are the World." Just five streets away, Leominster High School's marching band roots and toots across the soggy field.

I did want to toss a tassel and parade just as they do in matinee movies, but I can't bear to see Tom again. The sight of him switches off my galaxy.

Huddled at the desk, I divide pills into piles of five or ten. I fill fifteen Ziplock sandwich bags.

A clang clatters from only steps away so I stash the Ritalin.

Levi, only in underoos, cannons through, crashing down beside my roller skates. He thumps his chest, flapping and floundering.

"What's wrong?" I ask.

He bounces near.

"What the F?"

Crusty moans croak from within him.

"Are you choking?"

I whack Levi. Twice. Three times.

At once, the child gags, guzzling life. He pants endlessly. "*GOD!*"

"What *was* that?" I shout.

"A ring."

"*Man.* Stop putting stuff in your mouth. No buttons, no pennies, no tacks! You're nine now. You're a big boy."

"Sorry," he gasps.

"Was it her *wedding ring*? Did it have a diamond?"

My brother pinches his penis. "I think so."

"She'll go nuts if she finds out. You'll be on the toilet for a week."

At that moment, we both hear the nearby cheer as my principal whoops, "THE CLASS OF 1986!!"

Levi moves three steps closer. "Sonny... didn'tcha wanna go?"

"No."

"Why not?"

"Already got the diploma."

"But... don't ya think it would have been cool?"

I'm jacking with spite. "It's pointless. It's useless."

"But maybe you could have talked to Tom."

During *Creature Double Features*, I had twice explained. Levi, like always, asks again and again.

"I told you... *he shit all over me... and he ruined it for us*," I sputter. "I don't love him anymore. I don't love anybody."

Levi frowns. "What about me?"

"When you're not being a spazz, I love you. But no one else. And Tom's a mean stupid boy. *All* boys are mean and stupid."

"Well... *you're* a boy. So am I."

"Forget it. Go watch the *Flintstones*."

He staggers off, saying, "I know he's a bad guy... but maybe you could turn him into a good guy."

June 28, 1986

Roller Planet feels as though it is shuttling through the air. With drawn down eyes, I quake on the fringe of my own frenetic tempo. High once again, I'm shrouded by "Sugar Walls."

A seventy-nine dollar paycheck packs my acid-washed pocket and after every song, I squeeze my leg, nervously, thinking, "Still there." I know I should save. For plane tickets. For a convertible. For ear piercings. For my panther tattoo.

Then I see a gap-toothed girl coast closer.

"Hi Sonny!" she yells.

"Amber."

"How come nobody ever sees you out on the floor?" she asks.

I reply, "'Cause I'll bust myself into a billion pieces."

Her eyes are carelessly colored and she twiddles the pink feathers that fill her frizz.

"What'cha need?" I smirk.

"How much are they?"

"A buck a pill."

Unhooking the booth, I wave her in with a swoop of my hand. Laser beams and purple streams slice through Amber's broken smile.

"Everyone calls it Kindergarten Coke," she says. "Aint that funny? Some girl Tina thought of it. She's a total fuckin' mess, though. One night, she snorted eight pills, called her mom and told her she was having a heart attack."

I snag through my beach bag, hearing my inner gripes that zing. I silently say, *"Grow up... They're not even real drugs... They come from Osco... Christ."*

"Hey... Eddie B's kegger was awesome." Amber says. She pins a bill into my palm.

"I bet."

"Why didn't you show up? Tom was askin' for you. *Everyone* was askin' for you."

Heaving my head toward pinball alley, I shrug. "Had the runs."

"Grody."

Dirty One

The tenderness escapes me.

Yes… liberty. Yes… freedom

I've downed Tom's final dose of anti-biotics and I have no more seething piss, no more pink puss, no more stained briefs and all his ache is erased. .

Slapping my penis, I flog myself over and over again. I dream *Tight Teens 2*. Of armpits. Of stringy spit. Of snowballing.

At last, a gorgeous new glop jets out from my core. It spatters the storybook that lies, still open, beside my bed.

June 30, 1986

During Spring Break, I had vowed that, this summer, I'd be wrapped in nothing, but thin auburn skin.

Today, the sun sits, captive among clouds. I wait. I laze. I cough. I cuss. I paint each limb with Coppertone. At last, crowbar-shaped clumps sail sideways and the denim-like sky ignites.

"Ya look so… sparkly," someone says.

A boy looms above. Dodging beams, I see his big, bloated lips that shine, sleek and fine.

"What do you want?" I ask.

"I'm stayin' next door."

"Yeah?"

His eyes skim across my trunks. "Some girl from the rink said you deal. Got any weed?" he asks.

"No, man."

"Just those speedy pills, huh?"

"I'm all out."

"Oh… Well… I'm Seth."

"Well… you're blocking my UV's."

The boy tweaks, then sniggers. "Fuckin' *sorry*."

July 1, 1986

Levi has colored most of himself in green magic marker. Toes. Throat. Nose.

"That's permanent!" I yell, dropping into my bean bag.

"I know, Sonny."

A Stevie Nicks tape has spewed its crinkled, curvy guts and I crank my finger about, wheeling them back inside. "Mom'll get the enema."

"Naw."

"Why'd you do it?"

Levi rubs his streaky, stained skin. "I'm not tellin'. You'll just laugh."

I continue turning the tape. "Just say it. Don't be lame."

"Promise ya won't bust on me?"

"I promise."

"Well... ya might not believe me... but I *know* it's true. I aint what you think." Suddenly, he's hushed as though mom can hear. "I'm like... The Great Gazoo. Ya know, Fred and Barney's friend. From the planet Zetox."

"You're an alien?"

"Yep. But...not from *that* planet."

"Where you from, then?"

He totters about. "Uranus. And I'm goin' back."

I can only laugh.

July 2, 1986

She's spanking Levi in the kitchen again. "You're green! You're green all over! Why ya gotta test me?"

On most days, I'm in a California haze. Though today, I just shred off another Dannon lid. Cherry Berry Chunk. Low Calorie. If I gather one hundred covers and slip them to the postman, I might win a trip to the tropics.

"Did you take your pills?" she hollers.

"MOMMY! *YES!*"

"If you're lyin' I'll call Santa."

Tonguing a fruity dollop, I wrench around. "He took 'em," I say.

112

"Well... he bit me again. He bit my tit."

"Stop!" Levi screams.

I cluck my tongue. "Mom... he can't help it. Leave him alone."

My brother's cheeks are cloaked in tears. "Sorry!"

I drill down my spork, tap at the gooey, chewy bottom and this medley of cries and threats soon grows jumbled. Silently, I say, "*I hate you.* You're a bitch."

"Ya gotta learn!"

"Ouch!"

I scream out, "Mom! MOM! *I'll* do it! I'll finish spanking him."

She smiles. "Thanks, Sonny." She points toward the ceiling. "Upstairs, Levi!"

= □ =

"Now start yellin' like it hurts," I tell him.

Levi coils on my bed, clutching his green head. "Owww! Stop!"

"Don't be so stupid! Don't make mom mad!"

= □ =

"The prince was very very ill and there was no syrup, no pill. Plus, the disease was catchy. It could be spread. They feared the curse of a sleepy head..."

= □ =

I sit at my desk and grind three tabs with a cereal spoon. Quickly, they crumble to dust. I vacuum Ritalin, sniffing, sniffing, sniffing and soon, I blip and skip at the speed of light.

Beyond blinds, I see this boy from next door. *Seth.* He cannonballs into the pool and a spray spurts up, tickling the pines.

= □ =

113

My Reebox shoe box holds almost eight hundred dollars.

I'm drawing up more powder, sorting the bills and I think, "Maybe I could. Maybe."

July 4, 1986

I nod at Bryan B. and Kelly D. and shove up to my booth. Squalls of smoke pour from above while the glitter ball streaks through, launching off its violet spokes and, once again, I'm perched among the galactic glide.

"WELCOME TO THE JULY 4TH ALL-DAY SKATE!" I shout.

"Hey, *Champ!*"

My eyes dip.

Seth.

He grins and wobbles on his skates.

"What do *you* want?" I say.

"You don't like me, remember?"

Fumbling through LPs, I envision his dimpled face oozing, bruising after three blows from my fist. "I don't even know you, man," I spit.

"Well... hey... I don't like *you* either."

"And why's that?"

"'Cause... if *you* don't like me, *I* don't like you... and I've been thinkin'... that's lame. 'Cause... I *want you* to like me... then I can like you back."

His billion-watt charm hits like a cold cock. A Charlie horse. A bam. A slam.

This boy brightens. "You wanna come down and skate with me?"

"Can't," I say.

"Why?"

"Have to work."

"So... then play something for me," he says.

"What?"

"I dunno. You pick."

Seth rolls away. He is gobbled by the feather-headed crowd.

Soon, sweet sonics begin to pack the room as Stevie Nicks simmers from a half-dozen amplifiers. She's crooning "Stand Back."

Dirty One

July 5, 1986

I'm sprawled. I'm speeding. I'm goopy. I'm greased. "Cut the crap!"
Levi riots across the driveway, engulfed in a Glad bag.

"Come take your pill," I tell him.

He slits through the shiny sack and he careens closer, fully aflail. "It's like a black hole in there."

"You keep doin' that and you're goin' to asphyxiate."

"What's that mean?"

"It means you die." I dump a Midol into his palm. "Swallow it."

He growls with his best monster howl.

"You know... you gotta stop actin' up. If you be good then *mom'll* be good."

Before he chomps it down, the boy gawks at the pill. He starts jump jacking in place. "These don't look like my old ones," he says. "They're a lot bigger."

I tug on my trunks. "There's more medicine in these ones."

July 6, 1986

Seth sneezes and a warm speck of snot lands on my neck, yet I don't wipe this away. "Bless you," I utter.

"So anyway... it's tits. My Uncle's never home. Stays with his girlfriend all the time."

Porsche posters glaze each paneled wall... a certain sweetness sprinkles the room... bubblegum... cum... the innards of old baseball caps. We're in the basement bowels.

I ask, "Where's your Mom and Dad at?"

"My mom's dead. My dad's in Philly. He's loosin' it, so I'm stayin' here till school starts up again."

I free fall to the soiled, scratchy sofa. "College?"

"Yeah. U.C.L.A. I'm a junior. Aeronautics," he smiles. "I'll be an astronaut. So... where'd *you* get in?"

I won't reveal that Tom had promised to rescue us. I won't tell him that, over Shamrock Shakes, we had planned to sleep beside tides and tan until four. I will not speak about those paradise dreams.

115

"I'm goin' to Harvard."

"Wow."

"Yeah."

"Well… hey… you wanna go swimming?" Seth asks, shedding his tank top.

"*No*. No way. *No*."

He peels down bleached out jeans. Already stiff. Perfectly pink. "Wanna kiss my dick? I'll call him Sputnik."

I laugh, but in just seconds, I'm slurping, slurping, slurping.

"Good job. Good job. Come on… *make me bust a nut*."

July 7, 1986

Pushing Purple Passion aside, my fat eyes scan the ice box. There is no yogurt.

"Mom!"

I bash the door closed.

She still forbids a visit with Aunt Pam and Uncle Sam and she will not allow concerts or keggers or days at the beach and now, my mother has crossed me again because she rings around me like ribbon candy.

"Mom!"

When she emerges, she's strapped with two laundry sacks. Her bobby pins have lost their pinch. "What's the problem?"

"Where's my yogurt?" I snap.

"Oh… I was gonna make a list, but I forgot. I remembered the cottage cheese, though."

"I want my yogurt. I'm hungry."

Levi leap-frogs over. He hops around the foot-printed floor, squealing, "I'm hungry too! Mommy! I wanna eat too!"

"Hold on a minute," she says. "Sonny… I'll get it next week."

I'm shaded in anger. "There's a contest, Mom. I need the proofs of purchase to enter."

"It's probably just a scam."

"You don't know that. You just don't want me to win."

Dirty One

"I WANNA EAT! I WANNA EAT! I WANNA EAT!"

Mom drops the Downy-scented clothes, fracturing with defeat. "Fine, Levi!" She picks him up, pries out her left breast and, immediately, he begins to nurse. My mother pets Levi's neck. "It's okay, baby. It's okay. Get it all."

=□=

Safely inside his bedroom, I say, "No more milk."

"Okay."

"You're too old. You're a big boy."

He shrugs and buries his face in the landscape of linen. "Sorry."

I continue reading. "The beautiful prince dozed in a deep deep sleep. No one could wake him. Not even hot guys. He just couldn't open his eyes. It was like he had mono, but way worse. They all wondered if he would he be dreaming forever and ever."

July 13, 1986

Sometimes my aching atoms subside. Sometimes there are no visions, no memories, no pictures and it seems as though Tom and I had never slept forehead to forehead. Like now.

"Have to flip in ten minutes," I tell Seth, inhaling the last line.

He clicks on a mix while we loaf beside the pool, roasting in heat. Soon, Tom Petty pours from the boom box.

As I poke at my flesh, a pale print surges to life and then, new dark skin. I think, "Mint!"

"You're gonna turn black pretty soon," Seth says.

"Shut up," I laugh.

"It's cute. You're almost all brown… but then your ass is white as bread. *Hot.*"

My semen still taints his breath.

"This is tits," he sniffs. "Aint got nothin' to do."

"You psyched about school?" I ask.

He stretches. Moans. Burps. Groans. Seth swipes at the sizzling skyline. "Not really," he says.

"Why not?"

"'Cause then I gotta do papers and projects. I gotta get be up at eight. I gotta cram. I gotta study."

"Least you'll be outta here."

"This place is just like any other place," he snorts. "S.O.S. Same old shit."

"Leominster blows. Bunch of retards. Everyone's fucked from the factory fumes. I can't wait to get away. I can't wait."

July 18, 1986

"Don'tcha wanna play?" my mother asks me.

"No."

My mother pitches a purple lawn dart skyward and it tears through the air, quickly colliding with a maple tree. "Come on, Sonny. You can have some pina colada."

I'm hauling two trash bags to the curb. I tell her, "*No*."

"Please?" she begs, glugging on the whiteness.

"I have to shower. I have to spin."

"Just a few throws?"

I bristle, clomp closer and pick up a red dart.

My mother jigs about, holding her drink out. "Wanna sip?"

"Not now."

"Listen," she says, "for your birthday... I was thinkin'... let's go to Hampton Beach. Me, you, Levi."

I aim for the plastic circle that lies, in the dirt, ten feet away. "Naw," I say.

"But you love the ocean. Maybe we can get you in the water."

"I hate Hampton."

"Why?"

"It's gross. The water's filled with tampons and car batteries." I shut one eye and bend back my arm.

"Jesus Christ! I'm just trying to do something nice, Sonny. Something special."

118

Then, I shoot, launching my arrow.

"Mommy? Mommy?"

"Watch out!" I shout.

Levi appears. My dart lands, only inches from his feet.

"Levi," she says and sighs, "you're gonna get killed one of these days. Pay attention."

=ₒ=

I slither from my suit, full of Fruity Fruit.

Levi's shit is wading in the bowl, sparkling.

After one flush, her wedding ring swills into the sewer.

=ₒ=

Seth and I surf and slide off one another.

Tonight, he shines with a zillion volts. I think, "Maybe he'll do it. Maybe he'll take us along."

With such care, I stroke his scattered hair, only to find a stiff little lump.

"It's a shunt," he tells me.

"What's that?"

"Well... I have a thing... they call it 'water in the brain.' The shunt is, like... it's a valve that drains out all this extra shit."

I pet his bump. "Where does it go?"

"To my stomach. It's no big deal. It's nothin'," he says. He's decked in a sly sweaty smile. "I don't even feel it."

I continue stroking his skull.

"Fuck me," he whispers.

"For real?"

"Yeah." He pries himself open. "Do it."

My penis bullies through, forcing with friction. His skin almost burns. "Are you alright?"

He clucks. "Yeah... come *on*."

I begin to plug him in a fierce flux.

119

The basement and the town blurs away as we become sealed within our own dazzled stupor. Amid airy pops, I carve into this boy, thinking only one moment to the next.

July 19, 1986

Slowly, slowly, slowly, he unwinds from my grip. Seth whisks open patio doors and stares at the heavens above. "It's so quiet here," Seth says. "Kinda scary. Feels like we're the only ones awake. In Leominster. In Massachusetts. In this country. In this whole galaxy."

I kick off the sheet. "It's nice. Just you and me."

"Let's watch TV or make mac n' cheese or put in a porno," he says.

"Are you still speeding?" I ask.

"No."

I tell him, "Come here."

Seth teeters toward me, kneeling on the mattress. "What?"

"Lay down. Let's rest. It's almost morning."

Tugging on his tresses, he folds himself into three and nestles near my knee.

"Tell me something," Seth says.

"Like what?"

"I don't care. Whatever. *Anything*. Tell me your life story. Just… don't stop talking until I'm asleep."

It's 4:47 and I speak about being six… hiding away… the strip mall bathrooms… the arcade's photo booth… a whirlwind of freedom. "My mother gave me four enemas after that…"

=ₒ=

Levi stands in the backyard, scouting the caramel-colored sky.

"It's not even six. What's up?" I say.

"She's awake, ya know."

My high deadens. "Why you out here?"

With jam covered cheeks, my brother plucks his widow's peak. "Just lookin'."

"Levi... go back to bed."

"My real mommy's watchin'. She's out there and one day she's gonna fly down. She's comin' here. For me. Soon."

"I know," I say, punchy and worn.

=o=

Easing inside, I think, "Please be asleep. Please be drunk on daiquiris."

Blueness paints the room while mom fills the couch in mid-slouch and, on replay, Ronald Reagan's face looks as though it's slipping free.

"Hey," I whisper.

She's scratching her chin scabs. "President told everyone it's all okay. But... I *know* the Soviets'll cream us."

I shimmy from my O.P. tank top.

"Where you been?" she asks.

"Out."

She giggles. "Did ya fuck each other's butts?"

"Be quiet," I say.

"Did ya lick the shit off his dick?" She laughs louder. "He don't care about ya, Sonny. He just wants your hole."

July 24, 1986

Yes... this is bliss. Yes... this is splendor.

News at Four says today may be the first ninety degree day of 1986. Our town lags, fighting the fever, full of slack.

Half-draining a Bud Can, Seth stands before a box fan, immersed in its medium whizz. His arms reach east to west and he resembles a glossed lower case t.

I snort two rails, thinking, "We've been in the same room almost *all* day... but I don't want to eat... and I don't want to leave."

"How did you figure that shit out?" he asks.

"Huh?" I say, corking one nostril.

"How did you learn about the pills bein' like coke? How did you learn to sniff it?"

I'm tipped with tingles while my head slowly rocks and jingles. "This kid I knew... *Tom*... his mom... she was a total coke head. She was a *fiend*. After rehab, she started crushing up Comtrex, Valium, aspirin. And she'd steal his meds. So... I don't know... she just figured it all out. Then *we* did too," I say.

Seth mutters, "Crazy."

"I lied to you," I blurt.

"About what?"

"I'm not *really* goin' to Harvard. I'm not goin' anywhere. Just didn't want to sound like... a loser." I shrug. "Sorry. I'm... *sorry*."

He snicks. "So what. *I don't care*." His bangs toss and whirl from the fan.

"I've... got a plan."

"Yeah?"

"I'm getting out of here."

"Uh huh."

I see scenes of salted surf boys. Of freedom-filled days. Of golden chains. Of some California castle.

I say, "I love the sun and the beach. Maybe I could be a lifeguard... in Cali."

"Right."

"So... sometime I'm gonna take swimming lessons..."

He cranks his head back. "How are you supposed to save somebody if you can't even save yourself?"

July 26, 1986

The carport boils as a hot haze of coils floats up from the asphalt.

"Don't ya think ya might cook yourself to death?" Levi asks.

"No," I laugh.

We're stretched across a long lawn chair and Levi sits on my rump, peeling away all the dead white, sunburned skin. He pricks, then pulls on each piece. "You're gonna be like a piece of burnt toast. Like a pot roast."

"Well... I forgot to flip yesterday..."

"Ya keep fallin' asleep out here and you'll end up lookin' like fried chicken."

As an airplane streaks by, I tell my brother, "Seth got it even worse."

Levi halts his harvest. "Sonny?"

"Yeah?"

"Is he like Tom?"

"Nope. Not at all."

"Oh."

"Seth could be... great. Seth could be... everything." I stop speaking, but that word continues to tumble around inside my shut mouth. "Everything."

July 27, 1986

"Fuck my hole! Fuck my faggot ass!"

I spike this boy, driving with hard rocketry. Wet. Dank in sweat.

"Come on, man. Fuck the shit outta me!" Seth says.

We thrust toward our own baffled bliss.

"Stop..."

"Huh?"

"STOP! STOP! STOP!"

I feel his body revolt...a warm lava-like slush sprays my skin...freckles the sheets...I leap out of my daze...the foul whiffs ablaze.

"PULL OUT! PULL OUT!"

Seth is shitting.

"It's *okay*," I urge. "It's just an accident."

"Gross! Get the fuck off me!"

Unplugging, I ease back, smearing a wad of waste. "Don't worry," I tell him.

"This is... *fucking disgusting*."

The evening is soon punched up with his jeers and the whoosh of lawn hoses.

July 31, 1986

My mother is grinding grease from our turkey burgers and I see her choke as smoke funnels upward. "I'm going to mall sometime this week. Presents," she says and coughs. "What'cha want?"

"Nothing."

"Don'tcha want somethin'? A new boom box? Some tapes?"

"I don't know," I reply.

She tells me, "Think about it. Maybe make a wish list. Oh... and *don't* register with the Selective Services. If they drop a nuke, I aint lettin' ya get shipped off so some Russian asshole can shoot the shit outta ya."

I'm tight toothed. "It's the law."

"*Don't.*" she says, smacking down the spatula.

Every part of me suddenly becomes amped and I'm charged with courage, hate.

"I'll be an adult," I say.

"You're *still* a kid."

"No I'm not. Not anymore. I'll be eighteen. I'll be a grown-up. I'll be a man. And you can't stop me for doing anything!"

"Watch it!"

August 1, 1986

My mother is shouting in the bathroom, "Ya really got some nerve! Ya get what ya deserve!"

My brother is sobbing on the toilet. "Sorry, Mommy!" he shrieks.

This is his third enema and he lashes his legs, shreds up sheets of toilet paper.

"Ya gotta learn, Levi! Stop sucking on my broaches! Ya almost swallowed this one!"

"It keeps coming out! Owwww!"

124

Dirty One

In silence, I plead, *"No more."*

=₀=

My brother still clutches his chapped ass.

Turning the page, I read, "Up in the sky, a pink pixie fluttered by. The queen called out to her. "What will break this evil spell?" she asked. The pixie twinkled and sprinkled a rain of dust. She said, 'The prince can only be awakened by...'"

"I think I have to poop again," Levi says.

August 4, 1986

"Gotta call Doctor Rossi," I say.

Mom kicks her head toward the clouds. "Why?"

"Levi threw his pills down the drain again."

"Son of a bitch. Again?"

"Yep," I say, picking at the skin flaking on my shin. "I already spanked him. Two times."

August 5, 1986

The pool's filter hums and drums while the pines above spew more sap.

"Come on. I'll teach you," Seth says.

"No," I urge.

We're sitting on the concrete steps... naked and bare... bold black numbers hedge the water's edge... two... six... seven.

Seth softens. "I told you... just hold on. I'll swim for the both of us. Just have to kick your legs and... *float.*"

Terrified, I see me, blue. I see me, sunk by the ripped starfish lining. I see me, swallowed by gallons of cool bleachy murk.

He says, "Don't be a baby."

"I'm not."

"Don't be scared."

"I'm not."

"I won't let go, Sonny. I promise."

His eyebrows bounce toward the darkness above. I believe him.

"Okay."

Gently, gently, gently, we wade to number four, further, more and more. With my arms bolted around this boy, I feel all the fright fizzle. I am armored.

"See," Seth says, paddling, "it's easy."

"I just don't wanna end up at the bottom."

"You won't. Keep kicking. Good."

Amid splashes and spits, I ask, "Almost ready to go back to Cali?"

"I guess."

"You must be psyched."

"Yeah."

"Think I could come out and visit? Like soon?"

Seth sputters. His hair is soaked and skinned back. "Look... you're rad and everything... but... like... don't fall in love with me, okay?"

"Why not?"

"'Cause it's retarded. 'Cause we're fags and it doesn't work. *We aren't supposed to fall in love.*"

"Well... *I* am," I snap. Instantly, I see him with two puffed, purple eyes.

"Look at yourself," he says.

"*What?*"

"You're *swimming.*" Quickly, Seth grabs my torso. He tells me, "Start to flap."

I smack the water, chopping and cleaving.

And he releases.

In mid-flail, I suck up cupfuls of water. "Help," I yowl.

"Keep going. Keep it up."

"No!"

"Don't fuckin' freak out. Just *do it.*"

"Help!"

His eyes are flooded with failure and this boy tackles me and tows my body to the crumbling rim.

126

Dirty One

"YOU SAID YOU WOULDN'T LET GO! FUCKING ASSHOLE!"
Then, I punch his shunt.

$$=_0=$$

Chlorine clings to my skin. "So... F this. Right? We can do it. By ourselves."

"Okay," he says.

"We'll have to trick her, Levi."

"Why?"

"Because. Just... because."

"Will she try to get us back?"

I stare into his twitchy eyes. "Yes," I tell him. "And I could get in big big trouble."

Levi fingers his nose and flicks away the goo. He then starts hugging himself. "Don't forget my Transformers, Sonny."

August 11, 1986

Jupiter burns above... fearfully, I think of my world as punks shuttle, soar... a fanfare of laughter... wipeouts... Def Leppard... raised lighters.

For the first time since freshman year, I swirl among the teens that twirl and as I bobble on my skates, I'm dreading a spill.

My day is near. I'll be a free man, a grown up, a kidnapper, but, at last, I will have the chance to find what is happy. Is safe. Is warm. Is wonderful.

Tom suddenly slides up to my side, tan-faced. "Heard ya quit," he says.

"Yeah."

"What are ya gonna do?"

"Leave," I say. I wobble, swerve and skid ahead.

"Be careful."

"I'm okay."

"Wanna hold on to my belt loop?" he asks.

"Naw."

I rocket away, racing, racing, racing.

Michael Graves

Two trash bags are crammed with Jams and old cassingles.

My brother, still green, flits in. "Happy Birthday, Sonny," he says quietly.

"Not my birthday yet."

"I know… but still. Wanted to be the first one to say it to ya."

Gathering tube socks, I smile. "It's just a day away. You ready?"

He perks. "Yep."

"Like I said before, we'll just wait for her to pass out and then sneak away."

Levi jolts, then bolts in two circles. "What if she catches us? What if something goes wrong?" he asks.

"It won't."

He waggles in his Smurf night shirt. "I think… I think I feel scared."

Reaching beneath my bed, I grope for my Reebox shoe box and I find pens and a hard, cum-coated sock.

"I think I feel sick," Levi says.

I realize the money is gone. Immediately, my universe ceases to spin.

"Shit. She knows."

=□=

Checkerboard birthday cake dots the wall, the window, the stove and I can see one candle still burning in a frosty heap.

"Give me back my money."

Mom is atomic. Mom is nuclear. Mom is fiery. Mom is fierce. "Ya can't leave! Ya can't! I'll call the cops, Sonny. They'll take you off to jail! They'll put ya in prison! They'll fuck your ass every night!"

"We aint goin' anywhere," I say.

"I heard ya before. I heard ya through the door. Don't lie!"

"I'm not lying. I swear. I promise, mom."

She swipes at the air between us. "I can't be without my babies. Why? Why? Why would ya wanna leave me?"

Dirty One

Levi shouts, "Because you're a bitchy witch!"

My mother grabs the crock pot and launches it at my brother. It sails passed his head, crashing into the microwave.

"Run!"

=□=

As my brain blisters with fear, thunderbolts bust up the sky and I drag Levi across a dead Pansy bed. "Keep moving. Hurry!"

"She's gonna get us," he says, crying.

"Seth! Seth!" I scream. I slap at his windowpanes.

After a minute, he yanks open the deck doors. "What the fuck is goin on?" he asks.

"We need help."

"What happened?"

Levi says, "She's gonna get us."

"Who?"

"My mother," I whisper.

I see Levi wet his pants. Trickles of urine trail down his pale legs.

"She's just a little crazy right now and…"

Seth shrinks back. "I'm callin' the cops."

"No! Don't. She'll calm down soon. She always does. Just let us in."

"My uncle's comin' home soon," he says. "I'll get busted. Sorry, but… no way."

=□=

I think, "There is nothing left to do. There is nothing else."

Streamers of rainfall soak us while we stand on the patio, like warriors.

"Boys!" My mother stamps down daisies. She's crazed, clutching a golf club. "Boys! I see you!"

"Leave us alone!" Levi says.

She leers. "Boys! Ya gotta come back inside!"

I pluck up a rusted rake and descend. "Where's my money?!" I scream.

129

"You're not goin' anywhere," she crows. "Get in the house… now."

As I swing, my eyes pool with sadness. The tarnished teeth spear my mother's breast and she falls. Mom twitches while the wooden handle knocks on the concrete. Once. Twice. Again.

"Oh my God…"

"KILL HER!" Levi shouts.

August 15, 1986

I find my money inside the toilet tank and, after dusk, Levi and I lay each bill on the carpet and wait for them to dry.

I tell my brother, "We're going to have to wait for a while… but now I know we can do it now. We can. We have to."

August 18, 1986

As I wait by the water's lip, a bright inner tube hugs my hip.

I pencil-dive in, flailing for my life.

August 19, 1986

"The prince awoke. The evil spell was broke. After dreaming and dreaming for years, he finally dreamed of waking up. And he did. The nightmare was gone. Plus he had to pee really bad. Staring through his coffin, he could see planes in the sky whizzing by. The prince gave a Kung Fu kick. And, finally, the glass split all around him."

August 20, 1986

"Come on. Please!" Levi pleads.

"No way," I say.

"Please?"

Dirty One

Pledging the breakfast nook, Mom shoots me a barbed look. "Will you just take him? He's been buggin' me all day long." Then she scratches her bandaged bosom.

I throw my trunk to one side and scowl, "I got work soon."

"All the lunch meat's gone bad. Take the car and you won't be late. Okay?" she says.

"I WANNA HAPPY MEAL! PLEASE! I WANNA HAPPY MEAL."

I push in a Stevie Nicks tape while mom's Buick rips down Hudson Street. Spinning the wheel, I pass my brother some Ritalin. "Take one."

"Um... so... should I put it in my nose like you?"

I jab the brake. "For Christ's sake. No. That's bad, Levi. Just swallow it."

"Okay. Fine. Did ya remember my storybook?"

"No," I gasp. "Forgot. Sorry."

I see Levi chewing his tablet and he smiles, trembles.

We stoop, roaring down the ramp to Route Two. My brother holds onto my hand and, together, we shift to third gear. We blast on, fast as a space ship.

She's singing now, "*In the web that is my own, I begin again...*"

Seahorse

"God will get you," I whisper.

My mother is strung in tubes, quilts and corn-colored flesh. Still, she is void. She's blank. She's cool.

I had promised Woody I'd visit for one hour each week and right now, ten minutes remain. So I'm snapping through *Woman's World.*

Hurry. Hurry. Hurry.

Judy, the jumbo nurse squeaks in. About her: She'd gone to grade school with Mom and is always speckled with fourteen karat gold.

"How's our girl doin'?" she asks.

"The same."

"I know it's hard, Kiddo."

"Sure," I say, turning past a Pampers ad.

"She's in my prayers. Every mornin'. Every night."

I think to myself, "SHUT THE FUCK UP, LADY! You don't know *anything!*"

"Your Ma really does look terrible."

"Well... she's dying."

"No one deserves cancer. Especially in the *girly parts.*"

Know this: I've watched the illness gorge its way through my mother since last June and as time drips on, I gleam.

"Jesus Christ," Judy says and snivels. "This is just... *so* unfair."

"Um... I have to go to the mall."

≡□≡

"Mornin,'" chimes Clara, the saggy clerk.

Dappled in diamonds of sweat, I veer through checkout lane three. I plunk everything on the speeding black belt. I unload razors and deodorant. I set out a rabbit's foot and five discounted cans of red spray paint.

"Good deals," Clara says, tapping in each price.

"Yeah."

"Mall's crazy today, huh? Everybody's out gettin' ready for the holidays."

I sigh, but don't speak.

"Havin' a clearance sale next week, ya know."

Then my eyes catch the Speed Stick, glowing green. Her register says, $2.10.

"Everything's supposed to be a *buck*," I protest. "This *is* Buys for a Buck."

"Honey, it's just a name. Can't ya read all these tags?"

"That's retarded," I snip.

"I don't make the rules," the woman says. "Ya want me to ring it or not?"

"No way."

Spurned, oozing with glares, she begins to pack away my goods. "I *know* why you're always in here buyin' so much air freshener n' spray paint," she tells me. "I *aint* dumb. I know ya gonna go shove it up your face. That's what my son used to do."

"I'm eighteen. It's legal."

=o=

She wheels across the food court, K-Mart bags knotted to her stroller.

Gina's my best friend and one of the only girls I can bear. During tenth grade, I fed her Freeze Pops while she forced out a nine pound baby. We brewed formula, got high, stopped all the screeching.

"Did ya get it?" she asks.

"Yeah."

"No hairspray, right?"

134

I sink down to see the beautiful boy. "Hi, Babycakes."

Jesse just stares at traffic. He gurgles while thick slobber twinkles on his chin.

"Guess what *I* got," I say, pulling the purple foot free. "Look Jess... *fancy.* It'll give you good luck."

"What's *that* thing?" Gina asks.

"A surprise. A rabbit's foot. For him to play with."

"George... um... ya can't give a baby that kind of crap. They eat everything. He'll, like... choke."

In a huff, I cock my red head. "I was just being nice. What the fuck?"

"*Don't* have a hissy. *Don't* be mad. Let's watch all the cute boys walk by."

We both sigh and sit on a graffitied bench. Behind us, Johnny Appleseed's Memorial fountain spurts sadly. It once flowed, gushed, but now it barely trickles.

I plow through my pockets, snatching out coins. And I hurl them. Pregnant with hope, I watch pennies drown in the dead green water.

"Make a wish," Gina says.

Know this: God still seeks redemption. He has offered Woody and my perfect, new nose. He has offered Mom's death too. So I'm certain the Lord will grant me a pack of sons. Someday.

"Think it'll come true?" she asks.

"Yes."

Gina smirks, knowingly, "Ya could always adopt one. Ya could probably buy one... *somewhere.*"

"Maybe *I'll* just get pregnant."

She gags. "If ya do, *you'll* be the richest, most famous boy in the world."

"I'd love a big big belly."

"George... ya don't got an egg. Ya *need* an egg."

"Girl parts are gross," I giggle.

"Ya need a uterus too."

"So. Miracles happen all the time. You never know. What about the Virgin Mary?"

135

My best friend begins gawking at boys from Burger King. With a purse and a pout, Gina slides on sunglasses.

I tell her, "Cum is more important anyway. Maybe all I need is lots and lots and lots of cum."

"Betcha already got a name picked out."

"Ace," I say, busting with glee.

"Sounds like a porno name."

"Shut up. It's cool."

Jesse begins to howl as if he's just had five booster shots. He yanks on his shabby mane, wailing.

"What's your problem?" Gina says.

Our eyes plunge. The rabbit's foot lies, now drenched, on the glassy floor.

= o =

I'm at the sink, scrubbing skid marks from his Jockeys. I sing with Rufus and I'm happy since it feels like summer and I've already drunk two wine coolers.

Soggy coupons color the counters beside me. Each is cut, not torn. Some perfect squares say, "35 Cents Off Pledge," "55 Cents Off Luvs," "Buy 1 Six Pack of RC, Get Another *FREE!*"

Soon, Woody stomps through. About him: He once hid a heap of Honchos beneath the pull-out. After my blustering fits, he now knows not to waste.

"Hey, Gorgeous," he says and grins.

"No *Sentinel* today," I say. "Paper boy didn't deliver."

"Did ya call the office?"

"I don't want to get him in trouble. I just want more fucking coupons."

My boyfriend kicks off his beat boots. Squares of hardened mud crumble to the floor.

I'm thinking, "I *already* vacuumed!"

Then a bitchy smile splits across my face. "Can I get a kiss?"

Woody says nothing, just wiggles from his work clothes. He blows two wads of snot into the trash can.

"Yuck!" I squeal.

He's beaming, potbellied. "I'll kiss you now."

"Gross!"

"Come here!"

Woody tortures me with a quick round of tickles. He finally nips my chin. There's bristle and stink and peppermint schnapps.

"Um... what'd ya do today?" he asks.

"Nothing. Went to the mall. Saw my mom."

"How's she doin'?"

"Still can't breathe so well. Smells weird too."

His whole face softens.

I tell him, "She doesn't even know I'm there. She's practically dead."

"Really?"

"Yes. So why do I *have* to see her?"

"Think of it like this... if ya go, you'll get sent to heaven."

"I'm *already* going there."

Woody fake-punches my cheek. "Gotta do what's right."

I grope for my can of Kodiak. Fingering out a fat, minty bulge, I stuff it in. I suck and I suck.

"Ya still think about all that stuff?" he asks.

"No," I lie. "I don't even remember."

But I do recall month-long earaches. I do recall the olive loaf at Christmas. I do recall all those piercing cavities.

"What we eatin'?" Woody asks.

"Turkey pot pies."

=□=

Yes. Yes. Yes.

Red paint flecks dot my slick upper lip. I'm spritzing the washcloth and cupping my face. With a heave, I pull in sweet, clean vapors.

Gina's laughter falls like flurries. More about her: In May, she'd disappeared. Gina met a boy at Wal-Mart and spent the weekend slurping down Buds in his basement. So I took Jesse. When she returned, Gina was grounded for the first time since tenth grade.

137

"We shouldn't huff no more," she says. "But I love being wasted."

Wet coughs fire from my chest. Sputtering, I belly flop onto the twin bed beside her.

She stammers. "Remember... a few years back? On that New Year's? We drank a bunch of nips... and we danced on the highway?"

"I remember."

Gina jolts with a cackle. "George... I'm gonna kill myself. I swear. I swear to God," she says, joking.

I tease too. "Shut the fuck up."

"My life is like... It's... *the worst.*"

"Be quiet."

"I live with my mother. *Still,*" she giggles. "I don't got a job. I don't got a boyfriend. I don't got *anything.*"

"You have Jesse."

In a haze, she snorts and wipes away streams of chemical goop. Her smile is suddenly gone.

"I'd do anything to be like you," I say. "To have a little baby."

"Kids can be a pain in the ass, ya know."

I fold my legs. "Just isn't fair."

"I *know* I'm an asshole. When I think about it... if I didn't have a baby... I could have so much more." Now she's babbling louder. "And anyways, *I* ruined the kid's life. It's *my* fault he's messed up."

My damp eyes begin to flicker because I always forget Jesse's retarded.

=o=

"Do it!"

"Oh... *yeah.*"

Woody fucks me fast on the sofa. He drives in, disappears and then, three seconds later, slides free completely.

"I'm gonna' shoot," Woody snarls.

"Don't pull out."

"You're so fuckin' hot."

Dirty One

Right now, I'm inside a sweet slow dream. Beyond the squeals and hoots, my brain just fizzles. I think of bibs. Booties too.

"I'm gonna cum," he gasps.

"Fuck my pussy!"

Woody's drawing on the Lysol-drenched rag. "Ya want my baby batter?"

=o=

Couples strut across the dance floor ceiling. They boogie, clapping, clapping.

As an old Soul Train episode jitters, I'm flipped over in the midst of one long headstand. Quick pangs of pain shoot through my head like comets.

"George? George?"

Woody rumbles in. "What the fuck are you doing?"

"They're dripping out. It won't work if they get away."

With a squint, he utters something and bumps back through the darkness.

=o=

"The eczema's comin' back, darlin'," Judy says.

Sashes of sun pierce my eyes, but still, between the white hot bands, I see nurses smoking out back.

Boring. Boring. Boring.

Judy dumps Jergens in her palm and mashes both hands together. "The cream's so cold," she tells me. "You have to warm it up first."

"Oh."

She begins to rub my mother's hefty arm, stroking, squeezing.

Of course, I'm filled with sass. "*Why are you doing that, anyway?*" I hiss.

"Her skin's dry. Wouldn't you want someone to put cream on you... if you couldn't do it yourself?"

I say nothing. I think, "*Gross.*"

"George? Would you do me a favor?" she asks.

139

"Well… I have to leave soon."

"It'll only take a sec," Judy says. Now she's coating her own elbows with leftover lotion. "Why don't you give your Mom a hug? It's her birthday."

"She doesn't know what's going on," I say and snicker.

"She *knows* you're here. She *knows*. She was blinking and coughing last Tuesday."

Swiftly, the room begins to shrink. Faded flowery walls inch closer and Judy's just a breath away. I'm being squished.

"Come on, kiddo. Please?"

I tell her, "We hate each other, you know."

"That's not true!"

"Yes it is. You don't *know* me. And you don't *know* her."

"I *know* she's a sweetheart. I *know* she's an angel."

My rage spurts wildly. I almost begin barking about first grade when a swarm of ticks nearly killed me.

"She's sick, George."

"So are you," I say. "So am I."

"You're supposed to take care of your mother."

"*She never took care of me!*" I shout.

"Settle down. Sssssshhh!"

At that moment, I breach.

"SHE USED TO LIVE IN THE ATTIC, JUDY! AND SHE'D CRY AND CRY AND CRY! *All the time! Every day!* And she'd *never* come down!" I sneer, "She'd even pee in Tupperware bowls. And she'd shit in plastic bags. Because she was too scared to leave. *She couldn't.* Not even on Christmas! Not even on my fucking birthday!"

"Stop cussing! Quiet down!"

"No!"

Judy's enraged, her head shaking from side to side. "*You're* telling stories. And you *are* on drugs again."

=□=

140

Dirty One

I see my cupcakes tan. I sit before the oven, looking in, drawing up whipped- cream clouds.

And soon, the room flip-flops. In a frothy swirl of giggles, my hump rises, round as a kickball.

It's him.

Ace.

He's growing. He's swimming. He's squirming.

"Hi little man," I gush, so giddy.

═ᴅ═

"Thank God tomorrow's fuckin' Friday," Woody says. Stooped over his plate, he builds a chop suey mountain.

I tip back my wine cooler and tell him, "I'm getting a job at the mall."

"*Why?*"

"We're going to need the money," I say.

"No we won't. I make enough landscapin'."

"Well… kids are expensive. Have to buy diapers, toys, formula."

Woody stabs the saucy mound. Eagerly, hungrily, he scoops forkfuls into his mouth.

"Have to get clothes and booster shots and…"

"Georgie, *please.*" His big blistered hands slice through the air between us. "Just give it a rest."

For an instant, we stop and our strain soars, floating like a mist of Old Spice. I can hear the pipes thud. I can hear the Crowley's cursing next door.

Know this: I *will* have my son. I WILL! I WILL!

"Woody, we *are* gonna' have a baby!"

"You're so messed up. When you gonna' realize we aint gettin' a kid? No way!"

I slap the tabletop and a swift solid crack stings my hand. "I can do whatever I want."

He glares at me and glares at me.

141

"I want a baby!"

"Enough!" he thunders.

My fury ping-pongs, bounding throat to womb.

"You can't have no fucking kid, Georgie!"

"SHUT UP!"

"There *aint* no miracles."

"SHUT UP!"

"You don't got no cunt!"

=o=

As curtains of punch-colored clouds tumble above, I sit on Doyle Field's fifty yard line.

Of course, I'm raving. "I *should* get a job! I *should* leave Woody! I *should* move away! I *should* call Henry What's-His-Name!"

Then my torso tilts to life.

Ace.

I rub his full crowded bump, tracing hearts and swirls.

"Hey…" Woody starts to whisper from the sidelines. "I cleaned up the dishes," he says.

My belly rumbles around.

"Chop suey was good." He grins. "Think I'll take some for lunch tomorrow."

"Do whatever you want."

Woody drags himself close and drops beside me. "Georgie… don't be mad."

"Too late!" I fire.

"Why ya wanna a little kid anyway?"

I flick at the wind. "I don't want to be a movie star. I don't want to be a singer. I don't want to be a model. I want to be a parent. That's *all* I want."

"Yeah?"

"We could raise our kids to feel happy. We could raise our kids to feel safe. It would be *fun*, Woody."

142

"It *would* be fun. But... you and me... we're only boys. Only eighteen. We can't have no kid. Whose gonna give us a baby?"

"I'll just... have it myself," I say.

Blinking at a blank scoreboard, he snorts and says, "Right."

"Fuck you."

"George... stop it. Ya gotta come home so we can shave and shower and get to bed."

I snip reeds of trimmed grass, tossing them like New Year's confetti.

"Please?"

"I believe in all these things," I whisper.

He hooks his arms around my waist. "You're *my* baby. And *I'm* yours."

With a sputter, I begin to cry into Woody's lap. "Don't *you* believe too?"

= o =

Last Christmas, Woody gave the paper boy a card with ten dollars sealed inside, but still, he doesn't deliver and, soon, I just might phone that office.

Right now, I'm waiting by the storm window. A Tot Finder decal coils off its glass. The sticker is pale, bleached, baked on by years of sunlight. So I begin strapping tape to each corner curl.

"George? Hey!"

Gina thunders through, spangled in a new crown of sun-splashed hair.

I ask, "Did you see the Sentinel in the yard?"

"No."

"Fucking A!"

"George! I'm sick," she gripes. "My belly hurts."

"Why?"

"Got my period."

"Eeeewww." I flinch.

Drooping, Jesse hangs, lame on his mother's hip, yet in four seconds, the little boy begins to yowl.

"Stop it," Gina crows. She rests him on the floor.

"Hi, Babycakes," I sing-song in falsetto.

Jesse just licks the linoleum. He rolls around, burbling, burbling.

"I put his favorite toys in the purple bag," Gina tells me. "If he gets bitchy, just give him one. He'll cut the crap."

"Okay."

"So... do I look alright?" She orbits and fluffs her frozen bangs.

"Yeah."

"I can't *believe* Kurt asked me out. Weird."

"You'll have fun. He's cute too."

"I wish I could fuck him, George. Maybe he won't care. We could put some towels down or something."

Immediately, my forehead slinks toward the ceiling.

"Does that sound skanky?" she asks.

=□=

"Gross!" I shout. "*You're* smelly."

Jesse's diaper is crammed with loose gobs of shit. His stink strangles me. "Yuck!"

Skating across floorboards, I grab two toys off the table then, glide back.

"Which one you want, Cutie?"

Blankly, he digs at a sore on his arm shaped like Florida. The baby's scratching and pulling, dragging and clawing.

"Sweetheart, *no*."

He scratches again.

"You're going to *bleed*," I say, prying his fingers free.

Colored in spite, the child sniffles.

"Don't cry. Don't cry."

I snag a spit-soaked bunny from the floor and push it toward Jesse's grip. "Look, see." I offer him the toy.

He coos. He slips into silence.

I begin to wipe him clean. "I'm a pretty good mommy, huh Jess?"

Slowly, bit by bit, the baby lifts his head. As he gawks at me, a real grin curves across his face.

"Soon, *I'm* gonna have my *own* baby. A boy. Somebody *just like you*. He'll be really smart, really fun."

Jesse laughs out loud.

=o=

See: I often try to forget the unsigned permission slips and each lost weekend. I try to erase my mind, but all the mess remains.

Still, I press my mother's palm to my stomach.

"Feel that?" I ask. "I think there's a baby in there. I think he's *really* there."

Her cold, husky fingers twitch.

"I can feel him sometimes. Mostly in the morning. When I vacuum. When Price Is Right comes on."

"GEORGIE!"

My mother's head springs up from her pillow. "GEORGIE? GEORGIE?" she croaks. "I heard ya. Can ya hear me?"

Skimming backwards, I knock the tiny table and a mound of old *McCall's* slip to the floor.

"George?"

I'm draped in wonder. "*What?*"

"They're comin'. They are."

"Oh, yeah?"

She starts to yank on the hissing hoses. "They *still* find me. Every night they come."

"Still?"

"I'm *scared*," my mother moans. "I'm so scared."

"Well… soon you'll be dead," I whisper.

"I'm *sorry*." Now she's throttling with tears. "Please don't tell your baby… about the things I did."

It feels as if God just pressed pause because life outside is still and the nurses don't gibber.

"Tell him I was… *magnificent*."

145

My mother cannot see the sheen of tears that dribble down my cheeks. "I will."

=ᴏ=

I'm tipsy with hope. I swat through a CVS sack and scoop out my E.P.T. The box screams, "A woman's FIRST choice... CLEAR RESULTS... 99% accurate."

I glance up and see Clara, from Buys for a Buck. She waddles across the food court, hugging her handbag.

Quickly, I stash away the test.

"Hi," she says and slumps down beside me.

I don't speak.

Clara tells me, "Waitin' for my son, Derrick. Should be comin' soon. Said he'd be by round noon... but it's almost one."

I think: *"Who cares?"*

"Maybe he forgot," Clara says. "Derrick *always* forgets."

I say to myself, "Be quiet! Shut up!"

Then she thumps my arm three times. "Hey... uh... we got air freshener on sale, ya know."

"Oh."

"Some cinnamon spice stuff. If ya like that kind."

Looking at her, I hold my stare and, slowly, I tell Clara, "I quit doing that."

But a wet sour mist peppers our skin. There's slopping and cackles and clucks all around.

We watch school skippers hunt through the fountain. They're sweeping up handfuls of coins.

"Lord," Clara croaks. Bumbling, shaking, the old woman starts to rise. "Those are people's wishes! *My* wishes!" she hollers. "Now they aint gonna' come true!"

=ᴏ=

Dirty One

It's dark enough to switch on every lamp in every corner, but I don't because it feels snug. It feels secret.

I'm rocking in our beaten La-Z-Boy, whisking batter for another carrot cake. I dunk my middle finger and lap the sugary goo.

Beside me, Jesse's still snoozing, soundlessly.

There's a burst of thuds at the front door. Cradling my bowl, I shoot up and unclick each deadbolt.

It's Marion, Gina's Mother.

Fuck. Fuck. Fuck.

"Where is she?" the woman asks, rubbing her weary golden eyelids.

"On a date."

"I don't think so."

I blend three slow circles. "Maybe they went to the pool hall or something. Maybe they went to get subs."

Marion says, "She took her make up and some blouses."

"So."

"She took her birth control too."

"Oh."

With a smirk and a sigh, she unbuttons her coat. "Did Gina tell you about the pills her Uncle bought over the computer? The Zoloft?"

"No."

"Well they aren't working so well."

"She'll come back. Soon."

"If you see her, tell her I'm tired of her shit, George. I gotta work, okay. I have my own life."

"I'll keep Jesse. No big deal."

=ₒ=

"Is this gonna be okay?" he asks.

While my brow knots like a birthday bow, I dress us all in afghans. "What do you mean?"

"I dunno. We've never slept like this."

147

The baby is wrapped, bundled, nested between us. He's already dreaming.

"Should I put a shirt on?"

I shake my head, thinking, "Woody... you're *so* cute."

"What if I crush the kid?" he says.

"You won't. Jesse'd probably scream anyway."

Woody rolls closer and jabs a finger in his bellybutton. He sniffs it. "Ya think Gina's comin' back this time?"

"Yeah. By tomorrow. By Friday, definitely."

With a slow, drowsy wink, he folds the blanket over Jessie's shoulder.

"This is how it could be," I tell him.

=o=

See: I promised God that if Ace comes home, all will be settled. I'll be nice too. I'll donate to the State Troopers Fund and sweep the Crowley's crumbled walkway. I'll even attend mom's funeral.

Right now my legs are unlocked. As I drench the test wand, specks of urine hit my hand.

Please. Please. Please.

The cordless starts to sing its droning song. There's a crackle, then Woody's voice on the answering machine. "We'll call ya back," he echoes.

"Hey..."

Gina.

"Don't answer. If you do, I'll hang up."

Scowling, I bunch a wad of Charmin. I dab at my penis.

"I'm in Atlantic City," she says, beginning to sob. "I know that you hate my fucking guts. BUT I CAN'T DO IT! I gotta be... *alone.* Away from my mother. Away from Leominster. And Jesse. And you too."

I swish back down the hall and perch atop the whirling washing machine.

"I'm sorry. I know I'm a piece of shit."

Behind her blubbers, a girl shouts, "TWO HUNDRED BUCKS! TWO HUNDRED BUCKS!"

Dirty One

Gina's groaning, "I called my Ma. I told her that you'd take Jess. I *know* you'll do that for me George. You'll be a great Ma. Better than me. Better than..."

The box beeps.

Suddenly, Woody booms in. His face is crinkled and he clutches today's *Sentinel*.

"Hey, Gorgeous," he smiles.

My eyes dip down to the stick still in my hand. I can see a bright red plus sign, blurry and perfect.

Michael Graves

Photo by Kim Mooney

About the Author

Michael Graves' fiction has appeared in numerous literary journals, such as *Lodestar Quarterly, Velvet Mafia, Jack Magazine* and *Cherry Bleeds*. His work is also featured in the print anthologies, *Cool Thing, Best Gay Love Stories 2006,* and *Eclectica Magazine's Best Fiction, Volume One*. Michael's short story, "Seahorse," was nominated for the Pushcart Prize and the Million Writers Award. His non-fiction pieces can be found in *Lambda Book Report, Edge Boston,* and the collection, *Lost Library: Gay Fiction Rediscovered*. He earned an MFA in Creative Writing from Lesley University in Cambridge, Massachusetts. Connect with the author at www.michaelgraves.blogspot.com and www.facebook.com/michaelgravesauthor.

CPSIA information can be obtained at www.ICGtesting.com
Printed in the USA
LVOW111732091111

254245LV00011B/38/P